Other books

The White Wolf Prophecy: Book 2
The Hall of Records

This is one of the best supernatural book dramas to date -- for werewolf, elves, elementals, and vampire – crazed fans. Owing nothing to true legend and antiquity, The White Wolf Prophecy is unique in that it engulfs them all, changes the commonly excepted rules, and has just about everything in it, including sexual erotica, angst, dramatic tension, and plot solving.

The detailed, and well researched science behind Lycanthropy, is brought into the focus with four beautiful, and intelligent women, and their mates. An evil character seeks to take over and destroy the White Wolf Prophecy, and the women and their mates must stop this evil before it destroys them. A fascinating book where science, myth, magic, legend, and fact, all come together with a plot so brain - tingling creative and brilliant that it will have you enthralled from start of finish. I highly recommend this book for all readers.

Author Anita Meyer
In Search Of The Holy Language
And
Criminologist.
Religious Procurement Specialist.

Reviews

"I am only 1/3 of the way through White Wolf Prophecy, Mating and I am already hooked! It is the perfect combination of sensuality and supernatural. Kelley has you absolutely captivated with Kaitlan and Cordone, letting you see and feel every erotic moment between the two. The settings in every chapter make you feel like you are there. I was captivated by Cordone's Unique Estate and I longed to warm myself by the fire of the Main Room. So far every aspect of this book has me howling at the moon!"

Jennifer Lamb
Coldwell Banker Fleming Lau

~~~

I have read the book "The White Wolf Prophecy by LK Kelley. It is a well written engaging book. I was reading as quickly as I could to see what happens next. It was very riveting and exciting to read. If the reader is a supernatural fan, they will love this book. I can not wait until I get the other 2 to read and continue on with the trilogy. LK Kelley has a real ability to make the pages come alive in very vivid pictures. I will be recommending to all my friends who like to read about supernatural things.

Martha Cochenour
Administrative Assistant to the Superintendent of schools at Mountainburg
~~~

~ The White Wolf Prophecy ~

~ Mating ~

Book One

LK Kelley

DragonEye Publishing

Dedication

To my Husband & Daughter who encouraged me to write

"Thanks:

I want to thank all of the best people in the world who have been so gracious to help me with my book. I have had the best group of people in the industry!"

Photographers:

Erica Boniface,

Matt Mcclenahan

@ http://www.RazorbackFoto.com

ElleKelle Productions

@ http://www.ellekelleproductions.com/

Special Thanks to:

Anita Charlet Meyer, who, without her, this would never have been possible. Thank you so much, dear friend! (Check out her book)
    http://www.barnesandnoble.com/w/in-search-of-the-holy-language-anita-meyer/1113641675?ean=9781615000364

Curtis Meyer

Jennifer Lamb

OTHERS:

Jenece Amella http://www.stylesbyjenece.com/

~ Prologue ~

In an ancient Hall, built so long ago no one remembers its true age, a prophecy was found written on a small scroll. Through the years, it was interpreted by many, but as usually happens, it became obscured through multiple interpretations as time progressed. Another scroll was also found. But, it was forged to deflect from the true scroll.

Of the five races of Earth, Wizards disappeared long ago leaving only four of the five races still to survive - Human, Werewolf, Vampire, and Elf. These remaining four races have lived with a curse gone wrong for thousands upon thousands of years. Because this curse was cast wrong using the forged scroll, the fates decreed that it can be broken, but only by the one in the Prophecy.

The One, now, seeks to recast the curse. If The One succeeds, the Human race will be doomed. The others will be gone forever.

Only The White Wolf of the Prophecy is able to break this curse, and set right what once was. If The White Wolf does not succeed, the Human race will be doomed. The others will be gone forever.

Thousands of years have passed, and few believe, now. The prophecy has become nothing more than a "fairy tale" to the supernatural races while the humans know nothing of its existence. But, the prophecy will come true - when it is time, and it appears that time has now arrived....

<u>The White Wolf Prophecy</u>
(Forged)

When The White Wolf appears,
All that once was,
Will yet again be,
Beware that danger is not past.

Evil still present,
Will cause to suffer,
That which is,
To not last.

Find The One, who cursed our worlds,
Or succeed in task will he.
For if he wins, the second time,
Our fate, forever, will be cast.

~ ~ ~ And, so, the Prophecy begins ~ ~ ~

~ 1 ~

Fathers and Daughters have a Special Bond.
Enough Said.

"KAITLAN SENECA O'HARA! Get your butt in here right now!"

Kaitlan groaned, and rolled her eyes wondering what was wrong with her Dad this past week. Her Father's voice never needed an intercom. However, he had insisted that she have a direct line to him, and she was convinced that its very presence was to make her life a living hell.

Canaan O'Hara had steadily become more and more irritated with her lately. Well, that wasn't really fair. He had been a bastard to everyone in the entire building this week. What WAS his problem? Make no mistake; she loved her Dad, but sometimes - GRRRR! In addition, this whole week had been a GRRRR week for Kaitlan.

Canaan Marshall O'Hara was a highly sought after publisher who owned the Seneca Publishing House in St. Louis, Missouri. He owned the entire building, too. His reputation among the people in the city, and around the world, was unparalleled. He was generous to a fault, did business with a good, old-fashioned handshake, and everyone knew he was a man of his word. Neither client, nor friend, ever questioned, or doubted him.

Canaan had given the middle name of Seneca to Kaitlan, because it had been her Mother's maiden name. And the company, of course, was named after her Mom who had died giving birth to Kaitlan. Her Mother, Tara, had no family when her parents had met, and her Dad had fallen hard and fast for her. Kaitlan was very proud of her middle name, and her signature was well known to all in the publishing world just by her initials - KSO.

Every writer on Earth seemed to flock to Seneca Publishing House hoping that Canaan would publish their book, but few were chosen. Kaitlan was her Dad's chief proofreader and editor as well as helping him to choose which books were the right ones for the company. She had an innate sense about writers.

Kaitlan's entire life had been about books. She had started working for her Dad when she was only ten years old, because she had an almost perfect recall of anything she read. All through college, she had her own office several floors down from his, and she was still in that same office. Kaitlan graduated with highest honors in her major of English and Literature. She had several languages under her belt, as well, but most of her editing was primarily for writers who wrote in English. Her prowess for editing was unmatched in the world of Publishing.

"KAITLAN!" Yelled her Father, again. Sighing, Kaitlan had realized she was still in her office staring out the window. She pressed the button.

"Coming, Dad. You do know I could have been

in the bathroom, right?" No answer. Surprise? Not!

She shut the lid to her laptop choosing a good editing stopping point of the current book she was reviewing, and walked calmly out of her office to the elevator. Just pushing the button to the tenth floor caused her to sigh as it rose to her Father's floor at the top of the building. She was long used to his need for everyone to do what he said. Whenever Canaan yelled, "Froggie!", everyone jumped to his command. Not Kaitlan. Not on her life! She wouldn't give him the satisfaction!

The elevator opened. Kaitlan walked out, and down the hallway to her Dad's office. She looked at his secretary who was a woman about Kaitlan's same age of twenty-six. Lynne Rogers was very pretty, but always a bit shy. She had never married, but she was Canaan O'Hara's right hand, and extremely efficient. Lynne didn't even look up at her as she waved to Kaitlan to go into her Dad's office - all without missing a beat on what she was working. Yep! Lynne knew her Dad well, but Kaitlan admired her for not ever being intimidated by his moodiness.

Kaitlan opened his office door, and stopped. It never ceased to amaze her that her Father had actually done his own decorating for his office. He had such amazing taste in everything. It was a huge, corner office - sleek, modern, and minimal. He detested knick-knacks, which was another difference between them. Kaitlan loved them, and her office and apartment were loaded with lots of knick-knacks from her world travels. It was the colors he had chosen for his office which surprised most people when seeing it for the first time. The carpeting was looped, and was the color of white sand. While the rest of the room was modern, his desk was an antique that his own Father had made as a young man. It was a rich, solid mahogany, extremely ornate, and so large, it should have swamped the entire room, but somehow, it worked perfectly in an eclectic way. It would probably be worth a lot of money by today's standards, but he would never part with it for any amount. She had already been warned it was to stay in the family. The rest of the room was designed in chrome and glass, which was pretty typical of almost all successful men these days. The walls, in contrast, were painted in the color of a tropical sunset, because the corner two walls of glass, looking out on the city's skyline, faced away from the afternoon sun and its heat.

Canaan was on the phone, and waved at her to sit down. She walked over slowly to one of the two chairs in front of his desk. She was used to her Father's outbursts and gestures, but on one, rare occasion when he was being Daddy-ish, he had told her how much she was like her Mother. But, only once. Of all the things he had said to her in her life, it is what she cherished most. Her Mother had been beautiful, and Kaitlan had always had her photo on her nightstand. She would blow a kiss to her Mom every night before she went to bed. How she wished she had known her! Tomorrow marked Kaitlan's twenty-seventh birthday, and it was always marked with happiness and sadness.

Canaan O'Hara had never gotten over his wife's death, and still missed her. Nevertheless, his love for his daughter was unquestionable, even if he didn't gush about it all the time. In Truth, Father and Daughter were a lot more alike than even they realized.

Kaitlan sat, and waited quietly for her Father to finish his conversation. Her Father was an extremely hands - on publisher, and used a personal touch even if it meant sending his employees to the author - especially if it was one of their top authors - which is why the publishing house was in such demand.

"Yes, yes, of course! I will send someone right away." He turned with narrowing eyes, glaring at Kaitlan who flinched at the look.

"Uh-oh," she thought. "He's about to say something he knows I am not going to like!"

"Absolutely, Cordone. I have just the person to send to you." He had not looked away from Kaitlan, and was quiet for a minute. "I'll be sending Kaitlan today. She should arrive in your neck of the woods by this evening. Yes, um-hmm. Done. You as well. Bye, old friend. Keep her safe," he added quickly.

Oh, crap! He was talking to their biggest client, Cordone Valon! This is soooo not good! Kaitlan groaned. She and Cordone simply did not get along! She had never personally met him, but they had talked many times. He was another GRRRR in her proverbial side!

Her Dad sat the phone down putting his hands

together, and patted his chin with one finger. He buzzed Lynne to tell her to book a flight for DIA in Denver, Colorado. He would have sent her in the company jet, but it was picking up Anita Moore who was their Clan's doctor. She had gone to Italy for another of her research projects. Cordone lived in the mountains about four hours away from Denver. Way, way back in the backwoods of beyond. It didn't even have a zip code!

He was wary about sending Kaitlan due to their heated relationship, but he didn't have a choice. She was the best in the business, and Cordone deserved no less. More than that, it would keep her safe. Yes. She would definitely be safe with Cordone. He had full trust in him. After all, they had been best friends since day one. He looked back at Kaitlan, and moaned. This was going to be just a fun conversation.

"Kaitlan, I'm sending you to our biggest writer to work personally with him as he writes his next book. You will go home and pack, and fly out this afternoon at... Lynne what time is that flight?" He bellowed at her, tapping his fingers impatiently. "Thanks..." and then continued without a break, "...at 3 pm, to go to Denver, and then to Valon's home in the Rocky Mountains. Dan Wheeler is his personal assistant who will meet you at DIA. Once there, you will work with him on his next number one best seller until it is done."

Canaan tapped his chin as he waited patiently for Kaitlan to blow her stack. "Yep, here it comes!" Catching himself before he said it aloud. That would have been doubly worse.

He didn't have to wait long, of course. Kaitlan just glared at him. Had she heard him right? Seriously? Did he just tell her she was going to stay with a man she never had met - even if he was their top client - for an indefinite period? Oh, no, she wouldn't! Not VALON! She shot to her feet, and in an instant, the cool and calm Kaitlan everyone else knew, was not.

"Are you out of your friggin' mind, Dad? Seriously? How could you promise this without asking me first? Steven and I just got engaged!"

"Kaitlan, SIT THE HELL DOWN, and watch your language!"

Eyes wide in alarm, Kaitlan almost jumped back at the forcefulness of her Father's reaction, but she obeyed him immediately, and sat down without another word. OK. That was a new one! Her Dad actually cussed at her? HER? In her entire life, NEVER had her Father ever cursed at her! She felt her anger grow exponentially. Canaan wrestled with his emotions trying to get a hold of himself, got up, turned around, and put his arms behind his back. Then, he spoke.

"I understand that this is really an unusual request, Kaitlan, but Cordone Valon has requested it - personally. You know he always works from home. Nothing is different. He sends me his manuscript, I have it edited, and it's published."

"OK, so, why does he need me to come to him, now?"

Whatever was bugging her Father, well, it was really starting to worry her. She knew something was really wrong, now.

Cordone Tristan Valon was one of the most secluded, and eligible bachelors in the world. He was a real hunk of a man. Buff and built like a tank, most women would jump at the chance to be around him in any capacity. Her best friend, Sarah Collins, had already told Kaitlan she would be happy to do whatever he wanted as long as it was on her back! Geez, Sarah! That was just so wrong. Kaitlan, grudgingly, had to admit he was gorgeous. Take all the most gorgeous male models ever laid on a cover of romance books, and roll them all into one man, and they still wouldn't have the allure Cordone Valon had to the female sex! All, but Kaitlan, of course. She was in love with Steven Moss.

"Why me? I mean, we have tons of other editors around here. Send one of them." She jumped to her feet. "I am not going! I am staying right here!" Her Dad was not going to bully her into doing things his way this time! Kaitlan was just as stubborn as her Father was.

Canaan slammed his fists down on his desk, making Kaitlan jump back five feet. Her Dad had never done that before, and she found she was scared of him for the very first time in her life.

Canaan groaned as he saw her jump five feet behind her. Was it possible that she would change after all? She hadn't even noticed what she had done as mad as she was, thank the Creator!

"No. You. Are. Not. Kaitlan! Cordone wants our best, and that is you!" He waved his hand at her as he saw her mouth open in protest. "And, do not argue with me any more, because it will get you nowhere!" He looked at his watch. "It's 10 am, now. Get your ass home, pack, and I'll have Sam pick you up around noon to take you to the airport."

He held up his hand, again, for silence when he saw her mouth open. It was a move he had done to her, and others, many times before, and she knew better than to back talk him when he did this.

"There is no argument you can come up with to make me send someone else, Kaitlan. I have no choice, and therefore, neither do you. This discussion is over."

"Wait for it," Kaitlan said to herself. It was coming! She knew it was! And, yes! There it was. "The Look" her Father always used when his mind was made up, and nothing could sway him at all. Kaitlan doubted that if she were dying her Father would never have changed his mind! She also knew better than to argue with him when he was in this mood.

Slowly, Kaitlan stomped out of his office shaking with rage. Back in her office, she gathered up her computer along with anything else she would need, muttering every cuss word in the book at her Father. Forget "Neverland". This was a trip into Nowhereland. She hated the mountains! She continued to stomp out of the building in a huff. Why in the hell did she do what her Father told her to do when he told her to do something she didn't want to do? That was a tongue twister. It was almost a "pull" that forced her to obey him no matter what she wanted. Her feet moved without volition when her Father exercised his will toward her. No matter what, she just had no chance when he was like this. Only this was worse. She had been unable to speak!

"What is he? A friggin' vampire, or something!" She grumbled as she walked the short distance to her apartment.   Yes, unfortunately like other young women, she saw those movies, and read those stupid books, where the dull, boring, average, human girl got the really, hot vampire guy! So, where was HER hot vampire? She huffed. Right. Sure. Her Dad was a vampire working his mind mojo on her! She almost laughed aloud at the silliness of the thought.

~ 2 ~

Never, EVER Tell a Person Who is Scared of Heights They have to Fly!

Kaitlan, unwillingly, found herself packing for the trip to "Nowheresville". She looked around her apartment that she loved, which was decorated in greens, reds, and blues. It was loaded with all types of knick-knacks she had picked up during her many fun travels. This was her refuge from the world. She sighed, and then headed for her bedroom.

Kaitlan was an expert at packing light and fast when necessary. Checking to make sure everything was off and secured, she discovered that she was ready fifteen minutes early. So, she decided to give Steven a call to tell him she was leaving for a while, before Sam arrived to escort her to the airport. Steven was just so dreamy! Blonde hair, brown eyes, tall and muscular, he still wasn't a hot vampire guy, but he was hers nonetheless!

"You can't do this, Kaitlan! You just said yes to me last night! What about our plans for tonight? Your first time? What was he thinking sending you away, now? Does he hate me THAT much? Please, Kaitlan...don't go?" He begged.

As expected, Steven didn't like it much. Truth was her Dad didn't just hate Steven. He despised the ground he walked on! If she hadn't known better, she would have thought her Dad would have had him hog-tied, and put somewhere no one would ever find him! Part of her wondered if this was not her Dad's idea to get her away from Steven altogether.

"I'm sorry, Steven, but I just don't have a choice. Of all people, you should know this!   This is our biggest client, and I have to go. It won't be for that long. You know I'm the fastest editor in the west!" She laughed.

"I know, darling, but I just can't imagine you not being here! I had really GREAT plans for tonight, you know?"

Oh, yes. She did know what he had planned! A night of pure lust was what he had planned for them! He'd told her often enough what he would do to her when they had talked about her first time! The thought just made her even angrier that her Dad had ruined it!

"Damn! Sam's here. I love you, Steven. I'll call you when I arrive, OK? Gotta go, handsome!"

She shut her phone before Steven could answer. She didn't have time to argue with him any more. Kaitlan grabbed her suitcase, purse, locked her door, and ran down to hop into the car.

The door to the black SUV was open. Kaitlan threw her luggage in the back seat, then jumped into the front seat with Sam Knight who was not only her Father's driver, but also his very great friend. He looked over at her, and grinned.

"I see the big boss pulled rank on you, again," said Sam pulling away from the curb into traffic.

"Yeah. He did. But, it was strange, Sam. I don't ever remember him as ... well ... as violent as he was. It was almost as if he wanted me out of the way more than working with our largest client. I just don't get it." She turned to look at Sam. "Has he ever acted like that with you?

Without turning his head, Sam didn't really give her an answer, but he did tell her what he thought.

"Kaitlan, he's your Dad, and even his own employees know better than to question his decisions. You know, more than anyone, he didn't get where he is today without making the right ones. No one questions him on those decisions. Not them, not me." He turned to look at her seriously. "Not even you."

Kaitlan nodded in knowing agreement. Sam was right. No one EVER questioned her Father's decisions. However, well, she had never asked why...until now.

Crap! She hated to fly. She hated heights. Always had. She never knew why, though. She wanted to be down, on the ground where a person was supposed to be touching good old Mother Earth. The entire flight kept her so wound up, she almost found herself hyperventilating. Thank goodness, the flight attendant had come just at the right time. She ordered a tomato juice with lots of ice in it. It always seemed to calm her down while flying, and settled her upset stomach. She really wished she could drink booze like other passengers, but that just upset her stomach even more.

"Please prepare for landing," the Captain announced.

"Just a few more minutes. Just a few more minutes." Kaitlan kept repeating to herself.

She gripped her seat's arms as the plane's landing gear touched the pavement with just a slight jolt, then as the brakes were applied, she was pushed forward along with the rest of the people. That was another thing she hated. If it wasn't taking off, or heavy turbulence while in the air, landing always gave her the jitters. The plane landed at DIA almost thirty minutes early. Tail wind, or something. She didn't know the specifics of planes. Just stop already, and let her off! Finally, pulling to the gate, the door opened, and she waited for those ahead of her to deplane as fast as possible. They were way to slow for her!

With a sigh of relief that she was on the ground, and had exited the plane, well, it calmed her nerves better than anything. She took the train to the main terminal, then made her way to the luggage carousel to pick up her luggage. She grabbed the one piece of luggage she had checked, and started walking to the East exit planning to visit the facilities before she met this Dan who was supposed to pick her up, and whisk her away to who knew where for who knew how long. Before she even walked two feet into the main terminal, a man approached her, holding out his hand. Kaitlan automatically took it.

"Ms. O'Hara?" He asked shaking her hand in introduction. "I am Dan Wheeler, Mr. Valon's personal assistant. Are you ready to go? It will be quite a drive - about four hours."

"Ye gods!" Quoting to herself from her favorite musical, "The Music Man". This Dan was ready to drive her so far back in the mountains, she could be killed, and she would never be found!

"OK. Seriously, Kaitlan. You are really letting your imagination run away with you!" She admonished herself.

"It's very nice to meet you, Dan. If you will give me just a few minutes, Mr. Wheeler, to attend to some personal things, I'll be ready."

Dan Wheeler nodded without a word, and took charge of her luggage while she made a beeline for the ladies room. It's always hard to tell a guy you have to go - especially one you don't even know, so, she opted for the more formal information.

She just hated to use the restrooms in planes. They bounced all over the place, and trying to concentrate just to go was a pain in the backside! She also would never forget an incident related to her by a friend. The friend's Mother had been in a plane bathroom, and had flushed while still sitting on it. The problem? The suction had "stuck" her to the toilet, and they had to bring in something to pry her off of it! Since that time, if she had to go in a plane, she made absolutely sure she was up, washed her hands, and dressed before she flushed!

Her personal needs met, she let Mr. Wheeler

lead her to a black SUV Honda CR-V, and then loaded her luggage. She waited in the backseat preparing for a very long drive. She was not happy, and she hated people who sulked and pouted.

Kaitlan sat back, sulking and pouting, while she pulled out her phone to call Steven as she had promised. Waiting for him to answer, she thought what was it with the black SUV's anyway? Almost everyone in the company had one. Just to be different, she had demanded a red one - against her Dad's wishes. She came back to the present as Steven answered the phone. She forestalled him by speaking first.

"Hi, Sweetie! I just landed," she said to him.

"Hello?" Drawled a sleepy, seductive female voice.

Kaitlan's stomach and chest became tight with fear, and feeling her stomach roll, she said the first thing that came to her mind.

"May I speak with Steven, please?" She asked, her voice slightly shaky. Please, she prayed, let me have dialed the wrong number, or at least let the wires have crossed!

To her chagrin, Steven's voice came on the line.

"Hello?" Muttered Steven with a sleepy voice.

"Do you normally have sleepovers when I have to leave, Steven?" Kaitlan was madder than hell!

"Kaitlan? Are you all right, love? You made it?"

It was obvious that Steven had been asleep - and he was definitely not alone! That BASTARD! She could hear his nervousness even over the phone.

"Kaitlan? Darling, are you *OK*?"

As if she did not know that he had a girl in his bed? Was he seriously asking her that? Her best friend, Sarah Collins, had warned her hadn't she? But, no! She just couldn't listen, could she? She shook her head at her own stupidity, and it was the end of their relationship right then and there for her.

"When the cat's away, the jerk of a mouse will play it would seem! We are done!"

As she snapped her phone shut, she heard him say, "Kaitlan! I'm sorry! Let me expla...!"

Explain? What was he going to tell her? That he had invited an overnight guest to play tonsil hockey along with his very own form of "male plug into the female plug" as a bonus?

In seconds, Steven rang her back. She ignored the first two rings, and finally turned her phone off. Settling back in her seat, she felt a very dark mood invade her mind. How could he have done this to her? She really had believed that he loved her. She felt depressed, but she wouldn't let the tears come. Being confronted with the truth usually does that to a person. She wasn't going to cry over a cheater. Tears spilled down her cheeks in silence. Damn it!! Sarah HAD been right! She had warned her that Steven was a womanizer. Kaitlan just hadn't believed it, but believed Steven had changed just for her. Women always dream that they can change the worst of womanizers if they knew their perfect mate was them, but the truth is, they don't. Leopards truly cannot change their spots any more than a man can change his craving for women.

Sarah had told her that Steven only proposed so he could "get in your pants", as she had so colorfully put it. Kaitlan just didn't believe it, but then, she had to admit to herself that she had planned to let him "get in her pants" that very night before her Dad interfered. She shook her head as quiet tears streamed down her face at how stupid she had been. She looked up, and noticed Dan Wheeler looking at her through his sunglasses with understanding. She quickly looked down, taking her sunglasses out, and pushing them onto her nose.

"Ms. O'Hara. I am going to raise the divider between us so you can have some privacy."

Kaitlan nodded gratefully, and the divider rose between them. She picked up her phone, turned it on again, and dialed Sarah's number, but only got her voice mail. She checked her watch, and remembered that Sarah and Tom Foster, her fiancé, had a date. Tears fell, as she wanted so badly to have someone love her the way that Tom loved Sarah. So, she just left her a message.

"You were right, Sarah," and shut the phone off knowing that Sarah would understand. What was worse? Her Father had also been right.

Kaitlan opened her carry on, and retrieved some pain medicine, the bottle of water she had carried onto the plane, and swallowed the pills, then leaned her head against the seat back closing her eyes, and allowing the pain to consume her.

~ 3 ~

Why Can't Life Just be Simple?

Canaan O'Hara stood staring at St. Louis from the walls of windows that graced his office, but wasn't seeing the amazing view of the city he had made his own over the years. Damn! He hated cussing - from everyone else. He, however, usually cussed alone. He knew how angry Kaitlan was at his decision. Running his hands through his light brown hair, his guilt grew, because he had not told his only daughter who…no…what she really was, and why he would be sending her away. He knew he would never see her again, and this brought heaviness to his heart. It was imperative that she be kept safe, and anonymous, as to where she was. His very position brought danger to her life. Sam had informed him that Zanack had raised his head, again. And, Canaan knew he had been targeted. He had used the words that they had agreed upon long ago, warning Cordone his daughter's life was in danger, and that Canaan's own life was in danger. But, he wasn't afraid of death. He wanted to go to his mate he missed so much. He was afraid for Kaitlan's life.

His mind drifted back into the pain that enveloped him when his beloved wife, and mate, had died in childbirth, and her last words to him.

His Second, Cordone Valon, had come to the rescue when Tara had gone into early labor at their home. The doctor had been out tending to an accident which had severed a limb of a Clan member, and since Cordone had triage experience, and had delivered several babies through the years, he was the only one qualified to deliver Canaan and Tara's baby. Canaan had held his mate's hand as something went horribly wrong with her blood while Cordone had delivered their stillborn child. The pain and guilty look in Cordone's eyes as he held the tiny little girl in his hands, dripping with blood, yet away from his mate's view, told Canaan all he needed to know. He nodded to Cordone who had taken the child away. His mate had bled extensively. It could not be stopped, and no one knew the reason even years later. Even though she was so weak, she had begged to see her child, and Canaan had told her that the baby needed a bit of medical attention since it was born prematurely. This seemed to calm his mate down. But, he did not leave her side, and never would until the end.

When Anita Moore, their Clan doctor, had finally arrived, and taken over, she had told Cordone that even she could have done nothing. It wasn't until recently that Anita had discovered the cause, because several females in the Clan had been poisoned, and at least one had died of the same symptoms. Tara had been given a refined concoction through her IV bag made from Wolfsbane - a deadly plant in its pure form that kept blood from coagulating. Kaitlan had received a small amount, almost killing her.

Nevertheless, that did not ease Cordone's soul.

Cordone joined Sam in guarding their leader and his mate outside the door, but try as they might, they couldn't keep from hearing their last words. Both would go to their graves with what they heard.

"My love, please...keep her safe whatever you have to do," gasped Tara.

With tears in his eyes, he had promised her without reservations. "I will, my darling. With my life."

His mate was everything to him. It had been his choice to choose a human mate. As if he even had a choice in the first place. Once he had seen her, she was his forever. He did not regret it, until now, as he watched the life drain from her eyes. He had waited for over a thousand years for her, and in just a few minutes, he was losing her forever. He did not believe his heart could live after her death. No. He would shut down, and die as well. He had just been told his daughter was stillborn. He wanted to howl, and hit someone - no kill someone. He literally had to restrain himself to keep from doing so. Tara's eyes saw his struggle. He went over what was said that day.

Tara Michelle Seneca O'Hara reached toward him weakly with her hand, and he grabbed it holding it to his heart so she could hear it beating. For her, only for her. She smiled at him.

"I regret nothing, Canaan. You are mine, my life, my love, my mate, and my husband. You gave me an amazing life for the last fifty years. Never forget that you and I both chose this life together."

He nodded as a tear slipped off his chin, and landed on her hand.

He started to speak, but she said, "No. Let me finish before my life is over. It's very important for you to understand that Kaitlan is who she is - half you, and half me. The very fact that she is here is a complete miracle! We were never supposed to be compatible at all for children. She is extremely special, Canaan, and will change the Clan forever. I don't know how I know it, but the Creator does. Even though I will be gone, she will be here. Remember to have understanding with her. Canaan, Kaitlan is more than just you and me. I cannot explain this, but she is here for a real reason. Do not let her be hurt. She must complete her purpose for the Clan."

Canaan had nodded. He knew Kaitlan would have been in danger had she lived. Even though her words puzzled and surprised him as to how she could feel something so supernatural, he would not let his mate down. Life was so precious, and his mate's was the most precious. He also knew that Tara was right about her feelings, because he, and the others, felt it as well. But, she didn't know that the daughter they had made from their love was dead.

"Tara, how will I ever live and exist without you? You are the part of my heart I could never have believed possible. When we met, I remembered the draw to you was so strong, I could never have ignored it for very long, even if I had wanted."

She smiled, and gave him a weak laugh. "But

you did try, my love."

Even through his tears, he laughed aloud, as they both remembered together.

Canaan had taken Tara as his mate at the young age of seventeen. She was an orphan, and had no family. They had met by accident when Canaan had gone to deliver his yearly donation to the Orphanage he had created, because of his love of children. He had turned quickly to leave, and mowed down Tara, knocking her to the floor. Reaching down to help her up, he apologized, then looked into her brilliant green eyes, and he knew, immediately, she was his mate. His kind mated for life.

He had fought like hell not to mate with her, because she was so young, and human. He'd been horribly ashamed of desiring an underage teenager! Yet, he found himself picking her up, taking her to concerts, dinners, and movies. She was an amazing young girl, and he loved to tease her with "blonde jokes". Her long, "down to the waist" blonde hair, was gorgeous. Her body, lean and slim. Her skin was fair as the dawn, and flawless. He had longed to touch it.

He had finally told her what he was, explained what was happening, and told her of their mating bond rituals trying to drive her away from him. But, Tara would not be dissuaded from that in anyway. She didn't care. She loved him to distraction. She was his mate. He had insisted that they wait, at least until her eighteenth birthday, but Tara wouldn't let up. Her love was so strong for him, she kept insisting they were meant to be together before her birthday. She didn't know why, she just knew that they had to mate before that date.

And, then, the day came. On that rainy and stormy night, he was exhausted when he had entered his house. A business deal gone wrong always irritated him. He had gone upstairs to his bedroom, stripped, and was in his briefs before he turned to go into the bathroom for his shower. He stopped dead in his tracks. There, in his bed, lay Tara waiting for him covered only by a sheet. His wolf and human form were stunned to find her there! Candles were everywhere, and the light was low. In the lightning of the storm, he saw her beautiful face surrounded by extremely blonde hair that spilled down in front, and hung below her waist. It was only a month before Tara's eighteenth birthday. She sat up, and he watched as she deliberately allowed the sheet to slip down from her body, revealing her blonde hair framing her breasts. She was the most beautiful woman he had ever seen in his life, and his breath caught in his throat. She then had slowly pulled the sheet away from her body, revealing her nudity to him. She was prepared, and waiting to mate with him. Her first words had broken his restraint as he heard her use the special words of mating. Everyone's was different, but the words that came out of Tara's mouth were extremely unusual. She not only gave herself to him as his mate, but immediately after, accepted him as her mate. He'd never heard it done like that before, and because she did, he couldn't refuse. Tara revealed just how smart she was in that moment. She would give him no way out but to take her as his mate.

Mating was always done naked, because of the seriousness, and heavy desire that followed immediately after the Blood Bonding, when the urge to impregnate the female was so strong that the consummation of the mates was immediate, and fierce.

"Canaan O'Hara, I give to you, this night, myself for mating, and I accept you as my mate, my love, and my life. I give myself to you, tonight, in the Blood Bond as is custom through your heritage. I love you with all of my heart." She, then, turned her neck to him.

He realized in that moment that Tara was not a child, or a teenager, but a woman in his eyes. He had groaned, and relented as he stripped, and made her his mate that night, and all the next day. He had never regretted it. Tara, somehow, had the vision of foresight, and she had been right. There had been a reason for their mating. He, now realized, that it had been no accident. She had been fated to eventually become pregnant, and to give birth to their child.

"I did, didn't I? But, Tara, I knew it, even though I fought against it, because of the difficulty and danger that it could cause you - us. I still don't understand why it happened, but frankly, I don't really care. You are my reason for living."

He paused when Tara's face showed the pain she was suffering. Her hand clenched his as the pain increased. They were never compatible for a child, yet here they were...his mate was dying giving birth to that child. He wanted to howl with the unfairness of it all. He would be following her within a few days. As if Tara knew his thoughts, she issued her final order to him - one she knew he could not disobey.

"No, Canaan. Listen to me! You cannot follow me! Not yet. It's not your time, and I forbid it! You will raise our daughter to adulthood. You must keep her safe! Something bad is at work. Don't think I don't know I was poisoned." Canaan's head rose sharply. He had no idea that she knew! "And, don't think she is dead, Canaan. Kaitlan is not dead! Believe…me! I give… my life… for…….. hers……"

Her words trailing, Canaan jerked his head up. She knew her child was stillborn? They hadn't told her! How? And, then, Tara's hand relaxed as the pain receded, and Canaan knew it was almost over. She would have no more pain ever again in just a few moments.

"It is time, Canaan. I am being called by something…I do not understand. The light…is…just so…beauti…ful!"

Tara's free arm reached toward something Canaan could not see, and then, her beautiful, brilliant, green eyes slowly closed forever, and her smile was dazzling as she slipped quietly into death. Canaan collapsed across her body, and refused to let anyone near his beloved. He was left alone to grieve as he sprawled over his mate and wife, while both Sam and Cordone stood guard outside the door. No one would dare cross them.

Canaan stayed for a very, very long time. He had forgotten all outside that room. How long he stayed there, he didn't know, but he was ready to die as well. His heart could not take the grief, and he knew it. Mates could not live without the other. This was a fact. And, apparently, it didn't matter if one of them was human. But, strangely, she had given him an order - her last. Raise their daughter. She said Kaitlan was not dead! But, she was. So, he was not bound by her order. In that instant, he felt the bond between them break away at the same time somewhere outside the room, he heard the cry of a child. A baby cried waking him from the darkness that had engulfed him. His head rose realizing that the cry was coming from just outside the door. He stood as the door opened.

The door was thrown open by Sam who was stunned, yet grinning from ear to ear as he stood aside to let Canaan's best friend, and Second, walk into the room holding a tiny bundle in a pink blanket that was wiggling, and howling angrily. The sudden stop in her crying happened when she looked up into Cordone's black eyes. It was comical, and almost funny. Canaan saw that it was an obvious struggle for Cordone as he tried to reign in his emotions, but he walked into the room, and nodded his head in disbelief. Canaan stood, and walked to him. Cordone placed the tiny little baby into her Father's arms. Peripherally, Canaan saw Cordone barely shake with jealousy, and inside grinned widely. Even in that moment of grief, he had seen Cordone's eyes glowing which told Canaan that Cordone had gazed upon his mate whom he had delivered. Nothing could have pleased Canaan more, and he knew Tara would have approved with zeal, because she loved Cordone as if he was her own brother.

Canaan had lifted the blanket. He looked into her tiny, beautiful face, surrounded by blonde curls, and brilliant green eyes so like Tara's. She was the exact image of his mate. A smile broke across her face as she saw her Father for the first time. Startled by the smile, he lifted a finger, and stroked his daughter's face gently, and she giggled. He turned to his mate's bed, and leaned down as if Tara could see her. And, in truth, maybe she could.

"She IS alive, Tara! She's alive!!! Thank the Creator!! I will never let anything happen to this most precious of gifts, my beloved mate. She will be safe, and if ever there is something that will threaten her, I will make sure she is sent somewhere that is safe. This I vow to you my love."

With that, Canaan stood, kissed his mate's lips for the last time, and walked out of the room giving a sad nod to Sam and Cordone to prepare his mate for the final rites. He turned, and walked down the hall into the future with his daughter in his arms. No one had an answer how she had lived.

"Excuse me, Canaan, but Lon McClain is here," his private secretary, Lynne, told him which shook him out of his memories. He turned, and sat in his chair.

"Send him in, Lynne," and groaned. He didn't

like Lon McClain. Never had. He motioned to McClain to sit down, beginning their weekly updates on Clan business.

~ **4** ~

Into the Wolf's Den Rode the Platinum Blonde!

"We'll be at Mr. Valon's house in about fifteen minutes, Ms. O'Hara," said Dan.

Kaitlan opened her eyes, and stared around her in surprise, forgetting for a moment where she was. She must have fallen asleep from the terror of flying combined with the horror of discovering her fiancé had cheated on her less than twenty-four hours after he proposed to her!

Kaitlan wasn't the stereotype blonde who primped, and had to have her hair and makeup in place perfectly all the time. She'd never been that way, and she saw no reason to change now. She sat up, and wearily ran her fingers through her hair, not really caring how she looked. It had been a long day, and now, one of the worst days of her entire life thanks to Steven.

She pulled out her phone to try Sarah again, and realized there was no service. Damn it! She should have guessed that it would happen in the mountains. But, with a sigh, she started to put it back in her purse, then noticed she had no less than seven texts! Checking them out, six were from Steve which she deleted without reading. The last one was from Sarah who had very little text shorthand, so she always texted in full words.

"Sorry, honey. I really hoped I was not wrong. Tried calling. No answer. Figured you were in area without service. BTW…We broke up! Text when you can. Love you!"

She and Tom broke up? She really wished Sarah would expand on her texts more! She was eager to find out why, and texted her back. Two could play at that game!

"You broke up? WTF! That's it? Seriously, Pixie, more info! BTW…I'm going to edit a book @ Cordone Valon's house! TTFN!"

She sent the text, and put her phone back into her purse. Kaitlan grinned. Let Ms. Bubbly and Happy all the time, Sarah, figure THAT one out! Damn, but she was going to miss her! Well, it wouldn't be forever.

Now, to the man waiting for her expertise. Truth be told, she was terrified of meeting Cordone Valon. Her Father was always "kissing his ass". Why, for the Creator's sake?

Valon was an enigma. She knew what he looked like thanks to the jackets on the books, but she had never met him personally. Even Sarah had it "bad" for him. He was an enormously popular Science Fiction novelist. But, he wrote under the pen name of Jack Lawson. OK. Kaitlan admitted it to herself. Maybe she did had a crush on him - just a little bit.

"There is the house, Ms. O'Hara," said Dan

interrupting her thoughts, waving to the side of the mountain.

Turning, Kaitlan felt her mouth drop open. It was a mansion of enormous size and proportion - and built into the side of a mountain! It was totally unbelievable! Was she seeing things? It appeared to have five stories at the very least. Maybe six? Kaitlan wondered how he had managed building it! The entire front of the building was nothing but glass that reflected, and mirrored the view that it faced, almost giving it the appearance of invisibility.

She gasped, and Dan remarked, "It does take your breath away, doesn't it? I remember the first time I saw it. Still does." He smiled at her in the mirror. "That is nothing. Wait till you see the inside!"

Holy cow! Kaitlan had met the wealthiest of the wealthy, but this? This man, Valon, had to be beyond wealthy! There was no way that his books ever paid for a house carved into a mountain! She was so out of her element!

Dan turned onto the winding road leading upward to the house. And, finally, a humongous garage. Yep. No other word for it. Five garage doors? Gaping, as Dan drove in to park, she found the garage was filled with the newest cars and trucks on one side, and on the other, a collection of antique vehicles. She just stared as she saw Model A's and T's, Rolls Royce, Bentley, and other well-known cars that are exclusive to the very rich only. And, then, she saw her favorite car of all time...a Rolls Royce Phantom II!

There were only 1680 of them ever made between 1929 and 1936! Holy RR Phantom II, Batman!

Dan drove the SUV into a spot marked, SUV CR-V, and parked. She had barely even reached for the handle when Dan already had it open. Wait. How did he get over here so fast? It was a mere second since he had stepped out wasn't it? Maybe she had been staring at the RR a bit too long. Yes. That had to be it. Nothing else made any sense. Shaking off that thought, she stepped out of the SUV, and said, "Thank you, Dan, and please. Call me Kaitlan. I'm just not used to answering to formality."

He proceeded to get her luggage.

"This way, Ms. O'Ha...uh...I mean Kaitlan," he grinned sheepishly leading her to a door on the far side of the garage. Only it wasn't a door, but an elevator?

Seeing her eyebrow lift in question, Dan explained, "Cordone is very in tune with his friends and visitors to the house, and makes sure everyone has access to all parts of the property."

Friends? Visitors? Valon was rumored to be so secluded, he had no friends at all. This was a revelation to her. Her Dad never said anything about Valon having friends. He only dated on occasion when one of his books was published. Dan stood to the side allowing her to enter first, then pushed a button with the number "5" on it. The elevator was made of all glass. Valon certainly didn't want anything to obstruct his view, did he?

The mansion - a totally inappropriate name for it

- was five stories high, and looked down upon a five story atrium. The solid glass wall looked out onto the most amazing view, but it was the inside that had her mouth hanging open. The landings were designed in half-moon shapes leading to at least three rooms on each of the top two floors. Forgetting her fear of heights, Kaitlan looked over the railing and below, she saw three other graduated landings. Floors two and three were split in the center with bridges connecting the landings. A three story, natural rock waterfall flowed between them, and into a natural rock pool on the main floor. Outward from the pool, there was a fire pit in the central area with a solid copper hood over it larger than the pit, which rose through the glass roof ventilating the smoke. An open fire pit? Inside? Seriously? The roof was at least half-way glass for natural lighting to flow into the house making one feel as if they were outside. Her mouth open, she giggled when a picture appeared in her mind of the a movie that had a pendulum in it. Dang! What was the name of that movie? She forgot.

Aloud, she asked Dan, "Where's the pendulum?"

Dan gave her a puzzled look.

"Never mind. Bad joke," she laughed.

There was overstuffed seating in what she was sure was dark chocolate brown leather surrounding the pit, along with matching curved sofas and chairs. Other colors were in woodsy fall colors of golds, yellows, oranges, maroons, and dark wood furniture. They made the entire room look homey. Yep.

Definitely all male designed - and beautiful.

She turned to look at Dan who just grinned at her as if to say, "Everyone has the same reaction."

"Let me show you to your room, Kaitlan."

Dan turned to lead her along the landing. He stopped at the room directly in the center. There were at least three rooms on this landing, and each had a large, picture window open to the main room, and the view through the massive window could be seen. It was almost as if one was living outside instead of inside.

He turned the door handle designed as a branch, and opened it. "Each room has it's own personality, Kaitlan. This is the green room. I hope it will be satisfactory."

Kaitlan stepped into the room. She had yet to shut her mouth. She was in perpetual "awe mode". The room was beautiful, and decorated in her very favorite colors of greens, reds and blues. That was really strange! How did Valon know? Surely they didn't decorate it just for her? It was nothing but a coincidence, she thought, forgetting that she didn't believe in them. The room had to be no less than 1400 square feet! In the center, was a bed straight out of a spy novel. It was circular with white netting draping all around. The duvet was blood-red in color, and loaded with snow white pillows giving the false impression that they were just randomly thrown onto the bed. The bed was strategically placed so that one could see outside the window through to the main window outside. The glass was ingenious. No one could see inside the room, but it was clear to the outside! Just like the glass wall and roof in the main room. That was the reason for no drapes or curtains.

There was a huge dresser behind the bed, and a triple chest on the left with a huge mirror. A fireplace was to the right with a fire crackling happily in it. The mantel...she squinted. Was that...was that green marble? REAL green marble? The floor was of stone, obviously carved out of the mountain. As smooth as possible, it shined as if it had been polished by a special tool.

A thick, large, sandy colored rug was sprawled over the stone underneath the bed, and reaching out to cover most of the stone floor. The walls were dark mahogany wood, and beautifully paneled in a carved design she had never seen before. The wall over the fireplace sported a 65 inch flat screen TV. It was minimalist with a few paintings hanging on the walls. Lamps were scattered around. No lighting hung from the ceiling. There were real plants scattered around the perimeter giving the place a peaceful and relaxing feel, and yet they were set into a groove that had been carved from the stone so watering wouldn't be a problem. A more careful look revealed several drain holes to take the excess water away, while above were sprinklers to water the plants!

Dan placed her suitcases on the floor by the door, and led her to the back of the room where there was another door next to the dresser. He opened it.

"This is the bathroom," he stated.

The bathroom was huge - and carved out of solid

stone! All of it! It had a massive walk-in closet to the left that was lined with solid mahogany on the walls and ceiling. There was a built-in dehumidifier inside to keep out any form of moisture, and the door shut without a crack in it. To the back there was a sunken tub carved into the stone with at least two steps going down into it, and attached was a sunken shower at least twelve feet long, and eight feet wide which had a waterfall running in it combined with many shower heads inside! It even had a carved, reclining stone seat in the shower for relaxing on! To enter the shower, one had to navigate a glass, "S" curved entrance so no doors, or curtain, was needed. How did they carve all this? It was as if it was done by magic! To the left was a large, six foot long, green marble cabinet complete with at least two table top sinks along one entire wall including a vanity and chair. A cabinet was available for toiletries. There was a compartment specifically for the commode with a similar entrance as the shower giving total privacy. A sixty-inch flat screen television hung on the wall opposite the tub! Seriously? Is this place for real???

"Will this be satisfactory, Kaitlan," asked Dan, again.

She turned, and looked at him.

"Well, if it wasn't, I might be pretty damned hard to please!"

Dan threw back his head, and laughed outright.

"I like you, Kaitlan! I'll leave you to get settled. Cordone has asked that you join him for a late dinner about nine o'clock."

"Sure. That's fine," Kaitlan said absently, still absorbed in the room that was to be hers for however long.

Then, she thought of something, and ran to open the door to ask Dan how to get to the dining room. He hadn't been gone two seconds, but...where was he? He was just standing here, and now, he wasn't. That was just so weird...just like this house. And, just like her Dad who didn't give her any information about anything either. Her Dad also had the oddity of seeming to move fast as well. She had lived with it all her life, but she never really paid any attention to it - until now. She scratched her head, and realized she felt grubby and dirty. Shrugging her shoulders, she walked back into the room, and closed the door.

Grabbing her suitcase, she quickly unpacked her underwear, and almost skipped to the bathroom for a shower!   She couldn't wait to try it out!

That was the most AMAZING shower she had EVER had in her entire life! She had sat in the shower for at least an hour, letting the water run over her body. More than that, the water had smelled like lavender, and her body was bathed in it. No wonder she was relaxed!

She found a red robe hanging on the back of the door, and put it on. Soft and plush, she decided she could sleep in it if she wanted! Sleep. Suddenly, exhaustion took her over, and she stumbled to the bed. That concluded a "great" day. Her Father sending her to an unknown place to meet a client she had never met, while her fiancé - ex-fiancé, now - wasted no time whatsoever sticking his - well, way TMI. Yep. Best day ever. Besides, for some reason, she found she really didn't care at all. What would Freud say it meant? The bed was calling her. She lay down, and fell asleep in an instant.

~ 5 ~

"Never Say Never". It WILL Come Back to Bite You in the Butt!

A knocking was really bugging Kaitlan, and she just wanted it to stop. Her head was really killing her. She just wanted to sleep. To get away from the pain.

"Kaitlan?" A voice asked.

Opening her eyes, she realized she had passed out on the bed, and that Dan was knocking on her door.

"Yes?" She called sleepily.

"Dinner will be ready in about thirty minutes. Cordone asks that you meet him on the main floor in fifteen minutes, if that's OK?"

Kaitlan groaned. Time to meet the recluse with the amazing house. For whatever reason, she was really nervous about it. But, out loud she replied, "Sure. Will do!"

"I will tell Cordone. Press "main" in the elevator. There are no stairs. It will take you directly to the main floor," Dan instructed.

"Thank you. Tell Mr. Valon I will be there." Her eyes flew open. Did Dan just say there were no stairs? What kind

of house has no stairs? She must have misunderstood him.

She rolled out of bed, and stumbled into the bathroom. Looking into the mirror, she slumped her shoulders. Well, this was just great! Her hair was matted with tangles, because she had not taken the time to brush it out while it was wet. She really hated her hair, sometimes. She put her hands on the counter, and leaned forward.

What looked back at her, was a young, twenty-six year-old, platinum blonde girl with wavy hair that reached half way to her waist. Her eyes were the most brilliant green, and almost had a shine to them. She had light skin without blemish. Sporting a small nose, a perfect mouth, which did not need any lipstick (and she never wore it anyway), she was, well, cute? Kaitlan hated her height, and while she was proud that she was what some called "a real woman", because of her curves, most people would see that she was the perfect sized woman. At five-foot, four inches, her bust was a size 36C (why couldn't she have a larger one like Lynne's ample D?). Her abs were tight, her body slim, but her hips curved outward, and were the same measurement as her bust. Kaitlan sighed. At least she was not a "stick" like most other girls her age, and for that, she was glad.

All in all, she saw maybe not a "pretty girl", but she was cute, anyway. Maybe.

"Your loss, Steven!" Sticking out her tongue at the mirror. Not that he could see it, but it sure made her feel a whole lot better!

She looked at her engagement ring. She had

been so happy when he had slipped it on her finger, and it was extravagantly expensive, too. About three carats. But, now she questioned how she really felt. How did she feel? Humiliated came to mind, but surprisingly, that was about all.   Staring into her own eyes, she realized she really didn't care about him as much as she had thought. Kaitlan was over him, and if it was that easy, then her heart was never involved to begin with anyway.

Grinning with the truth, Kaitlan removed the ring, dropped it, and flushed it away. Real, or not, she wouldn't have cared. She grinned wider. If he ever asked for her to return it, well, she'd just have to tell him about the "accident", now wouldn't she?

Kaitlan brushed her hair to a glimmering shine as best she could, but it was still messy. She finally gave up, and pulled it into a pony tail. Not professional, but she was going to be here for a while any way, so what was the point? Cordone Valon may as well see her the way she really was. Sarah, and others may be all "ga-ga" about Valon, but she wouldn't let his good looks effect her into looking like a Barbie doll!

Looking at her watch, she only had just under ten minutes, and thanks to her day dreaming, Kaitlan darted quickly into the bedroom to her luggage, and whipped out a pair of jeans with rhinestones on the back pockets. Throwing off her robe, she looked for the bras she had packed. Where the hell were they?

She dumped the contents on the bed frantically trying to find them. She found her underwear, but not her bras. Shit! She must have forgotten to pack them! She was so mad at her Dad this morning, she wasn't paying a lot of attention to packing. She did find her exercise bra, though. She NEVER left home without it! Good thing, because her other bra she had washed out, was left hanging on the shower door, and still wet. While the sports bra supported her breasts when she was exercising, it did nothing to hide the points that showed at the end of her workout. But, it was better than not wearing one, and letting them bounce in front of a total stranger.

Putting it on, Kaitlan followed with a red, v-neck, long-sleeved sweater, then yanked her jeans up which parked about one inch below her waist.

Kaitlan just wasn't a vain woman. Yet, she really had no idea how beautiful she really was. In fact, she had always been insecure about her looks despite what her Dad, and others, told her. She didn't believe people, anyway.

Traipsing out the door and down the platform, she entered the elevator, yet again, but this time to join Cordone Valon in the dining room for dinner. She had no idea what she would find in Valon, and she was extremely nervous about this first meeting.

In his study, Cordone Valon had sat brooding, just before Kaitlan had arrived. He had returned Canaan's call from earlier. Lynne DeVane, Canaan's secretary, had told him that Canaan had Lon McClain in with him, and wanted him to hold. Gritting his teeth, he told Lynne that he would wait. He had no idea what Canaan wanted this time. It was Canaan's second call that day to him. He figured it was probably about Kaitlan, again. Earlier, Canaan had called to tell him he was sending Kaitlan to him for protection.

Cordone was one of the most popular science fiction writers in the world. For the last twenty-six years, his frustration at not seeing his mate needed an outlet, and writing had been just the right therapy. His very appearance, when he did make a public event, sent women into fits of melt-downs. But, he had no eyes for anyone but Kaitlan. His hair was short and peppered black and white. His deeply tanned body was due, mostly, to the Colorado's almost full year sunny days with little to no clouds, and toned by the result of hours in his personal gym. His writing was his outlet for his feelings, but his gym was there for his sexual frustrations always followed by an ice cold shower under his waterfall. His eyes were black as night, and sometimes, his pupils were completely invisible. His nose was regal while his mouth was all man, and a bit crooked giving him a wicked grin when he smiled. His abs were so well defined he almost had eight packs instead of the normal six. His hips were slender, his arms and legs strong, and extremely muscular for his six feet-three inches.

"Keep her safe," Canaan had asked of him. Canaan didn't have to ever ask him! But, this wasn't going to be easy on Cordone. Kaitlan was still his mate. He wondered how she would feel when he told her, because he had no choice, now. It had been forced upon him.

Cordone ran his hand through his hair, a habit he couldn't seem to break, thinking back to the night Tara had died twenty-seven years ago tomorrow. He had never understood why Canaan had picked a human for his mate. Nope. Still couldn't figure it out. But, regardless, he admitted that Tara had been the kindest person he had ever met, and she had won Cordone over along with the rest of the Clan. Almost immediately, Tara had gained their respect and loyalty. He would have taken a bullet for her. Hell! He would have died for her! She had been feisty, and if her husband went into a battle, so did she, regardless of the fact she was human. She proved to the Clan that she was Alpha, and able to stand, and fight when it was necessary, right by Canaan's side.

The night Tara had died, Anita Moore, their doctor, had not been available, and Cordone had been in Canaan's study at home, discussing Clan business when Tara had gone into labor. They had taken Tara to the infirmary in the Seneca Publishing House building. Because he had field training in medicine, Cordone was the only one qualified to deliver Kaitlan. The child had been stillborn, and Tara's blood could not be stopped. He remembered removing Kaitlan from the room quickly, giving the stillborn child to Anita's nurse, Teri, who whisked the baby away. Then, he had joined Sam standing watch outside the room, protecting them from any outsider who would dare to enter. He loved his friend without reservations. His respect and loyalty to Canaan and Tara was without question. He was Canaan's Second, and no one ever questioned Cordone - EVER. He could not help but hurt deeply for his friend as he said goodbye to his mate. While he may not have known what that felt like, there was no doubt in his mind that to be loved like that would be a true blessing. So many had never found a mate, and his heart had constricted when he heard Tara say her last words to Canaan. He and Sam had done their best not to hear, but with their hearing, it was impossible not to do so. Even in her death, Tara would not say anything evil about another person. Her kindness was so pure that she left this world in peace never knowing her child was dead.

Later, Anita would tell Cordone it wasn't his fault, and Canaan didn't blame him in the least. Eventually, Anita had discovered that someone had poisoned Tara with the one thing that could kill all supernaturals which was a refined chemical made from Wolfsbane. Somehow, it had been injected into Tara's IV bag, and that was what caused her to bleed out. Nothing could have stopped the child being stillborn, nor Tara from bleeding to death, because of the deadly plant. Watching Teri walking down the hallway carrying the tiny little baby away forever, his heart sank in his chest for his friend and leader. How the person got to Tara was a mystery. Cordone knew he would kill whoever had done this with his bare hands! And, no doubt, Sam would have his back when he did so. But, they never found the murderer, despite the intensive search.

Canaan had spent over 5 hours in the room after Tara's death. How horrible to lose the two people one loved most in this life at the same time.

Right then and there, Cordone had vowed to himself he would never, as in NEVER, take a mate.

As we all know, a person should "NEVER say never". It always comes back to bite them in the backside! So, naturally, the minute he finished that vow to himself, he saw Anita, who had just returned, sprinting down the hallway holding a tiny bundle in a pink blanket - and it was moving! The smile on her face illuminated the hallway as she reached Cordone and Sam. She looked up at Cordone with a smile so dazzling, he knew immediately what was in that tiny bundle! The child was alive! How was that possible? He looked at Sam whose lips turned up in the widest smile he had ever seen on Sam's face - before, or since. Sam just never smiled at all.

Cordone held out his arms, and the doctor placed the tiny, pink bundle in them gently. The Doctor lifted a corner of the blanket. The tiny little girl yawned, wiggled, and then howled in his arms as she opened her eyes. She sounded just like her Father, and he smiled. Cordone had been stunned when those same beautiful, brilliant, glowing green eyes of Tara's looked up into his, and the baby stopped yelling immediately. For what seemed like forever, their eyes were locked on each other. His world was rocked, throwing him totally off kilter as he stared into those green eyes framed with the round, porcelain face haloed with outstanding golden hair with waves. He felt his black eyes begin to glow.

Cordone had caught his breath, and almost choked, but somehow, he managed to keep quiet. Silently, he said to himself, "Kaitlan. Mate." He tightened his arms automatically in protection while trying to keep an unemotional face to the others. It was the hardest thing he had ever done in his life, and harder, still, not to tell Canaan that he had just claimed his best friend's daughter - the one he held tightly in his arms - as his mate! What kind of a man was he? To claim a mate on her birth? He never thought himself a pervert, but now he wondered. She smiled at him, and her green eyes held a beautiful, slight glow, as if she had claimed him as her mate! That slight green glow shook his soul to its foundation. He smiled tenderly back at her, but it would not do to let anyone see how much this little girl had affected him. Canaan would lock him away forever! He knew, one day, he'd have to tell him, but this was not the day.

He had never expected this to happen, not right after his own vow to himself a few minutes prior. He gained a bit of control, and without looking into Sam's eyes, nodded at Sam to open the door. Sam would know immediately what had happened if he saw his glowing eyes. Cordone struggled to stop the glow. Then, Cordone walked through the door to present the child - his mate - to her Father.

Canaan had looked up at him, his eyes streaming with tears, and saw a little bundle that was wiggling. With the best smile he could pretend on his face, Cordone's eyes were dimming, but not enough, so, instead, he nodded his head at the dazed look on Canaan's face without raising his eyes. And, then, almost with a growl, he passed the tiny baby to her Father. Cordone's emotions were totally inappropriate as he felt jealousy of another holding Kaitlan even if it was her Father. He knew it, but he couldn't help it. Now, he knew what Canaan had felt when he'd seen Tara. It didn't matter to him at all that she was part human. He watched Kaitlan's tiny mouth smile up at her Father with innocence and total trust. No...this was not the time nor the place. But, he knew he could not stay with the Clan without claiming her, now. No. Cordone didn't entertain the thought that he would do something like that when she was a child - ever. He only knew that when she grew up, it would be a whole different matter altogether. All he wanted, right now, was to protect her with his life, and know she was happy. And, to protect her against him. Slowly, he walked out the door, and shut it. He didn't look at Sam who was stunned as he watched Cordone walk down the hallway, and out the doors. He left, resigned his position as Second, and never returned. He couldn't stay without betraying his leader, or the tiny little baby he had just given away who was his mate, and that he would never do. His honor and loyalty remained intact.

He had boarded his jet, and left the area forever, and into the Rockies to his family home.

~ 6 ~

How Much Worse Can It Get? Don't ask!
Never ask!

"Cordone?" Canaan's voice had brought his thoughts to an abrupt halt. "Here, Canaan."

"Sorry to have kept you waiting, but you know how Lon can be."

Cordone closed his eyes. He sure did know how Lon could be. He had never liked the guy, and the only reason Canaan had put him on the council was because he was an outstanding researcher of the law.

"There are two things I need to discuss with you. First, Kaitlan and I have been targeted by someone calling himself Zanack."

Cordone's head had jerked up. It couldn't be! They'd gotten rid of him! He'd killed him personally! Cordone's hand grasped the phone hard hearing a slight cracking. Damn! He'd cracked another one!

"What the fuck, Canaan? I killed him myself. I took him apart, and burned his body while everyone watched!   How could Zanack be back?"

"I don't know." Canaan answered him. "If I knew the answer to that one, I'd have the answer to everything!"

"How do you know both of you have been targeted?" He asked sharply.

He stilled himself as he had tried to reign in his passion for Kaitlan to keep his friend from realizing how scared he was for his mate. He still felt guilty for having chosen her as his mate, although Canaan never knew it. He couldn't risk him finding out about it.

"A note somehow managed to make it to my desk without benefit of the Post Office. Both of us are in danger, Cordone. Her life has been threatened, as has mine. It was signed 'Zanack'."

Cordone had fallen in his desk chair while his right hand raked through his hair. This can't be happening! What the hell was going on?

"Shit! No Post Office." He said making a statement, not asking a question. "That means it could be internal."

"My thoughts exactly. I have to get Kaitlan away from here, Cordone, and I am sending her to you. Please, keep her safe. There is no one I trust more than you. She must be kept safe at all costs. My life is not my worry. I want to go to my mate. I will NOT let Kaitlan be killed! "

"She is coming today, then?"

"Yes. She's on her way. "

"Good. Whoever is claiming to be Zanack won't be able to get to her here."

Canaan cringed as he laid the rest of it on his friend.

"We can only hope, Cordone. This Zanack has killed several of my closest in the last month including Thomas. Kaitlan doesn't know he's dead, yet. She is the heir to all that I have, and all who are my Clan. You are still in my Clan, Cordone. It's a lot to ask, I know, but I have no other I can trust with this task. You are the only one!"

Thomas was - had been - Kaitlan's assigned, personal bodyguard. Zanack back, or someone masquerading as Zanack, well, it just couldn't get any worse! You know what they say? Never say it can't get worse, because it always does. And, sure enough, Canaan did have worse.

"The Second thing I need to tell you is that Kaitlan's twenty-seventh birthday is tomorrow."

Well, hell! Canaan was famous for jumping from one subject to the next in a heartbeat! Pushing Zanack to back of his mind, Kaitlan was front and center, now. Cordone had kept track of all her birthdays since the day she was born. All he could think of were those green eyes, and that dazzling smile that had never left his memory. Canaan had sent him photos of Kaitlan as she grew, and when she turned eighteen, Canaan had sent her graduation photo to him. Now, Cordone was able to desire her as a woman. It was as if a faucet that had been turned off for eighteen years had turned on with the photo. Now, it would never be turned off. He never expected his oldest friend and leader to contact him regarding protection ever again. Not after what had happened with Tara at Kaitlan's birth. He still blamed himself for Tara's death even though no one else did, especially Canaan. They were closer than brothers.

So, the combination of his claim and his guilt kept him from returning to the Clan's headquarters, and thus, he and Kaitlan never had to meet again.

"Anita has said that she doesn't know if the change will, or will not come tomorrow since Kaitlan is half human.   However, Kaitlan is showing the first signs of the change.   She is having horrible headaches that medicine can't relieve, She told no one except Anita, and Anita came to me, of course. Kaitlan even jumped back several feet in my office earlier when I told her she was going to stay with you, and didn't notice what she had done. I cannot have her here if she changes - not with her life in danger. It is our most vulnerable stage prior to the first change."

"Agreed."

Cordone remembered his own change, and how vulnerable he had been. No werewolf ever forgot it! The change always came at twenty-seven years-old. And, the first turn was not pleasant. Headaches, abdominal cramps, terror, and several other things accosted the new werewolf when it happened. But, usually, it was the parents who helped their child with it, not someone else. After the first turn, a werewolf would never experience pain again. Cordone groaned. How could he cope with a new werewolf's first change AND being her mate? Cordone closed his eyes. More than that, how could he ever explain to Canaan that his only daughter was his mate? After all these thousands of years, why her? Truth be known, when mates found each other, they did not have to ask permission from the parents. It was immediate and binding, but without the Blood Bond, she would never be safe. And, once two recognized themselves as mates, the mating bond was done immediately, without fail, wherever they were. It could never be put off for parental approval.

"Canaan, I'm not equipped to handle it if she changes! That belongs in your court! You're her Father!"

"True, but these are extenuating circumstances. Besides, why not you, my friend? You have helped more change than any other person in the Clan!"

"Yeah! MEN! Not women!" Cordone yelled. Canaan could hear the terror in his voice.

"Do I need to pull rank, Cordone? She's all I have, and I will do it if it will keep her safe! Do you not think I want to help her during this most crucial time of her life? But, I can't have her here! I can't be available for her! There is far too much danger, and I'll be damned if I will allow her to be murdered like Tara!" Canaan practically yelled at Cordone. Cordone didn't mind, though. It had taken a long time to realize that whoever killed Tara was behind all the other poisonings and murders in recent months. He'd do the same in Canaan's shoes. "Oh, and by the way? She has no idea who, or what, she is."

Cordone blinked. Then, anger clouded his judgment.

"Canaan, are you telling me that you have never told Kaitlan about her heritage? Nothing?" He almost screamed into his phone. And, there went another damn crack! By the time this was over, he'd have to call Lynne to get another phone. She would not be happy.

"No. I tried to raise her as a normal human. You know that. I believed I would have plenty of time to tell her everything, but hindsight never shows until it is past. If Zanack murders me, it falls upon you to tell her who she is, and her role as she steps into my shoes. She is feisty like Tara, has my recklessness, and she refuses to follow orders most of the time. You need to be warned. But, like Tara, she is fair and loving with our Clan. She is the most loyal, and one of the smartest, people I have ever met." Canaan almost sounded defeated.

"Canaan, you were wrong to keep her heritage from her, and you know it. She needs to know who she is. I had no idea you might never tell her! You have to tell her before you send her out here! The complications from the change to someone who doesn't know what's happening can be disastrous!" Cordone demanded. Not to mention the risk to his daughter's virtue from him, he added to himself.

"There is no time. Wait until you have a child, Cordone. Then, ask yourself how do you tell your daughter something like that? I was going to tell her three years ago, but Zanack reared his ugly damn head again!"

Cordone closed his eyes in irritation. And, yep! Another crack right across the screen!

"Three years??? THREE FUCKING YEARS AGO this unknown Zanack showed up, and you didn't tell me? You kept her in danger for THREE DAMN, FUCKING YEARS? Canaan, have you lost your mind? Why the fuck didn't you call me? Why in the name of Hades didn't you send her to me then? You should have called me before this, Canaan. Kaitlan cannot be allowed to be in such danger!" The thought of his mate being in danger angered him against his oldest friend.

"I know, I know, Cordone. I've been an absolute fool. But it's done. With her I am at my most vulnerable. I'm only concerned with Kaitlan's life, not my own. I have to ask this of you just in case Zanack succeeds in killing me. And, if he does, I need you to get her through it." Canaan's voice was grim.

Cordone gave in to Canaan. He could order Cordone, but Cordone wouldn't need it. Kaitlan was his mate, and his life. He'd avoided it long enough. He knew he couldn't resist taking care of her. It was what he was born to do.

"You know you don't need to order me, Canaan. We have been friends way too long for that."

"Sam just informed me that she's on the plane, now. Please, keep her safe. If something happens to me, I want you to know that I believe her to be the one from the prophecy. And, more than that, Tara believed it."

Cordone frowned. Kaitlan the one from that stupid, and ancient prophecy about The White Wolf? That was just ridiculous. He did not believe in prophecy. He certainly had no idea that Canaan believed in that drivel. Cordone dropped his head. He could not refuse his leader, and he would NEVER refuse his mate. Yes, no matter what, Canaan was still his leader. Cordone had never officially been replaced with another Second. That had never changed officially, nor in Canaan's mind, apparently. This was, indeed, the largest honor Cordone had ever been paid.

But, having her in his own home where he was born was a temptation to end all temptations, and could be just as disastrous. He realized it had always been inevitable that they would meet. He closed his eyes in resignation. He knew he would not be able to have her here in his home without taking her as his mate, and taking her to his bed. Silently, he apologized to his oldest, and best friend for what would happen to his only daughter.

"Of course, I will protect her, Canaan. With my life."

Canaan knew he didn't have to answer him. He was sure of Cordone. Canaan smiled knowingly on the other end of the connection. No matter how hard Cordone had tried to hide it from him, Canaan had seen Cordone's lightly glowing eyes when he had handed baby Kaitlan to him. Cordone knew that his mate was Kaitlan the day he delivered her, and brought her back to Canaan alive. He had not only seen it in Cordone's eyes, he had smelled it as well. There was always a different smell when one had found their mate for life. And, although Kaitlan did not know about such things, her head had turned toward Cordone to watch him with her tiny glowing green eyes, and smile at him as he had left the room while Canaan had held her. That simple gesture told her Father that she had claimed Cordone as her mate as well. Canaan respected Cordone enough to not acknowledge this fact. In the human world, he knew Cordone would have been considered a sex pervert. In their world, though, while it was highly unusual to find one's mate when a baby, it had happened a handful of times in the distant past.

Canaan was so desperate to save his daughter, he used Zanack and the danger to act. When her birthday and Zanack coincided, he devised a plan to throw Cordone and Kaitlan together. They were already chosen mates, but the fire in their relationship was like the magnet and steel. By Sending her to safety, he also hoped that their resolves would crumble, and Cordone would mate with Kaitlan by tomorrow. Cordone's possessiveness and love would be her best protection. He would never let anyone near her, because she was his. And, that eased Canaan's heart. He knew he could leave this world in peace no matter how he left it. Nothing in his life could have pleased him more at that point. Yes. His best friend, mate to his daughter. Couldn't get any better than that. He smiled as he remembered his own mating with Tara. He hoped it would be just as romantic and wonderful for Kaitlan and Cordone. Cordone had been waiting long enough, he thought.

"I will have Dan Wheeler pick her up, Canaan."

"Thank you, Cordone. I trust you with her life, and no other."

Cordone had hung up the phone, and called Dan with instructions.

Now, she was here...in his home, and he just heard her door shut. He groaned. He would be seeing his mate for the first time in twenty-seven years in just minutes. Her wolf would emerge in less than three hours, unless her human side was dominant. Dan knew everything, of course, and he knew that Dan would die before his good friend would suffer the loss of his mate.

Little did Cordone know that there were two others who knew that Kaitlan was his mate: Canaan and Sam. If Cordone would have known, he would have never gone into self-imposed exile! There would never have been a need.

~ 7 ~

Never Judge a Book by its Cover - or a Wolf!

Entering the elevator, and pushing "main", Kaitlan was trying not to be nervous about meeting Cordone Valon. The man dated little, but he did take a gorgeous woman when he had to show up at an event for his books. He may be a recluse, but she was sure he did venture out to get a piece! Kaitlan still never thought of herself as beautiful, or even pretty. Cute? Maybe, but never beautiful.

For goodness sakes! Why in the world would she even consider it in the first place? Like Kaitlan would be chosen by this hunk of a man. It wasn't as if she had a chance in hell anyway. She bowed her head, rubbing her temples. She had the worst headache she had ever had in her life right now. Tomorrow was her birthday, so did she just HAVE to develop a migraine now? And, for the first time, ever, she would not be with her Father for her birthday, and that made her very sad. She doubted Valon would know about her birthday, but then, why should he? It was depressing thinking she'd have to spend it all alone. Why would her Father send her away on her birthday? Her head pounded. Way too many questions in her mind. It made her head hurt even worse.

The elevator stopped, and the door opened. Kaitlan stepped out, and just gawked. Headache forgotten for a moment, she just thought she knew what "rich" really meant. By this standard, she and her Father were poor! This room was so beautiful. Looking at it from above was gorgeous, but standing in it? It was breathtaking. Her breath caught in her throat as her eyes followed of their own accord while she was gazing at the room in 360 degrees.

She stepped toward the fire pit. It was gigantic. It was designed to warm the entire atrium if needed. Her eyes raised to the massive window, and she took a step forward to look at the view. It was as if she could see the world from this vantage point. And, it was dark outside! That's odd. Why could she see so well in the dark?

"I love this view. Always have. It gives me such peace," said a soft, male voice just behind her.

Kaitlan jumped. She hadn't even heard him come into the room. He obviously moved just as fast and silent as Dan, Sam, and her Dad. Geez. Why couldn't she move like that?

Kaitlan took a deep breath, and smelled the most amazingly gorgeous scent she had ever smelled in her entire life. It was a woodsy smell and spicy. Shaking her head, she slowly turned around to face the most popular writer in the world's history.

When she stopped, her eyes raised slowly. OMG!!! He was a god! Or, as close as she had ever seen! Her Father was gorgeous, too, but Cordone Valon? His chest was strong - and bare! He wore a deep blue bathing suit that showed off his massive legs. That alone made her breathless! His abs, well, they defied description as they were incredibly toned. Better than six-packs. His skin had a hint of olive and sported a deep tan. His arms were muscles on top of muscles! What would it be like to be held in them? Unconsciously, she licked her lips as she raised her eyes to the man's neck. And, then his face, straight into his eyes which showed amusement. Crap! He had seen her lick her lips! She was mortified, and even that did not even begin to describe the sexy solid black eyes that met hers. They were coal black. She couldn't see his pupils at all! His lips were perfection, and she wondered what they would feel like on hers. His nose was just as perfect. His hair was sleek, and coal black peppered with white. It appeared to have a fire within it! She didn't have enough superlatives to describe him. It was one thing to drool over a book cover, but the real man in front of her exuded sexuality so strong, she found she had stopped breathing. He was hers. She knew it instinctively, but how, she had no answer. Wait! That's absolutely ridiculous. A man like this did not go for someone like her. And, yet...his eyes said something that she didn't understand. The term "sex on a stick" was the term most women would use for him.

Cordone's eyes looked into Kaitlan's green ones. They were the eyes of a woman, and bore the same eyes as the tiny ones who gazed at him at her birth. The same eyes that had told him that she was his. But, these eyes were full of beauty and innocence beyond anything he had ever known. Her mouth was naturally red, smaller, and she wore little makeup. Kaitlan's face was round, just as he remembered, and although her hair was the same gold blonde, it had been turned to platinum. It was exactly right for her milky skin. He continued looking her over as his eyes drifted, unashamed, to her chest. Her breasts were full, and he yearned to see them, and their rosy tips without anything covering them. He continued down as he looked at her waist, then her rounded hips that hid the most amazing secret from him. He looked back up into her eyes. She was gorgeous, desirable, and she was his mate. His mate who was half-were and half-human. Her eyes just stared into his while her face turned a beautiful bright red as he raked his eyes over her body. Slowly, Cordone smiled. Very soon. Yes, very soon, she would know it when he claimed her not only in their mating, but her beautiful body as he marked her as his forever. He had dreamed all her life of touching her body, and kissing it in the most intimate of ways as he moved inside of her. He felt his arousal stiffen. Then, just as suddenly, he remembered there were secrets surrounding her that she didn't know, and there may come a time when he was responsible for telling her all of it. Thank goodness, his hardened cock softened. But, there was no doubt that his balls were still full, and getting a bit painful. The very thought of giving her his seed was almost overcoming his sanity. Great. Another cold shower was called for after dinner. That wasn't something he was looking forward to, but as long as her Father was alive, it was his responsibility to tell her about who she was. Cordone would just have to wait his turn.

Zanack. Someone calling himself the name of an ancient evil. He was a threat to his mate. Over his dead body would he get to her! His face turned serious.

"Hello, Kaitlan," he introduced himself with great difficulty, as he offered his hand to her.

She looked at his hand as if it was a snake about to bite her, but she grabbed it. The second her hand touched his, a sharp surge pulsed over her body, and she felt warmth and wetness where she shouldn't just by the touch of his hand. Oh yes, she was definitely in trouble. Then, a tingle of warmth spread into her hand, and radiated all over her body.

They stared at each other's eyes during the handshake, and Cordone ended it himself. He had to, or he would take her here, and now, mating with her immediately.

"Mr. V-Valon. It's nice to meet you," she said breathlessly stuttering.

He grinned, and that was devastating to her. Oh, yes.   Danger was the word. Danger AND "sex on a stick"!

"Please, call me Cordone."

Kaitlan just nodded.

"I'm sorry I wasn't at the door to greet you when you came in, but my cell phone met with a slight accident. I'm waiting for a new one, and Dan forgot to call me."

Kaitlan just nodded not trusting her voice at the moment. She glanced over at the waterfall into the pool, and noticed that there was a large opening between the main room through the waterfall into what looked to be a gigantic pool beyond.

He offered her his arm. "I hope you are hungry. Dan is a fantastic cook! And, please, feel free to use the pool if you wish." He had noticed her looking at it.

He tucked her hand into the crook of his arm, and his other hand covered hers as he led them on a long, long walk to a small dining nook off the kitchen at the back of his "cave". It was beautiful, and fit the man completely. The table was black and glass with the chairs upholstered in black as well. The walls were solid wood painted white, and held nature photographs along one wall. Kaitlan decided to focus on those instead of the man.

"These are beautiful," Kaitlan remarked. "Who is the photographer?"

"I am," Cordone answered. Kaitlan turned to him in surprise.

"Really? I had no idea. Did my Dad know about these?"

Cordone laughed gently, and she felt her heart drop into her feet at the musical sound.

"Yes, he did, as a matter of fact. He actually put me in touch with a friend of his who publishes photos."

"You mean Uncle Denny?" Kaitlan asked.

"Uncle Denny?" He repeated.

She laughed, and said, "Yes. Well, I call him that. Everyone else calls him Matthew Morrison."

"Ah, Matt. Yes." Uncle Denny, he thought to himself. Never heard that one before.

Cordone turned as he saw Dan coming into the room carrying a tray of drinks. A beer for him, and a margarita for Kaitlan. Peach to be exact. He knew from her Father that it was her favorite.

Kaitlan said, "Thank you, Dan," and tasted it.

"Oh, my goodness, Dan! This is the best I have ever had!"

OH, GOD! Did I just say that? Closing her eyes to hide her embarrassment, she took another drink, and felt the cold drink drizzle down her throat.

"Thank you, and you are welcome, Kaitlan." He was clearly amused, and then, he turned to Cordone. "Dinner is ready, and I will bring it right out." He turned leaving Kaitlan and Cordone staring at each other.

OK. This was awkward, thought Kaitlan. Now what?

"My Father said that you wanted an editor with you while you wrote your current book. We have many great editors on staff, so why me?" Kaitlan asked, because she still didn't get it.

Cordone took a swig on his beer, then answered her.

"Actually, it was your Father's idea. The novel I am writing, now, is the longest I have written, yet. Because of this, he decided if I had an editor as I wrote that there would be less lag time between writing it, and publishing it. It would get out to the public much faster. I have always deferred to your Father's experience and knowledge."

That was a bolt from the blue to Kaitlan. Her Father had suggested it? Wait a minute! He had told her that Cordone had insisted she come. What the hell? Well, to be honest, her Dad's idea had real merit. Dang it! Kaitlan wished she had thought of that one. Not that she would have volunteered to be that editor, that is. Oh, who was she kidding? Of course, she would have come!

"Dad always seemed to have ideas of the best ways to publish faster. I wish I had thought of it!" She smiled at him.

His heart sank into his feet with that smile. It was the smile that she had given to him upon her birth. Grownup, yes, but the smile was the same. He felt himself harden at the thought of her in his arms whispering into his ear her love for him. And, suddenly, he had a vision of her lying in their bed with him beside her, their child suckling at her breast, while she offered Cordone her other breast for him to suckle. It was the most amazingly erotic thought he had ever had in his life. He growled under his breath as the vision ended with Dan bringing their dinner. He growled - again.

Kaitlan darted a look at him. Did he just growl?

Steaks cooked to perfection, baked sweet potatoes, and grilled asparagus with homemade rolls. They ate in relative silence with a few words here and there.

Kaitlan didn't taste a damn thing she ate. Basically, she was filling her empty stomach having not eaten anything since breakfast. It really wasn't fair to Dan, but with Cordone sitting across from her, she couldn't think straight.

A vision of her lying naked on a bed, Cordone next to her, watching their baby suckling at her breast, while she offered Cordone the other one to suckle popped into her mind. It shocked her to her core! OK. That was really strange, and she shook her head free of the vision. She'd never get it out of her mind! And, worse? She was wet!

Cordone didn't know that she had the very same vision as he did. More than that, he realized that she WAS drawn to him as well, and that's when she dropped her fork. It clinked on the plate, and Cordone looked up into her eyes. He knew, then, that she had felt him. Her surprise was a bombshell, to say the least. Their eyes met, and the vision returned to both of them, again, at the same time.

Kaitlan swallowed hard. She had to get away from him, now. Her confusion was apparent, and Cordone noticed it.

He rose from his chair, and said, "I think you must be tired, Kaitlan. Why don't you go to bed? We will meet tomorrow for our collaboration on the first three chapters that I have already written of the book."

Kaitlan rose, and nodded her head. She was tired. Very tired. More than that, exhausted. So, why did she want to throw herself into his arms, and rip his clothes off?

"OK. I-I-I'll see you in the morning, Cordone," she stammered. He nodded, and walked her to the elevator.

Cordone had to hold himself in place to keep from joining her in the elevator. Taking her to bed had never been so dominant in him as it did after that vision. He wanted that vision to come true, impossible though it would be.

Cordone retreated to his office, but he was distracted by the vision he had. He couldn't concentrate on anything. An hour later, Dan came into view, and held out the phone. Something in his face scared Cordone, and he knew it was not good.

"Thanks, Dan. This is Cordone Valon," he said into the cell.

"Sam, here." His voice was shaking, and somehow, Cordone knew that Canaan was dead. "Canaan has been murdered, Cordone."

Cordone sought out the nearest chair, and fell into it. While he was dreaming about a life with Kaitlan, his oldest friend and leader had been killed. Even though it wasn't on his watch, he felt that it should have been.

"How?" he asked.

"Zanack sent the Viper."

The Viper? One of the most deadliest assassins ever known. This was not good. This Zanack meant business. Deadly business. Thank the Creator Kaitlan was with him. He closed his eyes thinking that it could have been Kaitlan, and that would never happen. He would not allow it.

"Tell me everything," Cordone said, his heart breaking for the loss of his oldest friend, and his mate who slept under his roof.

Kaitlan took another shower hoping it would help her head. It didn't. She fished out her sleep set of mint green with sheer bikini panties and matching spaghetti strap top. She liked being comfortable in bed. Actually, she'd rather sleep nude like she did at home, but that might not be such a good idea here.

She was totally confused. Where did the vision come from, and how did it happen? And, if she hadn't known better, she would have sworn he had the same vision she had. Her emotions were totally out of control, but her logical mind set everything aside. Her head was worse than it was before. She had taken more pills which just weren't really helping, and she climbed into bed, and was out in minutes.

~ 8 ~

"I am here to tell you who you are, Kaitlan."

"Kaitlan," called her Father. "Kaitlan."

Then, another, gentler female voice called.

"My darling daughter, wake up!"

She stirred when she heard her name, and opened her eyes. She saw her Father and the most beautiful woman she had ever seen standing before her at the foot of her bed. Who was she?

"What Daddy?" She asked sleepily. "Is that you? I didn't know you were coming to Cordone's?"

"I am not there, Kaitlan. My darling daughter, I have departed from this life to be with my beautiful Tara," he nodded to the woman. "Although not by my own hand, but by Zanack."

"What? I don't understand, Daddy."

"I know you don't - yet. But, by tomorrow, you will. I entrusted the only man I could with your safety, and sent you to him. I come to you, now, because I am dead, and you must be ready to take over as female Alpha leader of the Clan."

Tears formed in Kaitlan's eyes. "No, Daddy! It's not true! You can't leave me! This is a dream, only a dream!" She cried out shaking her head hard! Not real! Not real!

Canaan rounded the bed, and sat down on it

taking her hand in his.

"I'm so sorry, my little one. Sometimes, we do not know when it is our time. This was mine."

Kaitlan's tears were increasing. She felt her bed give on the other side, and turned her head. She gasped at who it was.

"M-M-Mom?"

The same green eyes that stared at her were so like her own.

"Yes, my darling daughter. I am so proud of what you have become, and now, it is time for you to step up, and become what you were meant to be. You are the daughter of one of the most powerful men ever to walk this Earth. I was his mate, and his wife. When I gave birth to you, I never felt more complete. I am sorry that I could not be there as you grew up, but I have watched over you always. What you will be doing will be harder than anything you have ever done. And, your life is in danger from Zanack. That is why your Father sent you to the only man he could trust - his Second. Your future belongs with Cordone. Listen to Cordone. Let him teach you all he knows. Then, when that is done, you will take your place as the head of the Clan, and protect all who are yours. It is your destiny, and your curse."

Kaitlan's mouth just dropped open. Then, her Father continued, and she turned her head again.

"I am here to tell you who you are, Kaitlan. I regret I did not do so while you were growing up. In just a minute, you will be twenty-seven years old, and it's very important that you know the truth. You do not understand your position in the Clan as my daughter. I was Alpha to all. You will be the same as Alpha to all the women in the Clan. Your Mother was human, but I am not. I am a werewolf, and your Mother was my mate, and wife in the human world."

He paused to watch Kaitlan's teary eyes pop out of their sockets.

Her phone timer went off indicating it was one minute until midnight.

"The twenty-seventh year is the year in which your wolf will appear. Because you are half-human, no one knows what will happen since you are the only one of half blood."

Her Mother continued, "Your conception let alone your birth should never have been, Kaitlan. Humans and werewolves are not compatible in any way, and I had been totally content with that. But, somehow, some way, you were conceived in the love we had for one another. Some greater force stepped in, and changed the rules. No one knows why. But, you are destined to be the one to unite all Clans, and that is what you must become. Zanack is deadly, and has plans to destroy not only werewolves, but all supernaturals and humans as well."

Canaan finished. "You must learn everything that you can from Cordone. He will teach you what you need to know, and you must learn quickly."

Suddenly, her parents were holding hands at the foot of her bed, again.

She found her voice, screaming, "NO!" But, they both smiled at her.

"We love you, Kaitlan. Know this without doubt. Now, fulfill your destiny with Cordone as he must also fill his with you, and as Alpha to the O'Hara Clan. I chose him long ago as my successor. Protect your Clan."

With that, her parents faded out, and she sat up screaming and crying her heart out.

Downstairs, Cordone had just put the phone down when he heard Kaitlan screaming at the top of her lungs over and over. He looked at his watch. DAMN! Her birthday! Her wolf will, or will not make its presence, and from the sound of it, it was happening after all! She would be terrified, and like all new wolves, had to have someone to help her transition. It was the parent's responsibility to do this, but she had none, now. It fell upon him to help her.

Ignoring the elevator, Cordone jumped to the fifth story without effort, leaped over the railing, burst into Kaitlan's room, and froze.

Her heart was breaking as she screamed over and over, "NO, Daddy, NO!!! Mother!!!! Don't leave me!!!"

Kaitlan's eyes were wild, and she was literally lost in the beginning of the transition as her eyes glowed green. Cordone knew, then, that she was truly more werewolf than human. Her screams led him to believe she either dreamed, or saw, something. But, what the hell would cause her to bring on the horrendous pain she was suffering? This was far worse than any change he had ever seen, but then, she wasn't all werewolf, so for Kaitlan, who knew what would happen?

He leaped from the door to the bed in one bound over twelve feet of space, and gathered his mate into his arms holding her as still as possible so that she did not hurt herself. Her knuckles were bleeding from beating the metal headboard above her over and over. She felt horrible pain. He felt her struggle more as her wolf began to awaken within his arms. No one knew what a half-were and half-human would become if their wolf took over. It had never happened before. He was terrified beyond belief as he watched her suffer! He called to the Creator to help him contain her, and to be merciful to her. Tears streamed down his cheek watching his mate in such pain, and there was nothing he could do!

Cordone held her tightly looking at the clock to confirm his watch. It WAS just after midnight. It WAS her birthday, and this WAS when the wolf was always released. He looked down at her, and she looked wildly into his eyes. Her eyes were glowing bright green, and were the eyes of a wolf. Shit! She was changing in his arms without any control, because she had never been told what would happen.

Damn it! What was he going to do?

Kaitlan struck out at Cordone wildly, and pushed him away. She had an unnatural strength that even bested him! What the hell? She leaped out of bed looking in all directions, and then ran from the room. Kaitlan jumped over the railing to the main room while Cordone leaped after her, desperately trying to stop her. He couldn't lose her!

He looked over the railing not wanting to see her body slammed into the floor, dead. What he saw made him hold his breath, and he leaped over the railing as well.

Bloody HELL! She had turned in midair! Only mature werewolves could change in a jump! She ran toward the glass door below just as Cordone screamed "DAN!" Dan was already at the door with it open, and Kaitlan ran out. Cordone phased, and ran after her. This would be so good for him if they were together as mates, but she was a wild cannon, and anything could happen.

Tracking her was easy, because her scent was burned into his memory. But, she was fast. Faster than any werewolf he had ever seen. The combination of her mixed lineage must be effecting her more than they ever had realized. He kept her in sight, ready to take her over if she really got out of hand, but right now, he knew she needed to run as fast as she could in her pain. So he let her run, and he just followed her. She would tire soon enough.

~ 9 ~

Where, Oh, Where has My Werewolf Gone?

Kaitlan shook as she screamed. She knew her Father was dead, and with her mother without a doubt. But, she couldn't completely understand what they had told her. And, then, she screamed doubling over in sudden, excruciating pain within her stomach. Her entire body was racked with severe pain. It began to stretch, bend, and she heard her bones snap. Her screaming voice became stranger to her ears, as it was replaced by howling. The howling of a wolf. She did not know it was her.

She felt rather than saw her door kicked open, and Cordone stood there breathing heavily. Even through her rage and her pain, she saw him leap twelve feet right into her bed where he grabbed her, and held her tightly. Her Daddy was dead! How? Why? She struck out at everything including Cordone who continued to hold her despite the injuries she inflicted upon him. She barely could process the blood streaming down his face and arms. She felt him grab her hand, and looked down at her bloody knuckles. She remembered only that she beat them over and over on the metal headboard, but she didn't feel the pain. Zanack killed her Father! She was half-human and half-werewolf! No one had told her, and that was just one more thing that made her howl so loudly. Her entire world had been shaken, as if in an earthquake, in just a couple of minutes!

Suddenly, the pain was such that she totally lost it, and shook Cordone off of her as if he was nothing but a feather. Her insides were burning, and the pain was horrible! She had to get out of here! She had to get out of this house! She had to get out where she could run freely, and run off her pain.

The change to her wolf was happening, but she didn't know anything about it. Kaitlan ran toward the door, and leaped over the railing to the main floor.

Kaitlan felt her skin stretch, and alter in midair, and saw, in horror, her legs and arms change into fur and paws. She felt her face stretch into a muzzle, and her entire body shredded her clothes as it changed into some other creature. Terrified, she landed on all four feet, and shook her head as she streaked toward the glass door which led to a multi-level deck, and then freedom. It wasn't true! It can't be!

Cordone had yelled, "Dan!"

Just before Kaitlan crashed through the glass door, Dan appeared, and opened it. She jumped through it taking off at a pace that would have made any other werewolf envious. She ran to the woods without stopping. Totally focused on her internal pain, the loss of her Father, and the dream, she ran faster and faster. Her ears heard something following her. They tweaked up and back, and she turned her head spotting another wolf - a black wolf - behind her, but who was not trying to overtake her as she ran.

She turned her head back, her pain pushing her on faster and faster. Somewhere in her logical brain, she asked what was going on with her, but the logic did not remain, and she gave into the wolf, and let her have her way.

After what seemed like hours of running, exhaustion and grief was finally overshadowed as the pain ceased. Kaitlan slowed down, and stopped. She was now very, very sad. The other wolf slowed, and stopped as well. She looked for a place she could collapse, and found a huge aspen. Although she tried to get to it, she began to drop. Without warning, she was across a strong, black back that carried her to that aspen. He stopped suddenly, and gently laid her down on her side. Then, he dropped behind her. Neither were out of breath, but the sadness had weakened Kaitlan. Cordone put a paw around her, and pulled her into his stomach, then began stroking her back rhythmically. He licked her ear gently, which only a mate is allowed to do, and she fell into a deep sleep knowing that she was safe.

Cordone reached her, and stood by her watching. She shuddered occasionally, and a tiny whine crept out every so often. He watched her shake, not with cold, but with sorrow and terror. His mate. The woman he loved was in such pain, and there was nothing he could do about it but wait. He would comfort her whether, or not, she would allow it. She was more than just his mate. He was irrevocably in love with Kaitlan. Suddenly, he saw she was about to collapse. In an instant, he had crawled under her just as she slid to the ground. She fell on his back, and he carried her to an aspen that she had been trying to reach. He laid her down on her side, licked her ear, then he laid down next to her. Cordone placed his paw over her side to draw her next to his stomach, then began stroking, and petting his mate, trying to let her know she was not alone.

Kaitlan almost purred as the comforting strokes relaxed her body, and she passed out into the realm of silent sleep in the depth of night. She had never felt so safe in her entire life, and there, she dreamed.

She lovingly dreamed of her Father and Mother coming to her in her vision, and repeated everything to her. This time, she was not scared. Timid and a bit wary, but she was able to understand what they said this time. As they disappeared into a beautiful white light, she found herself standing in a meadow of flowers and grass. She was content, and very, very happy. She heard a noise, and looked to the left on alert, but without fear. In front of her, was the most beautiful black wolf. He was looking a bit frustrated at something, but at the same time, he seemed tender. Then, she saw two small creatures dart out from his legs. He turned, and huffed, but there was a grin on his face as he watched the two little gray wolf cubs playing together, nipping and rolling around in the grass. She felt his eyes grab hers, and the love Kaitlan saw there took her breath away. Kaitlan knew, then, that it was Cordone, her mate. That's what her parents had meant about their destiny together.

He was hers? This gorgeous hunk with black fur? Well, it was about the best description she had. Kaitlan looked down at her feet, and saw her fur was snow white. Then, those two little cubs saw her, and ran toward her. They jumped at her in play. Kaitlan had never felt as happy as she did at that moment.

The little cubs were a boy and a girl. The boy had Kaitlan's green eyes, and the girl, Cordone's. She sucked in her breath. These were her little babies! Their babies. When Cordone came to her, he stood tall and proud as he watched them roll Kaitlan around in play. Her beautiful family! Would her Mother's blood not effect her from having a family with Cordone? Is that what this meant? Kaitlan wanted it to be real. He lay beside her while she pulled her little cubs to her stomach so they could suckle her, and she sighed. Babies well fed, all four werewolves fell asleep.

In the early morning light, Kaitlan awoke as a human. She was confused at first where she was, but then she remembered not only her Father was dead, but the beautiful family wasn't real, and a sob was wrenched from the depths of her soul. She felt a hand stroke her back, and pulled her next to something warm. She also felt something hard and low pressing against her hips. She should run, but she didn't want to do it. So, instead, she curled herself back into the hand, her body accepting the warmth beside her, the hardness of something pushing at her, and let that warmth stroke her gently, lulling her back to sleep.

Cordone was relishing being next to his mate's naked body as he stroked her back slowly. She wiggled her bottom next to his hardness as she leaned back into his body. He was hard for her, but this was not the time for anything else, so he opted to just allow himself to go to sleep next to her. And, just before he went back to sleep, she wiggled that perfect ass next to his erection, again, and he pushed it into her hips.

And, there, the two wolves and mates lay together until the warmth of the morning sun was felt.

~ 10 ~

Waking Up Naked, Next to a Man, Can be Embarrassing.

Kaitlan felt the cool, morning air flowing over her heated body. She knew she should be cold somewhere in the back of her mind, but she wasn't. She really didn't know why. Something was poking her butt, and a hand stroked her body relaxing her, and comforting her. She had never felt so warm, or so comfortable in her entire life. There was also something about that hardness which was turning her on, but she was content to feel the breeze wafting over her body, letting that hand stroke her wherever it wanted to stroke. She really wanted it to cup her breast, but she didn't move to steer it there. For a few minutes, she felt as if she could lay there forever with that warmth wrapping all around her.

Kaitlan opened her eyes looking up into the leaves of a tree? She was under a tree laying in the dirt? And, more than that, she looked down, and saw she was naked! Why the hell was she naked???

Then, in an instant, everything came flooding back to her, and she began to cry softly. Her Father was dead. She was a werewolf - a real one. No one had ever told her this, until her parents told her in her vision. But, right now, the vision comforted her more than anything else. Her parents were finally together, and they were happy. Her Mother was so beautiful, and she wished she was as beautiful as her Mother. But, she had gotten to talk to her! Daddy was right. She was the most loving Mother, and that just made her cry more.

The rest of the conversation came flooding back to her. Her Clan was being threatened by something or someone called "Zanack". And, her Father had sent her to Cordone to teach her what he knew, and to help him fight against this Zanack. Why did her Father never tell her what she was? Did Sam know? Well, that was a stupid thought. Of course he did. Her Dad had never held anything back from Sam. In fact, everyone had to have known!

Wait a Second! Cordone! He was one of them, too!! Her mind just barely registered this fact somewhere in her haze last night. He had been trying to keep her from hurting herself, and tried holding her until she broke free from him, and leaped over the railing! She remembered the horrible pain she had suffered during her change. But, Cordone followed her. More haze, and she remembered a coal black wolf following her. It had to have been Cordone!

Uh-oh! Her eyes dried up quickly when she realized, again, she was naked! And, that hand was still on her back stroking it. Who belonged to that hand? She was almost afraid to look, but her Father had said that Cordone was the one to teach her what she needed to know. What did he mean by that? Teach her what? Sexarobics?

She gulped as she turned her head slowly to look behind her, and her green eyes met Cordone's amused, solid black ones. She stared at him for what seemed like forever. Then, her face flamed red as a beet. If she was naked, then, OH, NO! He was naked, too? Wait a Second. That hardness against her was...? Oh, shit! She was mortified, and dipped her head forward, horribly embarrassed. Last night, she had run into the forest with him on her tail. Literally. She had just woken up next to that man still on her tail - literally! Kaitlan ducked her head in her hands, covering her eyes. What would he think of her?

Cordone reached his hand up to her hair, and stroked it gently. So gently, tears welled in her eyes, because he was so tender with her. She looked back at him. His eyes were not those of a lover, but of a friend and comforter. She relaxed at this revelation, but that damn hardness of his was hard to ignore. In fact, if she were honest with herself, she felt wetness well between her legs. If that wasn't humiliating! Damn it! She moved her backside away from the hardness as best as she could, but Cordone just yanked her even closer to his body.

"I am so sorry, little one. How did you find out about your Father?" That had puzzled him all night long.

Without turning her body around, sobbing lightly, she explained, "Dad came to me in a dream."

She swallowed, and continued softly, "And, so did my Mother."

Cordone was stunned. There were myths in werewolf history that on very rare occasions, those from the after life came to those who were living in their dreams. It was rare that it happened. This was the first he had ever heard about it actually happening.

"You dreamed of them?" He asked surprised.

She nodded her head. "Yes. He told me who had killed him." She turned her head to look at him. "What's a Zanack?"

Cordone stood up quickly, and Kaitlan saw that he was, indeed, just as naked as she was, and she got a very, very good look! Redness streaked up her neck into her face as she realized she had slept with him all night naked next to his..um...well, never mind. That thought would just have to wait for later. As if he heard her thoughts, he grinned a crooked grin at her. Werewolf nudity was something that just couldn't be avoided easily. He never thought a thing about it, but for Kaitlan, it must come as a total jolt to her.

Why that insufferable son of a bitch was Kaitlan's first thought, drying her tears instantly. But, then, she backed off. He had kept her safe all night in the middle of the forest both as a wolf and a human. If he had wanted to take advantage, he had certainly had every opportunity. Part of her was grateful. The other part of her felt insulted that he hadn't taken advantage of her? She was really losing it!

"Zanack is evil incarnate. He is poisoning and killing some of our females. We believe he is the one who killed your Mother, too. Tell me everything he told you, Kaitlan," Cordone commanded looking down at her. He made sure he kept behind her so she wouldn't feel uncomfortable with him looking at her, but he stood straight and proud. He was her mate, and he had no problem with her seeing him.

"Really? He's on my hit list!" She said to him. Then, "They told me that I was never supposed to be born."

A tear slid down her face as he processed the words. Cordone waited until she was ready to continue. He was in no hurry to rush her. He knew she needed to take this at her own pace. And, Cordone had plenty of patience - except for anyone who would dare to hurt his mate.

"He said that he was Alpha to his Clan, and that now, I was the heir to that Clan, and I would become female Alpha. That I was to learn everything I could from you, and that you would teach me what I needed to know. That I was to protect the Clan, and to complete my destiny as you were to complete yours. Together."

Silence, they say, is golden. Cordone discovered this to be true, now, as he thought over what she had said. He sat back down behind her, and let his hand stroke her back again. In his unconscious, he knew her skin was soft to his hand. His destiny was to be her mate, and she his. He was a full werewolf, and his eyes had seen her pale fur as she had run in the moonlight, and he knew that this was absolutely unique. No other were had ever had that color. He remembered as he had stroked it how soft it was. He also remembered how he had hardened as he lay beside her in his wolf form. Now, he sat next to her in his naked, human form. He hardened earlier, and it hadn't softened one bit. He also knew it had been hard against her. When she had pulled away from him, he had pulled her back wanting her to feel his desire for her. He wanted nothing more than to pull her into his arms, mark her as his, let her mark him, and then to make love to her as they completed the mating bond. It was impossible to mate in wolf form for whatever reason, but that was alright with him. The human way was just fine. And, he wanted her to be the Mother of his child, if they were blessed by the Fates.

Laying back down behind her, Cordone stroked her face gently. She leaned into his hand. She knew this was wrong, logically, but, if truth were known, it felt right. She was his. She had known this the minute they met. She knew, now, without a doubt, that he was hers. Her mate. The man she was supposed to be with forever. Laying there together naked only enhanced these feelings. Between her thighs it became hot and wet. She wanted nothing more than to turn in his arms, and let him take her right there.

How far were they from the house? She looked around. Again, as if he had heard her thoughts, he answered her question.

"We are probably about 2 hours from the house, Kaitlan," he said with a real laugh. Walking back was going to be interesting with both of them nude. She blushed, and he had never thought he had seen her so beautiful. Just the thought of her waking next to him naked for the rest of their lives was the most arousing thing that had ever happened to him. Nope. He had to stop thinking about it. It wasn't time, yet. She was too new to this.

"We can phase, and run back if you want. It would be faster, and probably less embarrassing for you."

Man, what was wrong with him! He wanted her, and he could smell her wetness which would allow him to slide into her.   Yet, he cared more for her than his desire, and what they both wanted.

"We can do that? At will, I mean?" Cordone nodded.   "How do I do it?"

Cordone sighed as he saw her grin just to torture him. Thwarting him was apparently going to be an interesting experience.

"Yes. The first change is the only painful change. From here on out, Kaitlan, you can change at will. Think about last night. Remember when you phased the first time?   You let your wolf take over totally, even when you did not realize it. If you think about that, it is all you have to do. Don't fight her. Let her out. Let her take you over completely, and you will phase."

"But I can still keep myself and my sanity?" She

asked.

He gave her one nod. In an instant, Cordone phased before her eyes into a wolf with the blackest of fur. He rose behind her, standing incredibly tall and magnificent! The same black wolf stood before her that she saw in her dream. His beautiful black eyes remained looking at her. She could see intelligence behind those eyes. The wolf and the man were one and the same.

OK. Let my wolf take over. She closed her eyes. "Uh, wolfie? Are you there?"

Kaitlan felt the growl deep within her. "OK, wolfie. Let's do this," she thought. She felt her body change almost instantly.

When she opened her eyes, she was a wolf. Cordone drew in his breath as he was taken aback at her beauty. A white wolf? He had thought she was pale last night, but she was really snow white! Not possible! There was no such thing as a white wolf! The prophecy couldn't be true! But, there stood a white wolf before him!

Boldly, she nuzzled Cordone's neck. He growled in satisfaction as she did so. Strange. He could smell that her wolf was wet and ready for him just as she had been in human form. That was not possible. If only it could be true, again for the werewolves.

He turned, and gave her a knowing wolfie grin as if to say, "I know you're ready for me. Want it now?"

She held her head up tall, swishing her long furry tail at him as if to say, "Not yet buddy! We'll get there when it's time!"

And, believe it! She meant there was going to be the right time. And, she felt it would be very, very soon.

The two wolves, one snow white, the other black as night, broke into a run. She had never felt so free! This time, it was with joy she ran next to the man she loved, feeling the wind blowing through her fur. This was the man she wanted to make love to, to mate with, to have his children. She didn't know everything, but one thing she did know. She wanted it to be Cordone. He was HERS! And, then, she remembered a hazy time when she looked upon this same face who was holding her gently as he handed her to her Father.

That brought her up short, and she stopped. Cordone shot past her before he realized she had stopped. He turned, and trotted back to where she stood, looking at her with a question.

The memory was so strong, Kaitlan was mystified. But, there was no doubt. He held her when she was tiny. How, she had no idea, but she knew it was the truth. She turned, and grinned at him. The same smile that she had smiled at him when she was an infant, but in wolf form. Cordone thought his heart would jump right out of his chest. Then, Kaitlan started to run again, and he took off after her.

"Oh, we most definitely will NOT be talking,

and very soon," thought Kaitlan.

At the same time, Cordone was thinking the same thing. Talking was far from what he planned for them.   He grinned his wolfy grin as he thought about what he planned for the two of them on their mating night, or day. No preference.

The two of them entered the house, and Kaitlan headed for her room, but she couldn't use the elevator as a wolf. She looked at him in question. With a smile, he leaped five stories up, and flew right over the railing. Her eyes were wide. He smiled as if to say that's how it's done. So, Kaitlan backed up, and leaped - right over the fifth floor rail just as smooth and lithe as he had done! She grinned at him after she completed her first jump, then trotted into her room with her tail up and wagging, nudging her door shut. Cordone scratched the door, but she just grinned, and then growled at him. Grinning his wolfy grin, he shrugged his shoulders.   Jumping to the fourth floor, he trotted to his own room to change.

Resuming his human form, Cordone looked in the mirror at his toned, naked body. He grinned even wider as he thought, "Soon, mate, soon."

Then stepped into the shower.

Now...how did she phase back to human? Directing her thoughts toward him, "Thanks for telling me!"   Remembering how she phased by letting her wolf take over, she wondered if she just needed to let the human take over in order to phase back. She shut her eyes, feeling her body change. It worked! Where she had been standing as a wolf, now, she stood as a human grinning in the bathroom mirror. This was really cool! Then, reality set into her mind. Her Father was gone, yet he wasn't at all. He had come to her along with her Mother in a dream, and her shoulders dropped in sadness. Stepping into the shower, she let grief wash over her.

Kaitlan slept like the dead, pardon the pun, until five o'clock. She slowly stretched, then remembered her Father's death, her painful first change, trying to get away from the pain in her heart as she ran as a wolf, going to sleep with another wolf, and waking up next to the most yummy, perfect naked man in history!

Well, that was almost too much to start on her twenty-seventh birthday. Kaitlan knew that she had to make arrangements which meant she had to fly back to the city of her birth to do so. This made her even sadder. But, being realistic, she knew it would not be today. She also knew that Sam would take over in her absence, and would arrange all.

She dressed in a pair of jeans, and a very tightly fitted white t-Shirt. She only had one other bra, and her work out bra was shredded. For whatever reason, though, that made her grin. Yep. Cordone needed a bit of torture before she let him take her as his mate. And, this t-shirt should do the trick, especially when it left little to the imagination. Just the thought of Cordone seeing her with no bra, caused her nipples to harden quite prominently in the t-shirt. She donned a jacket, because she knew she would see Dan, and the t-shirt was only for her mate. She wore no makeup, but brushed her hair letting it hang down over her breasts. Yes, she was hot for him. She walked onto the landing feeling her breasts bouncing under her jacket. Her teeth bit her bottom lip as she looked over the railing. Did all that really happen, or was it just another dream? She saw Cordone walk to the railing just below where her room was, and noticed that there was a gate on the railing that was open. He stepped into mid-air, and dropped to the main room. Then, he turned his head, and looked up at her with a smile.

Well, that settled it. It was not a dream. She backed up, and noticed, for the first time, a gate right in front of her. Without a thought, she opened it, then she, too, stepped into mid-air. For a split second as she dropped, she thought she had made a mistake, but then, she felt her wolf laugh, and she dropped lightly to her feet next to Cordone. She turned, and grinned at him. Oh, yes! It was going to be a quiet, but interesting birthday for the rest of the day.

~ 11 ~

"H-H-How old are you?   Really?"

Cordone knew that Kaitlan was standing above him, and probably wondering if everything had been a dream. So, he grinned, and dropped to the main room easily. He turned, and met her eyes with the same grin as he watched her open the gate, and step off the landing, dropping quickly to the floor. He saw the momentary scared look, before it was replaced by a grin on her face as she landed just as if she had always been a part of the supernatural world. Most new wolves had to be taught even the most basic things, and it took them several years to learn them. But Kaitlan, well, maybe she really was different. The White Wolf is what Canaan had said her Mother believed Kaitlan was The White Wolf of that dumb prophecy all werewolves were forced to learn in school.

When she turned to grin at him, he felt his heart speed up. Her smile...THE smile that she had given him when he handed her to Canaan the night she was born would never cease to stir his desire for her. OK. That sounded a bit perverted, but he had never seen her that way when she was a tiny baby in his arms. He just knew that she was his mate for the future. No other woman had ever come close, and he would be laughed at had the rest of the males known he had not been with a woman since laying eyes on Kaitlan. But he would wait forever for her. Well, maybe not that long, but at least until she accepted him as her mate.

Kaitlan would never forget that moment when she looked back over the years. Then, her face turned somber, and he knew she was remembering her Father had been murdered. He was grateful that she had had a little reprieve. She had so much to learn. They would begin after the funeral, and after their mating.

They sat down for dinner in silence. Dan brought their food, and she just pushed it around on her plate. Cordone was patient, and for that, she was grateful.

Dan appeared to clean up the table.

"I'm really sorry, Dan, but I just don't seem to have an appetite right now," Kaitlan explained, because she didn't want him to think his meal was not good. She just couldn't eat knowing that her Father had been killed.

Dan nodded. "I understand, Kaitlan. Your Father was our leader; our Alpha. I, too, miss him. But, we will find Zanack...that I promise you." She nodded, and he picked up the plates, and went back to the kitchen. Stopping to turn around. "Oh. I have a little birthday surprise for you!"

He came out of the kitchen a minute later with a small cupcake with a lit candle on it.

Kaitlan's eyes widened, and looked at Dan.

"Oh, thank you, Dan. That's just the sweetest thing anyone's ever done for me!"

She blew out the candle, and ate the little cake, then Dan left to go clean the kitchen.

Her eyes rose to meet Cordone's. They were full of sorrow not only for her loss, but for the loss of a friend. She waited for him to speak. He just rose to his feet.

"Tell me about my parents, Cordone."

He nodded one quick nod. "Let's go into my office."

He held out his hand, and she took it. Together, they walked to the main room, and still holding hands, leaped up to his fourth floor office landing. He took them to a brown leather sofa in the corner. She grinned a bit as she deliberately shrugged out of her jacket. Cordone got a really good look at her breasts, full, nipples hard, and pushing against the thin shirt. He growled, and jerked her against him so she could feel his hard-on.

"If you ever appear in front of anyone else wearing a t-shirt like that but me, I'll take you right there! Do you understand me?" He pulled her tightly to him with his arm.

She nodded, thrilled that he had noticed. Like, how could he not? She just grinned, wiggled her ass, and moved next to him while Cordone watched her fullness bounce as she flopped on the couch.

Cordone wasn't sure how to start, but he knew she was waiting for him to tell her. Everything. He took a deep breath. How would she take the news about their ages, and everything else? He decided to trust her, and began.

"Kaitlan, first, you need to know that your Father and I were friends as pups, and we are very, very old." He stopped at the look on her face waiting for the question.

Very, very old? Exactly how old was Cordone? Inevitably, she asked him.

"H-H-How old are you? Really?" Kaitlan asked in a shaky voice.

He looked at her to make sure she could handle more, and even though her hands started shaking, her eyes never left his. He searched her face, and finally, nodded.

"You have to understand that being a part of this world is not the same as the human world, Kaitlan. We are not human, and the supernatural world has totally different rules for us."

He stopped, and watched as Kaitlan nodded, waiting for her answer. Nothing. He continued.

"Your Father was born two thousand years ago." Kaitlan drew in a gasping breath. He could see her shake some more. He knew she wanted to know how old he was, and he was a bit afraid to tell her. But, he plunged in with both feet.

"I was born 200 years after your Father."

Kaitlan's eyes still stared at Cordone, but her mind was running rampant with this knowledge. Her Father had lived two thousand years? And, Cordon, her mate, was eighteen hundred years old? Her mind could not process it.

"But, I don't understand. Shouldn't I be old as well?"

Cordone took a deeper breath.

"Let me explain. Wolves mate for life. There is only one woman for the males, and one man for the females. We know it immediately, and usually, the mating rites take place no later than the next day. Kaitlan, your Father met Tara fifty years before you were born. He had never had a mate, and no one could understand how, and why, his mate was a human woman. The power of mating is our biggest gift, and sometimes, our biggest curse."

Kaitlan interrupted with, "My Mother said something like that to me, too."

He nodded, and continued. "Your mother, was the most loving, and kindest woman any of us had ever met. She was absolutely beautiful. Your Father knew she was his mate instantly, and for whatever reason, Tara felt the same with your Father. She was only seventeen, but had no family. No one understood it, but it was out of anyone's hands. A mate must be accepted into the Clan no matter what."

Outside the house, lightning suddenly made itself known, followed by thunder. Kaitlan had always felt goosebumps up and down her body when she heard thunder. She snuggled closer to Cordone.

"A Clan is only as strong as its Alpha, and being with Tara made your Father even more powerful than he already was."

He paused waiting for her to process as he went along, giving her time for each new piece of information. The next, though, might throw her for a loop.

"A were and a human are not compatible, Kaitlan. They cannot have children. It's a flat out fact. There have been very few werewolf and human matings, but none have ever produced a child - until you."

"Me? You mean I'm the first cross-breed?" Kaitlan squeaked.

Cordone couldn't help himself, and he laughed out loud while nodding.

"We wouldn't call you a half-breed, Kaitlan, but essentially, yes. I remember it like yesterday. Tara had been feeling really sick for a couple of weeks, and Canaan was terribly worried about her. So, he called Anita Moore, who examined her. Since Tara had come to be in our Clan, Anita had had an almost obsessive desire to learn all about human anatomy. In fact, Anita is more versed on humans than human doctors, now! Anyway, Anita checked over Tara. The odd thing was that according to her studies, Tara had all the symptoms of pregnancy, but knowing that to be impossible, she never considered it. After about two months, Tara began to gain weight. Both she and Canaan were completely in the dark about what was going on, so Canaan demanded that Anita give her a thorough exam including both human and werewolf. Canaan called me with worry, and I sat with him while we waited. He wouldn't admit it, but he was terrified. He couldn't sit still. He paced back and forth, and quite literally, almost drove me insane!"

He stopped, and Kaitlan grinned. That was just like her Dad.

"Finally, Canaan had just had enough. How long did it take to do an exam you might want to ask?" Seeing Kaitlan about to ask the question, he continued with a smirk, and Kaitlan just squinted her eyes at him.

"After about two hours, just as he started to barge into the exam room, Anita ran out of her office after all her tests were done. Her eyes were wide and wild, and she was shaking like trees do when they lose their leaves in the fall due to a high wind. She came to a dead stop in front of Canaan, and her face scared him to death. Then, Anita said..." Canaan!!!! Tara is PREGNANT!!!"

Canaan, in his dismay, fell to his knees. I just sat there with my mouth open. It just could not be! His Tara had been unfaithful to him, and I just remembered growling to think that she would do this! I was almost ready to strangle her with my bare hands. Canaan jumped up, and started into the exam room in a murderous rage, and I had to literally hold him back. Anita jumped up to hold him as well, and the words out of her mouth next, froze us in our place.

"Canaan. Listen. To. Me. Tara is pregnant, but it is YOUR child! YOURS! Listen to me! You and Tara have somehow managed to conceive a child!'

Your Dad's eyes were wild as he tried to take in what Anita had just said. I had a tight grip on him, but like him, I was stunned.

"Impossible!" Yelled your Dad.

"Canaan...listen to me. Tara is going to have YOUR baby! YOURS! I have completed all tests -

both human and werewolf. There is NO DOUBT WHATSOEVER THAT IT IS YOUR BABY!"

The silence in that room was such that a feather could have dropped on the floor, and you would have heard it hit!   I felt Canaan's astonishment. I was busy thinking how this could possibly have happened. But, I looked into Anita's face, and saw truth in her eyes. Pregnant? Tara was pregnant? At that point, feeling your Dad's surprise, and then joy, I let him go. He rushed to Tara's side, and I heard them kissing and laughing together. Anita told me that there possibly must have been, somewhere in Tara's line, a werewolf gene. No guarantee of it, but there was no other explanation for it. As far as we know, though, she never found a werewolf gene in Tara. However, in truth, your parents should never have been able to conceive - not even with one gene. It was impossible, but it happened."

Cordone had looked off in the distance as he was relaying the story of her conception, and he turned to look into her eyes which were stunned with the revelation. She really wasn't supposed to have been conceived let alone born!   He hoped she was ready for more.

"I had never seen two people as happy as your parents were when they realized that they were compatible enough to produce a true miracle. Yes, Kaitlan. Your conception, alone, was a miracle. Your birth? Even more so."

He gave her a few minutes to absorb the information.   She was fascinated to hear all of this.

All those romance stories always combined a teenager with some supernatural being, who fell in love with each other. And, this reminded her those stories - and she was at the center of this one! And, there, before her was that supernatural being, and he was hers! Then, a thought came to her.

"Cordone? Were you there? I mean, when I was born?"

Why wouldn't he be there supporting his best friend?

The hardest part was coming for him as he nodded at her wide smile which disappeared slowly as she watched the pain on his face.

"What? Tell me, Cordone."

He nodded again. "I was more than there, Kaitlan." He looked up at her. "I was the one who delivered you."

Cordone delivered me? From my Mother's body? Cordone? She was speechless! She looked at his hands. Strong with a tanned, slightly olive skin. She reached out to touch them. These hands delivered me?

Cordone continued. "Anita was away on an emergency, and Tara was having a very hard time with her labor. I was the only one with the experience due to my battlefield days. When you dropped into my hands, you were stillborn. I blamed myself. Your Dad knew that you were not alive, but we did not tell your Mother. However some way, she knew it. Still, she insisted you were alive. I took you out of that room, and gave you to Anita's nurse, who removed your little body from our sight. I turned to stand guard with Sam. It was my fault. You were dead, and I couldn't stop Tara's bleeding out."

The pain in his eyes mirrored his heart, and Kaitlan's tears silently ran down her cheeks at the sorrow he must have suffered knowing he blamed himself for her death and her Mother's. She scooted to him, and put her arms around his neck as she wanted to be close to him - to comfort him. Then, she pulled his head to her breast as a woman would comfort her husband, or children. She held him there, and he didn't move.

"Cordone, you have to know it wasn't your fault you thought you had done something wrong. These things do happen in life. You did nothing wrong at all," she cried into his neck, while stroking his hair.

He sat up, and lifted his arms wrapping them around her. He clasped her tightly to his shaking chest as he remembered that she had been dead in his arms. Now, he couldn't - no - he refused to remember it. They stayed locked in each other's arms for several minutes, and then he gently put her away from him.

~ 12 ~

"Fate has a Habit of Biting You on the Ass Whether, or not, We Like It!"

One lone tear ran down Cordone's left cheek as he continued. Kaitlan wiped it away gently.

"I could hear what your parents said to each other as she died, and that will always remain with me, Kaitlan. It was a private moment between them that I will never abuse by telling anyone - not even you. Sam heard as well, and he would never tell, either.

I didn't want a mate after that. I never wanted to be mated. I didn't feel like I was worthy of a mate. Above all, I didn't want to feel what Canaan felt. I made a conscious decision to never take a mate, no matter what, on   the night of your birth."

He ran his fingers through his hair.

"Fate always has a habit of biting you on the ass whether, or not, we like it." Kaitlan told him.

Cordone nodded, and pulled her tighter to his body.

"We heard feet running down the hallway. Anita had just returned, and was running toward us with the biggest smile I had ever seen on her face over the long centuries. In her arms was a tiny bundle in a pink blanket...moving."

"It is our custom that all children born of an Alpha be presented to the Alpha by his Second. I was your Father's Second, Kaitlan. Anita placed you in my arms, and pulled the little blanket back. Your eyes met mine. In that instant, I had no choice but to claim you as my mate. Fate is shitty sometimes. But, I was helpless. You were my mate, my life forever. You were mine! I remember how jealous I was even just to hand you to your Father."

"Why, Cordone?"

Cordone turned to his mate, and stared into her eyes. He was happy that he was holding her, again!

"Simple. I didn't want him to have you. You were mine! But, I held back. Either I claimed a tiny newborn as my mate, or I left. I would have been lucky not to take you before you were eighteen! I felt I had betrayed my Alpha. So, I came back to my ancestral home to stay. I became a recluse. I thank our Creator for Dan, because if he had not been here, I would not have kept my sanity."

He turned to kiss her forehead. Kaitlan wanted so much more than that right now, but she knew he had to get it all out of his system first. So, she waited while he continued.

"Your Father never knew that you were my mate, and I never told him. Never did I ever think that I would see you again, let alone have you here in my own home next to me."

He looked into at her eyes, and did not waiver as he finished what he needed to say.

"You are my mate, Kaitlan." He stopped, and

waited.

Kaitlan's mind was trying very, very hard to take in everything that Cordone had told her. Then, she looked at him, and knew what her Father had meant. She stroked Cordone's face gently, then raised her lips as she kissed him gently. Cordone froze in surprise at the kiss. Then, she pulled back, and smiled at him.

"THAT was what my Dad was trying to tell me. Cordone, he KNEW I was your mate! He knew it! That's what he meant by our destiny together!" She sat up straight in sheer excitement, and looked him straight into his eyes.

Cordone raised his eyebrow at her. What the hell was she talking about?

"We are mates, Cordone. It was pre-ordained long before I was even conceived. Don't ask me how I know this. My conception was not a coincidence; my birth was not a coincidence. Claiming me as your mate was not a coincidence, either. You were born to deliver me. You were born to be my mate, and I yours. Whatever happens, we will do it together as mates, as lovers, and as equals. Daddy named you as his successor. You, Cordone, are the Alpha of the Clan."

Cordone's smile was as bright as the sun as he heard Kaitlan, his mate, tell him that he was hers! Dimly, he was humbled by being named successor, but it paled into insignificance when she claimed him as her mate!

"And, you, Kaitlan, are heir and Alpha female of

the Clan, my mate, my lover, my life."

His mouth came down on hers with all the longing of all the years he had waited for his mate. He crushed her lips under his, and she gave back to him kiss for kiss.The thunder outside paled to the thunder of love that was unleashed   inside the house.

"So," Kaitlan asked as she was curled into her mate, his hand just below her breast. She wanted him to cup it. She wanted to feel his hand on her. She wiggled a bit to see if he would catch her drift. Then, when he didn't move it, she sighed. Nope. Oh, well.

"What happens now?"

Cordone tightened his hold on her as he answered.

"Well, if you want your virtue intact, the next step is our mating immediately followed by consummation."

Kaitlan's green eyes were mischievous as she teased, "Who ever said I wanted my virtue intact?"

Then, he grinned devilishly as he felt himself hardening. He knew she wanted him to feel her breast. He'd let them both suffer long enough, and so he let his hand slowly slide up, and slightly forward, inching closer to her left breast.

Breathless, she said. "OK. I'll *bite* (ha ha). What happens?"

Cordone rolled his eyes, then howled with laughter. Kaitlan had no idea that she had said the magic word as to what happens in a bonding. Kaitlan looked at him as if he had lost his sanity. He pulled her even tighter as his lips brushed her neck -

with his fangs extended. Kaitlan didn't know about the bonding, so he guessed he had better tell her now. No more holding back. No more secrets.

"First, mating is done naked." He whispered.

He watched as she blushed a beautiful, bright red.

"Why?" She asked him timidly.

"Because the Blood Bond is so strong, an urgency to procreate comes immediately afterwards, and is an extremely strong emotion. It's immediate. Second, I bite your neck, and you bite mine taking a small amount of blood to swallow. This is what bonds us together permanently."

He looked at her with fangs descended, and waggled his eyebrows in amusement just waiting for it. And, here it came!

"Did you…I mean, did you just said procreate?" She squeaked out. Who talks like that? "We bite each other's necks? Swallow blood? What are we, vampire werewolves?"

He laughed out loud, again, and just pulled her tighter sliding his hand to the side of her breast. Close, but not yet close enough for him.

"Unlike human marriage in front of family and friends, the Blood Bond is completed in total privacy with just the two mates, and it is far more binding than human customs. It's the most intensely private act by mates, and it's how we mark each other so all others will know we are mated. These are the only scars that will never heal on our necks. They will remain there forever. It will not be, by far, the last time we nip each other through the years, but these are the mating marks. No other will ever come between us, because to do so would sign one's death warrant. A mated male is fiercely jealous of any other who would dare take his mate."

Kaitlan nodded, but inside was a bit nervous and scared - until Cordone added the next part.

"Then, my dear mate," he said, watching her face as he, finally, cupped her breast, hearing her sigh as his finger brushed against her hardened nipple. "We consummate our bonding immediately. As I said before, the urge for a wolf to impregnate his mate is so strong, the first act of consummation happens extremely fast. And, I am eagerly looking forward to our coupling!"

He laughed at her false, outraged face. He knew it was not real.

"Why do the males want to impregnate the females immediately?" She felt so dumb on werewolf stuff!

"Not just the males, Kaitlan. The females want it just as much. It's something in our genes. Anita could explain it better, but for the rest of us, it's nature at work to preserve our species. We have very few pregnancies, and they are getting more rare. But, the urge is still inborn into us. You will feel it as strongly as I do. You will want me to give you our child. Trust me."

Kaitlan was breathless at his admission he wanted her so much. And, the rest? Well, her nipples were already hard, but as his thumb began to tickle one of them, they hardened so much more causing wetness to flow steadily from her core. Her panties were already wet!

Her nipples, hardening even more under the cooperation of his thumb, were driving him insane for a taste!

She arched backward pushing them even tighter against her thin, white t-shirt.

"Now, that does sound great! OK, buster. Let's talk about the when." She was breathless.

"Perhaps after your Father's funeral?" Cordone did not want to wait, but this was still a sad time for her.

Kaitlan thought about it for a minute.

"No. I don't want to wait that long. Daddy's last command was that you protect me as your mate. He said as much. I don't think it would be wise to wait. I don't really know why."

"Are you sure?"

She nodded letting her hand, "accidentally", slip down to his lap onto his hardness. She grinned at him wickedly watching him flinch at her touch.

"I know Mom and Dad would not want us to wait. Besides, I thought you said once both realized they were mates, the Blood Bond had to be done immediately, right?"

"You are right. We are done with waiting. Twenty - seven years has been long enough!"

He grabbed his phone, and called Dan telling him what he wanted him to do - and fast.

"I have asked Dan to prepare where we will

mate.   It will take him about an hour. I suggest you change into something, uh, with less coverage. In truth, you will need no clothing at all, but this is new to you, so, it may make you feel a bit better about it. You will need nothing else. Dan is discreet, and is going to the city to stay for the next twenty-four hours, then we will take the jet back." He kissed her deeply. "Wear something easy for me to remove!"

"Whatever you want me to do is fine. So, yes. I will.   I just happen to have the right thing!" Then, "What do you mean, twenty-four hours?"

Well, he'd told her almost everything so far. She was really in for a huge surprise - pun intended. He grinned.

He pulled Kaitlan up, and patted her bottom.

"Well, and most mates think this is the best part. For the next twenty-four hours, we spend the time fully engaged in sex!"

"Is that even possible?" She asked.   Her eyes were huge as she looked at him.

"We are werewolves, Kaitlan. We have incredible strength, and most important of all in mating, stamina.   It's the way we were made. I promise you…it will be very enjoyable." His mouth turned up wickedly. And, then, he turned serious.

"It's to make the Blood Bond permanent. If the twenty-four hours are not completed, a werewolf will go rogue, and once done, can never return to sanity. They must be killed. Dan is the only one with the knowledge, and experience, to keep a wolf from going rogue, and the one who is called upon to kill them."

Kaitlan's hand flew to her mouth in horror.

"That's horrible! Is there any other way to go rogue?" She asked.

"Only one. If a werewolf does not allow their wolf out in a very long time."

Kaitlan nodded. And, then, color rose in her cheeks. She turned, went to the platform, and leaped to her room. She had just the thing for his "less coverage".

"Cordone Valon, you are in for one hell of a surprise!"

~ 13 ~

Subsection: Evil Never Meets in the Light of Day

In a run down building that looked as if it would crumble any moment, in a darkened room, in a basement filled with rats, three taller rats stood at a table cloaked in darkness except for a small lantern on the table. They couldn't see each other's faces, but Rat One had a black leather jacket on. Tall, but it was hard to tell how tall he really was. He stayed away from the light just enough so no one could see his face. Rat Two was also tall. His eyes glowed red, and the light revealed a toned and tight torso, but his face was in shadow as well. Rat Three was shorter than the other two. Wrinkled torso, face in shadow. Their features could not be detailed. They did not want anyone to see their faces. Rats Two and Three had their hands over their noses at the stale and rotten stench while the First Rat didn't seem to care at all. The basement was being used to dump waste, animal carcasses, as well as partially eaten humans and other supernaturals. Unseen blood on the floor and walls due to the darkness, just added to the smell.

"Geez, it stinks down here!" Whined the Second rat. "It was just plain, damn bad luck that Canaan sent his daughter away before we could get her. And, no one knew where he sent her anyway, and weren't

YOU the one that was supposed to have grabbed her?" Pointing an accusing finger at rat number three.

Rat Three pulled his arm back, and back-handed Rat Two sending him flying at least 15 feet where he hit an unseen wall in the darkness, and fell into a bunch of dead bodies.

"I'm going to send you to hell!" Yelled Rat Three.

Rat Two stood up, and sped to Rat Three moving so fast, a human's eye would never have seen it. Rat Two clutched Three's throat in anger lifting him high against the opposite wall.

"Do not ever touch me again! You are nothing to me, and I'll break your neck like the weasel that you are!"

"ENOUGH!" Shouted Rat One. "Drop him, now, Beta, or I'll kill you here, and now, making sure you are rat food!

"And, you," he yelled, "Mu, you so much as raise a hand to my Beta again, and I will personally have your body ground up alive in a wood chipper, and fed to the rest of the rats!"

Beta released Mu, and both growled at each other.

"This is business, and that's why we are here! Beta, you had better make fucking sure Viper has done his job, and Canaan doesn't draw one more breath in this life! And Mu, FIND HER NOW!"

The Alpha in the group was fed up with incompetence, and these two were the worst choices he could have made. But, he needed to make sure that he had full cooperation. That's why he had to bribe them. These two were as about as honest as a politician! Once they had served their purpose, he would kill them both!

"Alpha?" Mu began. Alpha turned, and looked at him in disgust.

"What?"

"Well, I just had a thought...if Canaan was dead, will that not bring the girl back to arrange his final rights? She would come to us, wouldn't she? "

Beta agreed with Mu who was still rubbing his throat. "Wherever she is, O'Hara's death should be enough to bring her back here. We won't have to look for her."

Beta and Mu stood shaking as they waited for Alpha to answer. Alpha turned, and walked into the dark, then turned back to the small light that only illuminated bared fangs, and a snarling grin. These two were incompetent, but quite frankly, every so often, they could be a help to him. Otherwise, he wouldn't keep them around at all. He'd kill them in a second. But, in this, he nodded to them in agreement.

"Yesssss," he hissed. "Make sure you get her this time!" Alpha ordered.

Beta and Mu skunked into the darkness of the basement, and out into the night.

He called himself "Alpha" because he believed he should be Alpha of the O'Hara Clan. If Canaan died before he named his successor, then he would be ready to take over immediately. He grinned as he casually walked down the street in the worst part of town. No one would ever guess that the downfall of the O'Hara Clan was about to come to fruition. Yes. This was going to go perfectly. Once he mated that bitch, Kaitlan, he would, personally, kill her himself, and that would free him to take over the Clan.

Looking around, he realized that he was hungry, so he wondered what might be on the menu for a late night snack? A couple of hookers standing under a corner street light was classic. He had no need for human hookers. He found enough women eager to spread their legs for his cock, and he didn't want to bang them right now. Maybe later? A snarl lifted his lip at his own joke.

For a minute, the thought drew him to his next move after he had his hands on Kaitlan O'Hara. He would carry out the mating rites followed by raping her. He was certain she would never consent to his cock in any way. She was a bitch, and he hated her guts. Raping, beating, then raping her on their mating, would be the only fun he would have. And, that made him laugh out loud at just the thought of the pain he would inflict upon her! All his anger and hatred would pour into the acts, he vowed to himself! Just the thought of having to even be inside her body let alone biting her and having to swallow her blood disgusted him so much, he gagged out loud. A half-breed! But he would do whatever he had to for the power - even it meant being inside the body of a half-breed. He doubted he could ever remove her stench from his body, even when he plunged his dagger into her, slashing her body until she died - slowly…very, very slowly! Slicing her up alive is what he would do. Yes! Skinning her alive, maybe! He licked his lips at the thought of her blood spurting out all over his naked body as he sliced her over and over. And, after that, he decided he'd drain what was left, and bathe in her blood before he showered it off! He snorted loudly with happiness and glee at the thought. He wondered if he could get a tattoo with her blood mixed into the ink? The thought of mating with the half-breed at all almost made him too sick for his snack, and he refused to let that bitch deny him his midnight treat!

Pushing her to the back of his mind temporarily, he continued to observe around him. A drunk came staggering out of the bar across the street. Hmmm. Nope. No booze tonight. He needed a clear head for the next few days. He looked around getting a bit depressed at the very few who ventured out in the street at 2:15 in the morning. A gang strolled down the street looking for action, but finding none. Nah. He'd had enough of those idiots for a while. His last, he admitted to himself, was the worst he had ever eaten! He continued to look, and his eyes fell on his snack! Ahhhhh! Perfect, he decided as he saw a homeless man sitting in the darkness of the alley. His fangs descended, he phased.

~ 14 ~

How Do You Give Yourself, without Reservation, to Another?   Love.

An hour later, Kaitlan was ready. She had brushed her teeth, shaved, but put on no makeup. If there was going to be a twenty-four hour marathon, she didn't need it. For some reason, she had put a joke gift she had received from Sarah two years ago into her luggage. Sarah never wore underwear, and Kaitlan hadn't known it until then. Sarah told her the reason was she hated the confinement! So, she pulled out a very, sheer lace. It was mint green, Kailan's favorite color, of course. Green made her eyes pop. It also left very little to the imagination it was so sheer, but this was the only time she would mate, and she wanted to be beautiful for Cordone. Made sense, actually, to wear little with the biting thing. She put it on, and it softly fell to just below her hips without clinging to her body. It was loose and flowing as she moved. It was almost totally see-through with no matching panties. Just another barrier, and she knew she wouldn't need them anyway. She always believed that "less is more". Moisture begin to form between her thighs in anticipation. Spaghetti straps held it up, but the neckline plunged deeply to just above her nipples, barely covering them. She took an excited breath. Then, nervous, she phoned Anita.

While Kaitlan was talking to Anita, Cordone was preparing himself as well, and pulled on a pair of coal black silk boxers with nothing else. He wouldn't need them later, anyway. He didn't want to be confined by briefs. His erection was hard, and needed freedom. He remembered this morning when Kaitlan awoke with his hardness against her back, how beautiful her blush had been when she realized it. Her naked back was fully open to him, and it was beautiful, right down to her perfect hips and legs. He had become hard before he woke, and he wanted her to know it. He stared at those hips that held the secret and promise of ecstasy. But, what stirred him even more was the birth mark on the bottom of her right hip. It was a wolf. This was on all who were members of the O'Hara Alpha Clan throughout history. How he had wanted to place his finger there and trace it, then reach that same finger down to her soft, creamy, wet folds feeling her readiness for him to take what was his.

Cordone rubbed his head. He felt like a horny teenager with his first crush! How corny did that make him?

He looked at his watch, and knew it was time. Dan had finished Cordone's instructions by now, and had made himself scarce. He'd heard the sound of the car leaving the garage a few minutes ago. Dan had told him he had never been happier for his friend. That had meant a great deal to Cordone.

Cordone's life was about to change forever, and

he reflected upon a time in his life when he vowed his loyalty to Canaan.

Canaan and Cordone had been inseparable. They had done everything together. Dan, Anita Moore's best friend, had joined them making up three best friends. Sam had been injured from a fall off a bluff, and the three had become four. Finally, Richard O'Malley had made them five. No five men had ever been more loyal to each other. They all trusted each other with their lives.

Sam, Dan, and Richard had pledged their undying loyalty to both Canaan and Cordone. When Cordone had to leave, Dan went with him to protect the next Alpha, unknown to Cordone. Sam and Richard had stayed to protect Canaan. In these few seconds of thought, Cordone elevated Sam to his Second, and Dan as his Third. Richard, already on the council, would be elevated to the chair to the Alpha's left.

On a run when they were young wolves, Cordone and Canaan had a serious talk. Unknown to either, Dan, Sam, and Richard were always around, always unseen, giving the two privacy.

Canaan and Cordone stopped as they came to a high bluff overlooking the O'Hara Clans' homeland. It never ceased to awe either of them from this vantage point. It was the their favorite place to be whenever their wolves were able to get away for a run. Canaan phased to his human form surprising

Cordone who followed his lead.

Nakedness was part and parcel for weres, so much so that the neither male nor female noticed. But, if a male and female phased together who were mates in the presence of unmated males? That was an entirely different matter! An unmated male who viewed a mated female, could easily cause fights, and even deaths between males. Werewolves followed the laws of nature, not man.

Although Alphas, Seconds and Thirds could easily speak to each other telepathically in wolf form only, this was too important to Canaan. He had to say it aloud. Furthermore, the terms, Beta, etc., had been dropped three hundred years before in favor of the more current terms of Second and Third.

"Wonder when we will find our mates, brother?" Canaan had asked Cordone.

"No idea, brother," Cordone had answered. He had also wondered that himself. A male was never complete without his mate.

"Our Dads say it could come today, or a thousand years from today."

"I take it you haven't felt the pull, either? I dream of that day, though. We just aren't right without a mate."

"Speak for yourself!" Cordone had laughed, elbowing Canaan in the ribs.

"Cordone? I need to ask something of you," Canaan continued trying to put his request into the right words.

Placing his hand on Canaan's shoulder, Cordone vowed, "As your future Beta, and best friend, you can ask anything of me, and it shall be done ."

Canaan nodded.

"If I am ever lucky enough to find my mate, and even more so, to have a child," he started, then turned to look at Canaan dead in the eyes, "and, if that child is ever threatened in any way, I will say three words to you alerting you to trouble within the Clan. It will between you and me. No one else will ever know our signal."

Cordone had nodded. "Say the words, Canaan, and it WILL be done! In this, I make my vow as your Beta. No harm will ever come to your child."

"Thank you, my friend. It will be these words - 'Keep him/her safe'. Do you understand?" Cordone kneeled in front of his Alpha to be.

"It shall be done, Alpha," he had repeated his sacred vow.

Now, he remembered his last conversation with his dearest friend.

In the midst of being thrown for a loop that his half-human mate was being sent to him, followed by Canaan's death, Kaitlan's phasing, and the revelation that she was in danger, he had totally forgotten. Now, the words came back to him like a sledge hammer!

"Keep her safe!" Canaan had said.

Cordone was overwhelmed about becoming Alpha. Oh, he knew he could do it, but he never, really, thought it would happen, and certainly not the way it had. Canaan had been the Clan's most important, and finest leader. He could never hope to fill his shoes.

Kaitlan had said her Father had known all along they were mates. Apparently, so did both Sam and Dan since Canaan never withheld information from Sam, and Sam and Dan shared all important information. How could he have missed this? He shook his head at his obvious ignorance. He should have seen it. But his fear that his best friend might not accept him as an appropriate mate for his daughter scared him so much, he ran. He had been a coward, yet Canaan had respected Cordone's decision. But it seemed that Canaan had plans, already, to throw them together when Kaitlan's twenty-seventh birthday rolled around, and Cordone didn't get down to business before that happened.

No one would ever harm her, he vowed again to his friend.

Cordone realized he had stopped at his bed. Kaitlan was right. Her Father had said that he wanted them mated, but what Kaitlan didn't realize was that it was an emergency. She already knew about it, but he didn't want to say anything.

All his thoughts disappeared in that moment. He had a vision of Kaitlan laying there while he made love to her. As excited as he was, it was time to take his mate. He'd waited long enough.

He stepped onto the landing, and dropped to the main floor. He looked up. Kaitlan stood there with the light behind her dressed in what looked like - almost nothing! His breath stopped as he watched her step off the platform. When she landed next to him, she smiled devilishly. He looked her over. Why had she even bothered to put anything on? She was almost as good as naked already! She was beautiful! He could see her breasts very clearly through the thin material, and a hint of curls, but no panties? The little Vixen! She had dressed that way deliberately! And, DAMN! He loved it! His cock hardened even more. Her eyes had dropped down to look at his boxers which were doing a pretty bad job of hiding his huge erection. She even licked her lips! That just made him grow more as he thought about her mouth on him! Then, he felt his mouth water with the thought of his own mouth drinking from her most intimate place, and he licked his own lips! Her face blushed!

But, this was a solemn moment, an important moment in their lives, especially hers. He would make it beautiful just for her. He tamped down his desire for her, and held out his hand. She placed her hand in his, and they linked fingers.

"I have a special place on my property that is mine, and mine alone. No one goes there. You will be the first to ever enter it, and today was the first time that Dan was there. He has prepared it for our mating."

He led her out the back door, down the multi-leveled deck, and out into the woods.

"Is it far?" Asked Kaitlan.

"No. It's about a ten-minute walk."

They walked, hand in hand, out the glass door

into the wild, and into their future.

~ 15 ~

"The Heart Expands with as Much Love as it can Hold."

Cordone and Kaitlan walked in complete silence with their fingers interlaced. Just touching her like this was sending him into waves of desire.

Kaitlan had been nervous, not knowing what to do about mating. She finally had broken down, and called their Clan's Doctor, Anita Carol Moore. Anita was thrilled to find out that Kaitlan finally knew about everything.

"Anita, I don't have anyone else to ask," Kaitlan began.

"I'll answer if I can," Anita had replied.

"I'm mating with Cordone Valon, tonight. Can you tell me what I'm supposed to do?"

Anita had sucked in her breath. Kaitlan was Cordone's mate? She had no idea! She smiled from ear to ear, and for reasons Kaitlan would never guess!

"Oh, Kaitlan! I am so very happy for you! Congratulations. I can't think of a more ideal mate for you!" Anita had exclaimed. And, then, she told Kaitlan what she needed to know.

Now, Kaitlan was glad she had asked. She was ready for him to mate her.

The moon is never so bright as it is away from the distraction of lights within a city. The stars were brilliant as well, and her eyes easily saw a solid rock wall with an arched opening, exactly where Cordone was leading her. She also knew that even if the night wasn't bright, her wolf eyes would have been able to see it. The arch was obviously hand-carved, about two feet deep, and at least ten feet high. It opened to the most beautiful place she had ever seen. Before her eyes was a large pool carved out of a solid rock with multiple waterfalls. A surround of solid rock revealed no other opening. It was as if she had stepped back into an ancient time. The water was green caused by the reflection of the green leaves hovering over it as if protecting this beautiful place. The clarity, even in the moonlight, was such that she could see the bottom which was absolutely smooth. Tiny little fish were darting around in it. With the moon and stars bathing it in almost daylight, it was, by far, the most beautiful place she had ever seen in her life. It was perfect.

"Like it?" He smiled.

"It's beautiful! How did you find it?" She smiled widely up at him. He thought his heart would stop.

"I found it exploring the land in the early days of my youth. I loved it so much, I never told anyone at all. It was harder to see in those days. I let the twigs and heavy vines keep it a secret, and I snuck out for a swim constantly. Eventually, I cleared it out, and had the rock on the bottom of the pool smoothed out. I'd cut my feet several times over the years skinny dipping. It's as smooth as a baby's bottom, now. Makes swimming much easier in the nude." He smirked at her.

"Skinny dipped a lot, did you?" She blushed, but that devilish look was back in her eyes. Now, they had begun to glow. His breath almost stopped.

"Yep. Alone, though." He pulled her to him kissing her with a long, drugging kiss. "From now on," he whispered, "you will be the only other person allowed to skinny dip with me!"

Laughing, Kaitlan wrapped her arms around his neck as he pulled her to him drugging her with another possessive kiss.

He released her gently.

"It's time for us to mate, Kaitlan."

Kaitlan was shaking inside with both a bit of fear and excitement, but far more with desire. The emotions rolling inside of her were unlike anything she had never felt in her life. It wasn't butterflies, but damn pterodactyls!!

Cordone guided her to what lay to the right of the pool. Now, Kaitlan could see a bucket with a bottle of champagne, two crystal cut glasses, a plate of chocolate candy, cheeses and grapes, and just beyond, next to the waterfalls, a lush, soft green grass area where a large, thick, fleece blanket lay with pillows piled high.

She turned to look at Cordone who was gazing at her in wonder and worship.

"I called Anita. I wanted to know all about the mating bond, Cordone. She gave me a crash course in it!"

He smiled. Anita was the perfect person for her to talk to, and he didn't know why he had not thought of it earlier. He was also secretly thrilled Kaitlan had discussed it with their Clan Doctor for reasons of his own.

Anita had told her that matings were done naked, because, as Cordone had told her, the desire to procreate was immediate after the Blood Bond.

So, now, knowing what she needed to do, Kaitlan stared into Cordone's eyes as she pushed the spaghetti straps off her shoulders, and the thin wisp of nothing fell to her feet.

Cordone sucked in his breath, and let his eyes travel down her body. He'd already seen her naked back, but seeing her this way was perfection. His eyes met hers, and he saw her surprise as they glowed. Then, his gaze stopped at her perfect, swollen breasts as he watched their peaks harden more under his gaze. His mouth watered, and he licked his lips in anticipation of tasting them. Further down, he drank in her flat, toned stomach, her long legs, and then up to the curls hiding what he sought most.

Cordone looked back up, all traces of embarrassment, or shyness, had disappeared as he gazed into the glowing green eyes. She smiled at him with the left side of her mouth slightly raised along with her left eyebrow. She was enjoying his inventory!

It was his turn. Lowering his black boxers, he watched her eyes grow wider as he stripped them off, revealing his hardness to her.

Her eyes stared at his huge erection, and couldn't move them from the sight before her. He was glorious! *"OMG!"* Kaitlan thought. He WAS larger than a human male! His large testicles were hanging low, and very full, between his legs. Anita had told her that male werewolf anatomy was half again the length and thickness of human males, and that male werewolf testicles, when full, would distend to three times the size of human males. This was nature at work insuring the survival of their species. The size was because the males carried both human and wolf together. When Kaitlan had asked her the question, Anita explained that the female werewolf, in human form, was designed to fit with the male's human form. Before Kaitlan could ask, Anita told her no. Werewolves could NOT mate in human form with wolf form. That was impossible, not to mention disgusting! Then, she had continued.

"The female werewolf cervix is higher up." Anita had told Kaitlan. "Unlike human females, a female werewolf's cervix allows full, physical passage of the male werewolf's penis. It enters the womb, directly, allowing the male's semen to thoroughly fill, and coat it. Again, all for the survival of our species."

Another question. Yes, Kaitlan had the female werewolf anatomy even though she was half-human.

The biggest problem, though, for thousands of years, was that they could not mate in their wolf form. They could long ago. And, it was usually in their wolf form that babies had been conceived in the past. But, now their wolf form could neither mate, nor conceive. No one knew what had happened, but in the female wolf form, the anatomy became just a bit too small to support the male wolf form.

Kaitlan had been blushing hard as she heard Anita tell her everything. She was really glad no one could see her right then.

Then, Anita told Kaitlan the best thing she could do.

"Kaitlan, just relax into the mating, but be aware that it will be the most intense moment two mates will ever feel in their lives with the exception of the birth of your child, if you are lucky. Werewolf babies are just far too rare."

The two mates were only for each other, and like wolves in the wild, they mated for life. Anita had always had a bit of a crude streak in her. And, now, it showed up.   "Kaitlan, nothing the two of you can do between you in private is forbidden, and I want all the details of your mating!   For research purposes, of course!" Anita had told her while giggling. Honestly! The woman had no tact!

Kaitlan shook her head remembering their conversation. Now, she looked into the smiling face that held wicked, glowing eyes that were filled with amusement as he saw her take in his size.

"Then, come, mate." Cordone said to her.

No embarrassment. This was just the two of them. It was intensely private, and he was hers forever just as she was his.   Why should she be embarrassed by something that was between only the two of them? There would be no holds barred, nothing they could do together that would not be blessed by their Creator. It was how He had made them.

Kaitlan grinned at him, turned, and laid down on the fleece on her side with her head propped on her hand. She was ready.

She held her hand up, wiggling her index finger as it motioned for him to come to her. Cordone's eyes were burning with love and desire for his mate as he lay down beside her, leaning on one elbow.

She reached out to take one of his hands, and gently placed it on her breast. His fingers automatically brushed the nipples, teasing them to harden even more. Kaitlan's body increased the wetness that was flowing from her entrance with every brush.

His eyes couldn't move as he stroked her. She was beautiful. Her breasts were so perfect, he had to indulge in a sip of them. He leaned his head over the one he had been stroking, and took the tip into his mouth. Moaning came from both of them as he gently suckled it. Kaitlan had never felt so much like a woman in her life. Her tomboy days were completely over! She felt more of her liquid pool at her opening, the excess running onto the top part of her thigh, and then, sliding down her thigh onto the fleece. It couldn't be stopped, and it just excited her more. Surprisingly, she could also feel her cervix swell larger as it softened, readying her body for her mate.

Cordone lifted his head.

"You are so beautiful, Kaitlan. I never thought this day would come."

Kaitlan smiled, and put her hand over his as he continued to stroke her breast. It was a very cool night, but werewolves' temperatures ran warmer, so it was wonderful with the cool breeze caressing their hot bodies.

And, the mating words were finally spoken in the silent of the night with just nature around them, waterfalls gently pouring over the rocks into the pool, light from above, the candles' fire, and a gentle cooling breeze.

Kaitlan gently pushed him back to lean over him pressing her chest to his. She rested her arm on his massive chest, and looked at him in the eyes.

"Cordone Tristan Valon. I claim you as my mate, now, and forever. I know, now, that when I looked into your beautiful black, glowing eyes on the day you delivered me, you were mine…my mate. You were never shamed, nor was I when I chose you that day. I may not have known about who, or what I was, nor do I know why I remember it, now. You were my mate at the beginning of my life. But, we were already to be mates before I was conceived. You are my miracle, Cordone. My world. Only death will separate us, and then, only shortly. Daddy blessed our union from the beginning. Our love will grow as time passes, but it will never stop growing. The heart expands with as much love as it can hold. Cordone, my mate, my love, my life, and my Alpha, I am in love with you so much, my heart hurts. Will you accept me as your mate?"

Cordone had never thought to hear words like that spoken to him. She was right. She was conceived for him. He was convinced that both Tara and Canaan had known this, now.

"Kaitlan Seneca O'Hara, I accept you for my mate from this point forward. You are my heart, my love, and my life. I love you."

Cordone lay back. Kaitlan lowered her lips to his taking her kiss of mating. Cordone turned his neck to her.   She lowered her lips to his pulse, and kissed it. It was beating hard for her. She raised her head, and felt her fangs descend piercing his pulse with them, and blood appeared. She took just a little bit, and swallowed the surprisingly spicy and sweet liquid. Raising her head again, she licked the wounds that would mark him for all time as hers. More biting would happen through the years, but these were the only wounds that would never heal, because they consistently would release a scent telling others he was her mate.

Cordone turned his head back to her with his glowing eyes, and looked into the glowing green eyes of his mate. She lowered her mouth to his, and took her kiss in the final step of mating.

Cordone stopped stroking her, took her hand, and held it over his heart. This was his moment.

"Kaitlan Seneca O'Hara Valon. I claim you as my mate, now, and forever. For the last twenty-seven years, I have waited for you unknowing that your

Father knew we were mates. I left, because I was ashamed of looking upon you as my mate - you, a newborn baby. I felt I must be a pervert, because while it is not normal for it to happen, it has occurred in the most distant past of our history, and then, only to a few. You don't know what that means to now know he blessed our union even as I held you, and your brilliant, glowing green eyes met mine that day. Yes. They glowed for me, telling me that I was your mate. It is overwhelming to me that he approved of our mating without reservations the day I delivered you, and placed you in his arms. Now, all barriers of my shame are gone. I am free to love you the way I have always wished. Kaitlan, you are my heart, my love, my life, and my Alpha."

From underneath the pillows, he brought out a very old velvet ring box. Inside were two rings.

"First, I give to you, the ring given to me by your Father when your Mother passed from this life. It was your great grandmother's engagement ring, and is always presented to the heir of the O'Hara Clan by the Alpha of that Clan, or given to the mates of the Alphas and heirs. I have held it in trust since your Father gave it to me for you, and now, as your Alpha and mate, I give it to you. I also present to you my Mother's mating ring which she wore until her death."

He took her hand, and slipped the rings onto her finger. She was surprised. She didn't even know they existed. Tears filled her eyes as she gazed upon the rings her own Mother, and his, wore. They were beautiful.

"And, now, Kaitlan, my love, will you accept me as your mate?"

Two tears slowly slid down his right cheek. He had no idea how emotional this was. No one had ever truly prepared him for it. Every word he meant with every part of him.

Silent tears ran down Kaitlan's face at the most beautiful words she had ever heard. Anita had told her it always began and ended using the words "claim" and "accept", but everything in between came from the heart of two mates as they said the words aloud to each other. She had told her how intense it was, but nothing had ever prepared her for the stirrings of love that burst into her body as he spoke.

Cordone had touched her heart with his words that no other could ever do. A warmth, a bonding was spreading through her body, and she realized the mating was what she felt. It was something she couldn't explain, but she felt him inside her warming her heart, mind, chest, stomach, womb, core, all the way down to her legs. It was a warm tingle so strong, she felt if anyone saw her, she might think that they could see her glow from the inside out. Yes. It was time as the full meaning of being a werewolf exploded within her.

Cordone saw her eyes glow to a point that they must be lighting his face. He waited for her response.

"Cordone Tristan Valon, I accept you as my mate forever. You are my world, my life, my love, and my mate.   Take me, now, and for always."

Kaitlan lay back, and Cordone leaned over her taking his kiss of mating, then she turned her neck to him.

Anita had told her that the bite didn't hurt at all, but would be erotic, each mate having a specific taste within their blood. Cordone slowly lowered his lips to her pulse, kissing it. His fangs descended, and he lowered them to the pulse. Kaitlan groaned when she felt them pierce her skin as he took her blood. It was spicy and sweet. It surprised him. After having taken the correct amount to seal the mating, he raised his head, and licked the only wound that would never heal.   It was his mark. The fangs of werewolves were as individual as fingerprints, and a scent came from the mark continuously, thereafter warning all others she was his mate.

His glowing, black eyes stared into hers as she turned back to him, and he lowered his head to take his final kiss of mating from her lips.

~ 16 ~

The White Wolf Prophecy Begins!

Heat. Scorching. White-hot flames spread through his body almost instantly as he raised his head from the mating kiss. His balls filled with even more semen than he had, now.

"How is that even possible?" His desire surged, stunning him with the need to impregnate her. Even though he expected it, he knew this heat wasn't part of it. What the hell was happening to him? This was the most intense thing he had ever felt, and secretly cursed Canaan for never having told him how intense it really was. This, though, was nothing at all like he had ever heard from any of the mated males. None of them had described this burning!

Kaitlan's body was filled with the same scorching, white-hot flames. Her heated womb throbbed with constant contractions, desperately needing to be filled. She wasn't prepared to feel this searing need for her mate to impregnate her. The burning Anita had not mentioned. A fire inside her womb was driving her desire higher than she could believe. All thought and reason started to drain, robbing her of her ability to think. The need - an almost clawing need - grew in her to the point she would go insane if he didn't take her now! Oh, God!

What was happening to her?

Cordone turned Kaitlan over quickly.

"Wrap your legs around my waist, Kaitlan!" Urgency making his voice sound raspy.

The need to release the searing pain that was gripping him was pushing him to react more like his wolf, but still in human form.

Kaitlan felt that same desperate need. She lifted her legs, and wrapped them around Cordone's waist as he had asked. Her need was overcoming all thought, now. Just a furious urge for him to be inside her, wanting him to release his seed within her. Her wolf demanded it!

All thought and rationality disappeared from Cordone. He had to take his mate, now. He let loose, and latched onto Kaitlan's mouth kissing her with a desperation that seeped into his very soul. Both of them were on fire with an unexplainable heat. Both were burning inside almost to the point of scorching them alive. They were without thought. A primal instinct took them over, and he slammed his erection into her body without hesitation.

Kaitlan screamed his name as she felt him enter her for the first time. Not in pain. Female werewolves had no membrane to break. But, with an animal instinct she never knew she had. He moved fast and furious within her. She stretched wider and longer for him with each thrust, taking him even deeper. Her body was releasing an amazing amount of liquid that continued flowing from her like water. Cordone threw his head back taking his mate, driving himself harder and harder within her.

His release was coming fast.

"Kaitlan!" He cried out.

She gasped with the ferocity of their love as she felt his heavily filled balls hitting her with every massive thrust of his body.

"Cordone!" She screamed. She was desperate. "I - I need your seed inside me!!! OH, PLEASE!"

Cordone's body sped up with her words, and his thrusts came with an unbelievable power he didn't know he possessed. Her words were all he needed to let loose all the pent up years of desiring her! Of needing her! YES! He desired to give her his child more than anything he had ever wanted in his entire life! He knew the only way to cool the fire was for him to spill his seed inside of her!

Kaitlan was flying high with each hard, speeding thrust feeling her mate reaching his release! She met him thrust for thrust; speed for speed. She wanted him deeper, harder, and she demanded he give her what she needed! One thought, one need was all she could think of - she wanted his child! She realized only his seed, flowing deeply inside her, would cool the fire in her womb!

"CORDONE!!!   She   screamed   loudly. "PLEASE!!!"

"KAITLAN!!!" He screamed loudly, as he felt his seed explode into her.

It was like a pressure washer on full force! Like white water rapids. All speeding his seed to her womb! Oh, God!   It was overwhelming him to a point where he couldn't think!   His body shook with his release! Over and over he spilled his hot liquid inside of her, emptying his balls that had been painful for so long! Sanity began to slip slowly back to his brain with each release of his love into his mate. Somewhere in his mind, he was asking what the hell was happening, but he wasn't sane yet.

Kaitlan had no idea how she could lift her hips so high as she felt his cooling semen flood into her womb, filling it full.   Her womb began to cool down. Sanity resumed.

Cordone's thrusts finally started to slow down as he emptied, and he was cool, again. Sanity resumed.

Then, quiet. Nothing was heard except the beating of two massive hearts, and two lovers breathing hard, trying to take gasps of air deeply into their lungs. Minutes passed, maybe an hour, or more, for all they knew, and finally, the last step uniting them as mates - the consummation - was completed.

Cordone had buried his head into his mate's neck where he had bit her as he slowly came down from the white-hot heat. Kaitlan's arms that had been a vice holding him to her as his liquid flowed into her, lessened.

He raised his head to look into her eyes, and saw her wolf's eyes glowing back at him.

Kaitlan look into his eyes as he raised up from her.   Surprised, she saw his wolf's eyes glowing instead of his human eyes.

They both blinked, and their human eyes returned.

"Cordone? What just happened?" Kaitlan asked him. She had never felt so satisfied, so deliciously replete.

"I don't know. I never heard of it described as white-hot heat," he told her.

"Then, why? Why did we feel that heat? And, I so want your child!"

"Wanting our child is normal, Kaitlan, but honestly? I never heard of any mated male saying anything about the white-hot burning, either." He looked at her. "But, I do know I desired nothing more than to give you my child. I NEEDED to spill my seed inside of you! It was a need so strong, no other thought entered. Almost primal. I lost all sanity with you."

He rolled off of her, both of them sweating and dripping from every pore. Kaitlan's body was overflowing with their liquid. It was like water as it flowed out, and down her onto the fleece. Cordone closed his eyes, and sniffed. Their fragrance was driving him to want something so badly, he was having a hard time not to act on it. He hadn't heard of that happening either. What would Kaitlan say if he asked?

"I had that same response, Cordone. My sanity disappeared, too. Anita didn't tell me about the heat either. Certainly nothing she described matched this!"

She leaned up on her elbow putting her head in her hand. This was her mate; her lover. There was definitely no doubt about that now.

"Cordone, the fire?"

He shook his head. He had no answer. The scorching fire was quenched, but would it return?

"It's not supposed to happen like that, Kaitlan. Not the heat."

"Is something wrong with us?" Her hand lazily traced his chest with her fingers causing him to harden with each stroke.

"I don't think so. We'll check with Anita when we return."

He turned his head to look at her. His hand brushed her damp hair out of her face. She was beautiful. Her hair matted and tangled, the flush of love making on her face, was causing desire to rise in him again. What? After all that he still wanted more without a pause? He was growing again - and fast. He felt his testicles filling up again. Her breasts were engorged, and so big he doubted that she could put her bra on without it strangling her let alone stretch around her. Her nipples were huge. Suckable. This desire felt normal. The other wasn't. The desire for what he wanted was far too great, and then Kaitlan asked him a question.

"Cordone, would you be sorry if you did give me our child just now?"

She had to know. Her need for him growing again.

Cordone pushed the hair out of her eyes, and

pulled her on top of him so she could feel his desire.

"Never, Kaitlan. Never. Whatever just happened, I wanted to place my child within your womb. We both wanted it. I don't know why the desperation, but I do know I should never have been that full. If you do become pregnant because of it, I'll be thrilled beyond measure."

"Really? Because, I'm almost sure you gave our child to me. I just know it!" Her hand slipped to her belly as if she was ready to cradle it. His hand covered hers.

"It's impossible. Humans can't have werewolf babies. Even full werewolf females rarely have them. You are only half, but you have to realize, it is probably just wishful thinking."

Kaitlan shook her head, her breasts bouncing with the movement. God! He was hungry for them!

"You're wrong, Cordone. Your child is growing in me, now."

He flipped her over, and kissed her thoroughly. His mouth slipped to her nipple, and he suckled it slowly. His tongue circled her nipple, and flipped it, causing Kaitlan to arch her hips upward as she moaned.

"If so, I'll be the happiest werewolf on the planet. And, if not," he murmured between sucks, "I guarantee you I'm willing to work some more on it." He grinned. "Oh, just so you know…I forgot to mention that mating causes us to form a bond so strong, we can talk to each other through telepathy."

Her eyes widened.

"Kaitlan, it's one of the biggest perks of being a werewolf. We can talk to each other wherever we are even when parted." He thought directly to her.

"Huh?" Was her first thought.

"Can you hear me now?" He laughed

"Hey! This might turn in handy!"

"Yep. Because I plan on giving you orgasms over and over this way! And, when we are in public!"

Kaitlan started.

"Oh, really? Well, watch it, buster, because two can play that game!"

"Oh, her nipples taste so good!" Cordone thought.

"Oh, his mouth feels so good on them!"

"Funny, Kaitlan. Funny." He laughed.

Amused, she answered. *"Do you want to know what I want to see someday?"*

"Sure," he answered, still happily sucking first one nipple, then changing to the other while slipping his fingers into her wet folds. He hardened more as he listened to her gasp with desire, because his thumb gently tickled her clit.

"I want our child to nurse at my breast while you nurse the other one," she told him as she held his head to her breast. It was something that was so very erotic to her, wetness flowed even more from her. This time she didn't need to be ready for him. She already was. Right now.

Cordone let go of her breast with his mouth staring at her in surprise.

"Did you have the same vision I did earlier?

That vision?"

She stared at him in understanding, and then, nodded her head.

"Yes, I did. Cordone, nothing would give me greater pleasure than to see our vision come true!"

Her hand had reached down and wrapped around his hardness. His tip shining with wetness. She used her finger to spread it over the head, and gently ran her hand down his hardened, velvet shaft.

Cordone couldn't stand it any longer. The scent from their love flowing from her was driving him insane. He leaned down to her, kissing her.

"Kaitlan? I need to drink from you." Cordone whispered between kisses.

She jerked, and looked at him. "What?"

"I need to drink our cream from you that we made together. I really don't know why I have this urge. But, the scent coming from your flow is driving me insane! I'm desperate to drink from you!"

"Do you mean what I think you mean?" She responded, and the thought of his lips against her excited her more than ever. At his nod, she simply said, "Yes. Drink from me."

She laid flat, and spread her legs for her mate. He slowly slid between her legs, and she watched as his face dropped to her opening. His lips touched her, and she arched her hips in excitement. His tongue licked her gently, causing her womb to throb again. He circled her swollen nub with his tongue as she felt his lips suckling the white cream that flowed from her. She didn't know if she could survive this great pleasure. His hands lifted her hips so it was easier for him to suckle her.

Cordone's face, lips, and tongue were wet with their love. He didn't know why he needed it, but he did. He felt an incredible strength flow from her as he drank. And, that same strength flowed into his mouth, and down his throat. The scent and taste of their love was unbelievably incredible! He was craving more, and more he would give to her.

Her hands gripped his hair keeping his head pushed into her heat. His tongue was doing things to her she never felt before. It was as if they were truly animals. And, she adored it! The more he drank from her, the more her body made for him. This was a part of heaven she never expected in her life! She grabbed his head to pull to her lips, and his lips sank onto hers shoving his tongue into her mouth as they shared their love together.

Then, it was Kaitlan's turn.

"You drank from me. It's my turn to suckle you," she whispered to her lover.

She pushed him flat, and moved down to his hardened shaft. Her tongue licked the wetness spilling from his tip. She took its head into her mouth, and slid it up and down the shaft slowly, suckling hard when she would reach the tip. Her tongue licked its way down to the bottom of his shaft, and then slowly slid to lick his heavily laden balls full of semen. Then, back up from the base to the tip, only to swallow it again. It flexed constantly while it was in her mouth, and the harder she suckled it, the stronger it flexed with his desire.

Cordone's hands grabbed her hair, and he wrapped his fingers in it. He was calling her name as he felt her mouth move on him. Drink from him. Heaven had nothing on this! Her mouth felt incredible to him.

Then, Kaitlan slowly straddled him, and lifted her hips as she slowly slid her wetness over his tip taking him inside of her. Her breasts dangled just above his mouth, and he leaned up to suck a nipple hanging in his face.

"OK. I guess we'd just better work on making sure your belly swells with our child, don't you think? And by the way, I have a whole lot more positions to show you!" His thrusting movements were driving her wild with desire.

Suddenly, Kaitlan cried out in pain. She scooted off of him, and in just the blink of an eye, she phased. Cordone didn't know what to do.

Kaitlan's wolf looked at him, and cocked her head.

"Can we talk this way, too? I wasn't even trying to phase. What the hell?" She wanted to know.

"You didn't try to phase?"

"No, I didn't. I didn't even feel her! Oh, crap! Not again!"

That all-encompassing fire hit her, again.

"What?" Cordone asked her, still in human form.

"Cordone? Uh...we can't mate in wolf form,

right?"

Cordone nodded.

"I don't think that's true any more."

"What do you mean?"

Kaitlan turned her back on him, and in an instant, he saw why she had asked. Her wolf was extremely wet for him - and plenty big enough!

Kaitlan turned her snout. *"Well? Am I right?"*

His disbelief must have shown on his face, because she knew she was right.

Cordone thought back to The White Wolf Prophecy.

"When The White Wolf appears, All that once was, Will yet, again, be."

Kaitlan heard that. *"What are you talking about?"* she asked.

Just the thought of him looking at her rump increased her desire.

"It's called 'The White Wolf Prophecy', and says when the white wolf appears in werewolf form, werewolves would, again, be able to mate in both forms, and to have children. No one knows what happened to stop us from being able to mate in wolf form in the first place. The female wolf has always been smaller than the male - preventing sex between them. But, now…I don't know what to think with what I see!"

Suddenly, that same white-hot fire hit him again. He felt his cock growing harder. His balls filling even more after her mouth had done its magic on him.

"Well, let's see if I am the prophecy - that is if

you want to?" She laughed, wiggling her butt at him.

"Well, OK. If you insist. I have to admit to being highly curious!" He phased to his black wolf form.

He placed his front paws on her wolf rump. It seemed absolutely right to him even though he had never known it to happen.

The fire became hotter. It was beginning to scorch him alive as it had in his human form.

"Kaitlan, I'm starting to lose all reason again. The fire is too hot! That same desire to impregnate you is taking over!"

"I know, Cordone. The fire is...oh, God!! I need your seed inside me again! I can't...can't think!"

Cordone proceeded to sink deep within her body. The first werewolves to mate in wolf form in known history had begun. The fire consumed them both as she opened her body for him to pound into her as hard as he could. The single-minded desire for them to create a child overwhelmed them. This time, their wolves took total control of them, and their mating was no different than those of wild animals. Her orgasm was coming, and she began to howl to let her mate know. He howled back at her as he pushed as deeply as he could, and let his seed flow from his body into hers.

As before, when his semen met her womb, it cooled the fire. As before, when it left his body, it cooled the fire. They stayed locked together until he softened, and moved out of her. Reason returned to both of them again.

He went to her side, and stood with her as their breathing calmed down. Kaitlan nuzzled his neck with her snout, then laid down, and turned over as if seeking a tummy rub. Cordone laid his head down on her belly. They stayed that way for quite some time until desire reigned again.

They phased back, and looked at each other, both having that same, questioning look. The fire, and that strange desire to make a baby. They still didn't understand.

Again, their desire peaked. But, this time, it was completely normal, and the fire never again returned in either form. They both sighed with relief. They didn't want to be mindless like that again.

She was ready for him again, and pushed him into a sitting position straddling him. She teased him rubbing her wetness against him. He grinned devilishly as he lifted her hips to set her on top of him allowing him to push inside of her.

They stopped just a moment to wait for the fire that didn't come.

"I hope you are ready, because we are going to be very active for the rest of the day!" Cordone teased her as he moved inside her.

He grabbed a nipple into his mouth, and suckled. His erection, huge, and his balls were filled to capacity, again, but were back to normal werewolf size. He was relieved.

"I'm more than ready, mate! More than ready!" Feeling her mate inside her moving faster and harder

was the best! Cordone, again, released his semen into her that had built up again, and yelled her name as he did so. She threw her head back as her orgasm hit, screaming his name into the night.

~ 17 ~

And, the New Alpha is............?

Kaitlan awoke feeling lusciously refreshed. It was late in the evening, and she was curled into his side feeling his cock pushing into her from behind.

With a wicked laugh, he began to move slowly, deliberately. She arched back against him, and thought how wonderful it was to wake up like this. He reached around to fondle her breasts.

"I agree. It feels great to wake up like this, my love! And, I promise you, there will be many more to come."

"No privacy, I guess?" She panted as they came to their climax.

"I doubt we need any privacy, Kaitlan! We share everything, and are not only open to each other through sex, but we are open to each other in our minds. Call it our getting to know each other period."

He pushed harder as he felt his release flow inside of her.

"Getting to know each other, huh?"

Kaitlan and Cordone knew every inch of their bodies. They had explored every indentation, every line, every place, and in every way possible with their mouths, tongues, and bodies all night long. There had been nothing left unexplored, or untouched. She throbbed when she remembered his tongue inside her wetness in both forms while hers had explored his hardness in both forms. His tongue was a whole lot longer in his wolf form, and she loved it as a wolf! More than once, they had bit each other's necks, drawing strength from their blood to continue their "sex-a-thon".

As Cordone exited her body, Kaitlan turned to him. Her womb held so much of his love that the excess had continually flowed out of her for hours. She never wanted it to be empty again.

"I wonder why we haven't felt the fire, again?" She asked, shuddering as her post-orgasm washed over her. He'd given her so many, she had lost count of them. And, yet, how was it possible for her to want more and more as the hours slid slowly toward when they would have to return. She didn't want to return. She wanted to stay right there. Wanted to be alone with him for ever. Just like this. Both of them always ready for each other.

"If it were within my power, I would keep us here, Kaitlan, naked, and making love, or lust, forever." He dipped his head, and kissed her.

She stroked his face with her hand. "How about a bit of both?"

He nodded as he took her mouth in another one of his soul-numbing kisses. Cordone had never known such happiness. He was content to hold her, and make love to her in every way he could think of just to satisfy their craving for each other. She was his equal in the sex department - giving as well as taking.

This amazing, beautiful woman was his. He sighed, and got up.

"Is it time?" she asked.

"Yes. Damn it, Kaitlan, I don't want to go anywhere else!"

"I know, my love. But, you are now Alpha, and it is your responsibility just as it is mine. Uh…how much time do we have before we have to leave?"

"Dan is getting the jet ready. We should be able to take off by the time we get there. We probably need to leave in about an hour."

"Hmm. And, four hours to the airport, right?"

He nodded. "Just what do you have in mind?" He grinned.

In answer, Kaitlan rose on her knees as if she was her wolf presenting herself to him. Cordone needed no invitation, and falling on his knees, he gave her what she wanted.

Arriving at the Seneca Publishing House the next morning, Cordone and Kaitlan entered along with Dan, and took the elevator to the council chambers next to Canaan's office. Sam was waiting for them, and he saw Kaitlan's one tear roll down her cheek as they passed her Father's office. Cordone kissed it away, and she smiled up at him.

They had managed to make love two more times before they had left.

"I just don't want to leave! I love it here, Cordone!" Kaitlan whined to her mate as he held her.

"Neither do I. But, I guarantee you, we will come here frequently, my love."

They had packed quickly, and an hour later, jumped into his blue SUV to which Kaitlan almost jumped up and down!

"YES, FINALLY"!

Cordone had turned his head puzzled. She laughed, and told him why she had said it. Cordone had just shook his head in amusement.

"You get this excited over an SUV that is in any color other than black?"

She looked at him grinning while she nodded her head excitedly. Her hand, amazingly, had found its way to his lap where it proceeded to make him hard again.

"You know, I need to stop off to put on a bra, before we go to the office."

"I noticed you weren't wearing any after you got here. Why?" He had asked her.

"Well, I could say I wanted you to see my boobs easier, but the truth is, I was in such a hurry packing, I forgot them. And, then, when I phased, I destroyed my work-out bra, and the one bra I did have? It wouldn't go around me!"

He roared with laughter reaching over to flip her nipple through her tight t-shirt.

"Well, damn! I'm glad you did forget them! Makes everything so much easier!" He had squeezed her breast in fun.

They had stayed at her Father's home the night before after landing, and remembering the conversation about her bras, Cordone had a hard time waiting in the car and not following her when they stopped off at her apartment before they reached the office. Kaitlan had darted inside to put on a bra, and change her clothes to something more appropriate. Then, she joined Cordone, and they continued to the office.

Kaitlan, Cordone, Dan and Sam entered the council chamber together which was next to Canaan's office, now Cordone's. The council consisted of no less than nine members: Alpha, Second, Third, the Alpha's mate, and five other members of the Clan chosen by Canaan. The five at the table stood as the four entered.

Richard Morton O'Malley, the oldest member spoke first.

"Kaitlan, it is your right to take your Mother's place at this time. Please." He said, indicating the chair that had been empty since her Mother's death.

Kaitlan broke off from Cordone, reluctantly, and took her Mother's place.

"We will begin to induct our new Alpha." Richard tuned to Sam.

"Sam, do you accept the responsibility to announce to this council Canaan's choice of successor?"

"I do, Richard." Sam walked, and stood behind the Alpha's chair.

Dan stood guard at the door. Kaitlan was fascinated to see all this in action having never known she was in a den of werewolves. She looked around the table at the men she had known all her life. Besides Richard who had been on the Council, for who knew how long, the other members consisted of Lon Alvin McClain who was just so damn creepy, loud, and obnoxious, she couldn't stand him.

Ceasar Stefan Cecchi was from Italy who was the Clan's head of accounting, and a total whiz at numbers. Nothing got by him, and no one had ever cheated the Clan while he had been in charge.

Next, was Roland Millard Tanner (where he came from, she had no idea),and was their oldest member. Even Older than Richard. He had been on the Council since her Great Grandfather had appointed him. No one knew much about him, except that he was a complete skeptic when it came to someone trying to harm the supernatural world. In fact, he would laugh at the idea when someone brought it up.

Last, but not least, came Wayne Daniel O'Kelly (who was a sweet man with a lovely wife - uh - mate). Quiet, but his penchant for Clan relations was unparalleled. Everyone loved him, and he could do no wrong. Therefore, he was head of their PR Department as well as for all their businesses around the world. Canaan had trusted him implicitly. Other Clan had tried to woo him away from the O'Hara Clan, but he was loyal to a fault.

"You may proceed, Sam." Richard declared aloud. Sam dipped his head, and began.

"First order of business is the induction of our new Alpha. As the duly recognized acting Second, I have been charged with the elevation of the new Alpha when a Clan's Alpha has passed into the next life. My authority comes directly from Canaan."

All gasped! He was the ACTING Second? All the members looked at each other in disbelief while Sam continued.

"The last new Alpha appointed to the Clan was Canaan Marshall O'Hara who was elevated to Alpha in the year 2023 B.C., upon the death of his Father, Dillon Canaan O'Hara who was elevated to Alpha in the year, 3500 B.C., upon the death of his Father, Rudolpho Canaan O'Hara, the first Alpha which was formally founded in the year 6000 B.C.

"Whoa, seriously, Cordone? Just what is the longevity of a werewolf?" Kaitlan thought to her mate!

Her eyes met Cordone's. She knew that he wanted to answer her as she heard all this.

"A long, long time provided they do not get killed," he answered her.

Her eyes widened at the answer, then turned back to the business at hand as Sam was explaining more.

"...is the duty of the Second to keep, and record, the rite of passage to the next Alpha, and to name the successor. Since this hasn't been done in a very long time, and deferring to our Alpha female, and heir to the O'Hara Clan..." he nodded at Kaitlan, who automatically nodded back to him. It just seemed right. "...we will keep this short and sweet. We have a great threat facing us, now. The one who murdered our Alpha, and threatened our Alpha female and heir who calls himself Zanack."

All around the table nodded. Everyone had already been briefed by Canaan.

"Before I name the successor Alpha, do you agree to my authority?"

"Aye," all members said together.

"OK. Each Alpha of their Clan chooses, and passes a specific token to his successor at an appointed time which is secured, and held by his Second when needed. This is an ancient rite to insure that the next Alpha will be accepted as the successor chosen as our laws dictate, and without question. Canaan Marshall O'Hara chose the ring which belonged to Kaitlan's Great Grandmother, and worn by Tara Michelle Seneca O'Hara, as his token. He gave this ring to his successor twenty-seven years ago to hold for his proof of leadership. As is custom, there were two witnesses to this act. Myself and Daniel Marcus Wheeler. The successor does not know he had been chosen."

He continued as he watched the tight faces staring at him around the table.

"It is important for all to know why Cordone Tristan Valon has returned to this council chamber. I attest, now, that Cordone was never replaced as Canaan's Second."

Gasps, then silence met his announcement. Fury showed on the faces of the five council members.

They held their breaths knowing a huge change was coming.

"No questions? Good."

He turned to Kaitlan, and asked her to stand which she did immediately with a little smile on her lips. She knew what was coming, and so did Cordone.

"Kaitlan Seneca O'Hara, will you, as heir to this Clan, recognize Canaan Marshall O'Hara's choice of successor?   Will you, heir to the O'Hara Clan, promise to obey, and serve, the Alpha of the O'Hara Clan until the Creator deems him to leave this life?"

She looked around the table, and her eyes stopped on Sam. Was she supposed to say something formally?   No one had told her, so, she winged it.

"Uh...yes, I do accept the choice of Alpha of the O'Hara Clan made by my Father twenty-seven years ago."

She just couldn't wait to see their faces when they found out who it was. Geez! Holding back a huge smile had never been so hard!

"Very good. Please, will all stand and remain standing as the formal announcement is made."

He beckoned to Kaitlan.

"Kaitlan Seneca O'Hara, I now ask you, heir to the O'Hara Clan, that you present to the council the token given to you by our new Alpha which belonged to your Great Grandmother, Lily Nareen O'Hara. It is, now, your duty to tell all who held this token, and who presented them to you.   As I am only acting Second, it is my right to ask you to name our new Alpha."

Kaitlan looked around the table at the stunned look on everyone's face. Slowly, she lifted her left hand for all to see the rings. Both rings situated on her left finger identified the man who would be Alpha, and that she knew who it was.

"I bear these rings as proof of my Father's choice of successor to the Clan of O'Hara. The engagement ring was my Grandmother's. The mating ring belonged to my new mate's Mother. Our new Alpha stands before you, now, as not only my Father's best friend, and Second, but who is now, also, my mate. Gentlemen, may I present to you our new Alpha. Cordone Tristan Valon."

Five pairs of male eyes shot up to her neck, and there they saw Cordone's mark proving she had completed the blood rites and consummation of the mating bond. The same eyes turned to Cordone who bared his neck to all showing his mating marks as well.

The council sucked in their breath! That meant that the Alpha had not only be chosen by Canaan, but that his daughter had been chosen as his mate by Canaan directly!

Kaitlan felt like she was in a cage in a zoo at that moment.

Sam looked straight at Cordone. He stepped out from the table, walked past all the council members, and kneeled in front of Cordone as was the rare, and age old custom raising his eyes.

"Cordone Tristan Valon...as acting Second, I, now, officially recognize you as the rightful, chosen successor by Canaan Marshall O'Hara in front of all assembled. Do you accept the position as Alpha of the Clan of O'Hara?" He bowed his head, and lowered his eyes in submission, signifying that he accepted his Alpha.

Cordone answered, "I accept, Samuel James Knight, the honor bestowed upon me by my best friend, and Alpha, Canaan Marshal O'Hara. I will endeavor to do all that is right and necessary for the O'Hara Clan, to keep it safe, and I shall remain honor bound to do so. I do, here and now, also pledge my honor, my sword, my life and my love to my mate, Kaitlan Seneca O'Hara Valon, for all time until death parts us." He paused.

Their eyes met, and everyone disappeared for that moment as she saw, in his eyes, he meant every damn word! Kaitlan was all dreamy-eyed. Well, what do you know? She WAS the plain girl who DID get the hot werewolf guy!

For some reason, suddenly, Kaitlan knew she was to answer. She didn't know why. She had shuddered when she heard him speak her mated name for the first time in public. She stood and walked past the council members, next to the kneeling Sam, and she, too, knelt in homage to her mate. Kaitlan raised her head to meet his beautiful black eyes looking at her with such love, it brought tears to her eyes. She almost choked up as she pledged her loyalty and love to her mate in public.

"I, Kaitlan Seneca O'Hara Valon, heir to the O'Hara Clan, accept you, Cordone Tristan Valon and mate, as my Alpha of the Clan of O'Hara. I have presented my Mother's ring, and your Mother's ring given to me on our day of mating, after having held them in safety and reverence until this day. I also pledge my honor, my life, my loyalty, my love, and myself to my mate, and Alpha for all time, until death parts us."

Kaitlan bowed her head in submission as had Sam.

Cordone's eyes showed his pride as she spoke the words necessary to acknowledge him as Alpha, but he didn't know how she knew what to say.

Lon McClain jumped up yelling, "NO!"

He addressed the council members.

"It was decided that I should be successor by the council! There was never a Second, nor "acting" Second appointed!"

Richard, grabbed Lon by the throat lifting him off his feet.

"No, we did not, Lon. We did NOT acknowledge that you would be Alpha. That was in your own mind, and you know it!"

"ENOUGH!" Sam shouted.

Richard turned to look at Sam, and took his hand from Lon's throat, dropping him on his ass. Lon jumped to his feet, and started to rush Cordone, but was intercepted by Dan who back-handed Lon, and sent him flying across the room into the glass. Good thing it was not that easily broken.

Sam was very angry, and demanded, "Do you, Lon McClain dare to challenge the rightful Alpha? If you so do, you know we have rules for the challenge. You have overstepped your bounds."

Lon struggled to stand, but he shook his head rubbing his neck.

"Good. Now, you all must kneel, and pledge your loyalty to Cordone in acknowledgment that he is the rightfully chosen Alpha. I will NOT tolerate any more outbursts. Do I make myself clear?" Sam looked at the faces in the room, and all nodded.

Each of them kneeled in front of their Alpha, as Sam had instructed bowing their heads in submission.

Cordone accepted their pledges, then they all stood, and took their places remaining standing until Cordone walked to the head of the table, and offered Kaitlan her seat, first. He had decided that things were going to change more than just in prophecy, and that from now on, his mate sat before he did. She was the heir, after all, and the first child ever born of an Alpha since Canaan.

~ 18 ~

Second and Third are now known

Cordone sat down, then waved everyone else to sit.

"Now that the right of succession has been completed, the second course of business will be to name my Second and Third as is custom. My Third will guard my family from this point forward as will his family until my death. One of you will be replaced. The council will draw lots, and the one who draws the black ball will be replaced by my Third. Is this understood?" Everyone nodded.

Sam prepared the lots, and then stood behind his Alpha. Dan remained at the door as guard. His time with Cordone was about over, and he was saddened by this. What would he do, now? Cordone began to speak.

"First, I will name my Second. There is no one I know who is not fully versed in all laws of this Clan. He will never abuse this position, and he has remained loyal to this Clan without reservations. All will turn to him in matters of Clan law. And, if I am absent, he will serve in my place, and you will obey him as you do me. Therefore, Samuel James Knight, will you accept the position as my Second?

The council was very restless. One of them

would be asked to leave the council. Cordone had made that clear. They knew it, and they were not happy about it.

Sam dropped his mouth in surprise. What an honor he had been given! He knelt in front of Cordone.

"I am honored that you would choose me, Alpha.   I accept the position with great humility."

Cordone nodded to him to place the drawing of lots in the center of the table. This was only one of the duties of the Second.

"Next order of business will be the council will be chosen by lot. The one who draws the black ball, will leave the council chambers immediately." It was not a question. Sam was not asking them.

Each man silently drew. No one had replaced a council member since Canaan had been named Alpha.

"Good. You will place your draw in front of you simultaneously."

All reached out, and placed their balls on the table in a carved, tiny indentation that was designed for the purpose of lots.

The black ball belonged to Lon McClain who growled loudly.

"Lon McClain, you have been chosen by lot to be replaced at the table by Samuel James Knight. Please, collect your belongings, and leave the council chamber."

McClain stood up, pushing his chair to the floor.

"You have NOT heard the last of this!" He

yelled startling Kaitlan.

McClain went to the door where Dan opened it for him, and closed it behind him with a smile. It had a note of finality about it. Something about McClain had always annoyed him. He made a mental note to check into his life.

Cordone continued. "Please, Richard, will you take the chair to my left?"

Richard was happy with his new position. Besides, he was thrilled that McClain was finally gone! The guy was a bastard.

"Caesar, will you please take Richard's vacated seat? The seat to my right is now Sam's."

Kaitlan was so damn proud of her mate!

"You are just soooo good, mate!   I'm so proud of you!" She told him.

"Thanks, Babe! I am proud of you, too!"

"BABE!!! Did you just call me BABE??? Oh, I'm gonna get you for that one!"

"I'll be looking forward to it, Babe!" Kaitlan almost choked when Cordone responded as he sent a picture of what he was going to do to her.

Cordone stood, but Kaitlan did not. She was, to all intents and purposes, their leader, and she stood for no one.   Cordone would never let her bow to him, or anyone else, again - not even himself. The other council members also stood.

Cordone smiled at Sam, proud he could elevate him to the place he should always have had. He waved Sam to take the first chair to his right.   Sam did so. Finally, the council was balanced.

"I have one more position to charge."

The position of Third was very important since this person would protect Cordone, and his family, for as long as he was Alpha, and would serve as the Clan's head of security.

"No wonder Canaan hated council meetings! These are so damn boring! I'd rather be back home!" He told   his mate.

"So would I, Cordone, as long as I get that wonderful stick of yours inside me!"

She never turned her head, but he saw a tiny grin on her lips.

Cordone almost came right then.

"My STICK? What is this? A whole new name for it?"

"You'd better believe it, buster. I have all kinds of new names for it - and where it is going to be! What's the matter, mate? You know I can smell you. I'm so hot for you right now, I'm going to have to change my underwear!   Or, I could take them off.   I do have a dress on, you know, it could make things easy for you under the table!" Kaitlan almost laughed out loud.

"Mate, careful. I'm a wolf, and I might just take you in front of all the council members, and let them watch! Oh, yes! I have always had a fantasy of taking you with an audience!"

"Oh, shit!" The very vision of that caused Kaitlan to have an orgasm right there - in front of all these council members!

"Mmmm! You smell so good when you orgasm,

Kaitlan!"

Cordone was damned pleased with himself! *Not bad if he could get her to orgasm in the council chambers, of all places. He'd rather have been in her, though. Well, that will come later. Good thing only mates could smell each other's arousals!* This time it was Cordone who had a slight grin on his face.

"Just giving you a taste of what's coming later, love!"

Kaitlan shifted a little bit in her chair, her wetness making her horribly uncomfortable. *Damn her mate! She was going to get him for this! But, with a subtle, sneaky grin. She was already making a plan to do it. She also had an appointment to see Anita after the meeting to confirm if she was pregnant. Cordone didn't know it, though.*

Aloud, Cordone was saying, "As you know, Daniel Marcus Wheeler has been with me for years as my guard as well as my friend. I trust him with my life, and now, with the life of my family from now till I see death." He looked at Dan's surprised face, and grinned at him. "He will also serve as head of security. Do you accept the position as my Third, Daniel Marcus Wheeler?"

Dan was almost speechless! *To be the Third, and guard of the Alpha of a pack was second only to, well, the Second!* He had never felt so honored in all his one thousand years!

Dan preened a bit, and stood a lot taller as he stepped away from the door, and walked toward his

Alpha and friend.

He knelt in front of his Alpha and friend. "I am, indeed, honored, and pledge to you to keep you, and your mate safe. Also, any child that is born to the Alphas."

Dan's eyes met Kaitlan's who was startled. He couldn't possibly know, could he? How?

He smiled at his friend, and motioned for him to take his place behind Cordone's chair. Dan would be on guard constantly. The Third always stood above the Council table.

"We must now arrange the funeral of Kaitlan's Father."

The members agreed, and nodded. Kaitlan began to cry softly.

"Anger and hatred are the conduits by which evil seeks revenge" ~ LKK

Beta and Mu entered the door to the rat infested basement where they always met their Alpha.

A chair came flying at their heads, and they barely made it out of the way before it hit them! What the hell?

"DAMN IT!!! DAMN IT!!! DAMN IT!!!" Screamed their Alpha. "How DARE CORDONE TAKE MY RIGHTFUL PLACE! MINE! I am Alpha of the O'Hara Clan! He took her from me! I will kill him if it's the last thing I ever do!" He picked up anything, and everything, sending it all crashing to the walls.

By the time he had nothing left to throw, he leaned on the table fisting his hands breathing very hard. He would NOT be denied his place as Alpha! HE WOULD NOT!

Beta and Mu slowly skulked into the room.

"Uh, Alpha?" Beta cautiously ventured.

"WHAT THE HELL DO YOU WANT?"

"If I may…? Perhaps you might think of it this way? I mean, uh…." He continued warily as the Alpha turned his hatred on him. "I mean…you don't have to mate with her, now. That would have been disgusting let alone degrading to you."

His Alpha glared at him through eyes of hate. Then, he stood up.

"Perhaps you are right. The thought of being inside her let alone taking her blood is repugnant to me."

Mu nodded agreement. "May I make another suggestion?" He looked at his Alpha in terror. "Kill one mate, you kill the other. Would that not be much simpler than the first plan? I-I-I mean…you could gain the power faster, right?"

Alpha calmed down as he stared at his two incompetent morons. He hated to ever admit they had a good thought, but this time, they really did.

"That is a good plan, you piece of pathetic filth."

The human funeral for Kaitlan's Father went smoothly. Little did most know that his body was not in the coffin as they buried it, but the body had been removed, and placed aboard the Clan's jet.

Cordone had set aside an area on his property, long ago, for the burial of Kaitlan's Mother, Tara, and they were taking him to rest next to her.

Once she had endured the human burial customs, they headed directly for the jet, and flew back home. She already considered it her home. She loved the mountains, now, where she didn't in what seemed another life. Cordone had laughed at her nickname for it - The Black Wolf named for his wolf. She had felt that if she was The White Wolf, then, something had to be named for her sexy husband's wolf!

Cordone, Sam, Dan and the council accompanied them to the burial as well. She had not been happy with the council coming. She had wanted to join the Mile-High club! On the way back, after their mating, they both had collapsed, and slept the entire way missing their chance.

Cordone had heard her thoughts. He showed her, in pictures, what he would do to her when they did join it, and it had, again, triggered an orgasm. She was so wet, she would have to go dig a pair of underwear out of her tote that was in the jet's bedroom. She hadn't been able to cause him to orgasm from her thoughts, but, she would find a way soon. He was just so damned smug about it!

Her other friends, Sarah Collins and Lynne Devane joined Anita at Kaitlan's request. No one else knew that Anita was their for two reasons. One of those being Kaitlan's great friend, and the other was in case something went wrong with her pregnancy. She didn't believe it would, but it was still comforting to have her around.

After her first council meeting had adjourned, Cordone had to begin his Alpha duties. Kaitlan begged off feigning a sick stomach. Then, she had gone to Anita for a checkup. She really wanted to know if she was, or wasn't. She couldn't believe how much she wanted to be carrying Cordone's child. Their child. It was so deep within her, it had become a part of her. It was as if it went gene deep. As if it was what was supposed to happen. If she was The White Wolf, and it was real, then her presence, and mating with Cordone, would have changed everything for all werewolves. By mating in both human and wolf form, and if she was pregnant, it would indicate she truly was The White Wolf of prophecy.

While Kaitlan had removed her clothing, and put on a gown so Anita could exam her, she wondered whose idea it was to make gowns from cheap, rough material with all the ties that didn't cover one's backside.

Anita had taken blood, urine sample, and checked her female parts. But, Anita knew something else was going on. Kaitlan had to ask the question.

"Anita," she began, her feet in the really cold stirrups. Good thing she no longer felt the cold as a werewolf, because in past exams, her feet almost froze!

"Hmmm?" Anita responded.

"Uh. Is there a difference in the gestation period

between werewolves and humans?"

Without looking up, Anita had told her.

"Well, the gestation period for just wolves is about sixty-three days." Anita told her, scaring Kaitlan to death. "Oh, stop being silly, Kaitlan. The werewolf gestation is around 120 days, or four months."

That, too, scared Kaitlan. Anita had continued by saying that gestation was much shorter for werewolves than humans. And, a female werewolf would know a lot faster if she was pregnant. Usually the signs were almost immediate after Blood Bondss, and once determined, birth would occur within four months.

Anita had stood up, pushed her chair back, and tossed her exam gloves in the trash. She had seen something very odd, and it was time Kaitlan "fessed" up.

"Kaitlan, what are you not telling me?"

Kaitlan didn't know what, or even how, to tell her the other part. How was she going to tell her that they had mated as wolves? It didn't happen in the werewolf world. So, she asked Anita about it, again.

"Anita, didn't you tell me that werewolves cannot mate in their wolf form?"

"Yep, I did, Kaitlan."

"Ever? Why? I mean, I know you told me before, but can you detail it down for me?"

"Well, that's pretty simple. As I told you before, the female werewolf's anatomy is, half again, smaller than in our human form. The males, however, are larger in wolf form. As you can guess, that just doesn't mix. It's really not all that complicated. Werewolves, in the beginning, were able to mate both ways, and pregnancy could result in either form, but somewhere along the line, something stopped the werewolf matings. It cut down on werewolf pregnancies when the female wolf could no longer accept the male. After that, mating in human form was the only way pregnancy could occur, but was, and is, very rare. Our population dwindled drastically almost overnight. That was long before I was born, of course. I've been trying for years to find out why." She looked up at Kaitlan.

"If it wasn't for the fact that we live a long time, our kind would have been extinct long ago. It's as if something interfered with the wolf part of our lives, and only partly as humans."

Kaitlan closed her eyes, and sighed. Why was she hesitating telling Anita?

"Kaitlan? I've known you for years.We've been friends for a long time. You can tell me. Whatever is worrying you, I'm here." Kaitlan nodded.

"Anita, I think you need to exam me."

"I just did."

"No, I mean in my wolf form," Kaitlan said, and looked up at Anita.

"Why, Kaitlan?" Anita asked cautiously.

"You'll understand when you see me." Anita nodded for her to change.

Kaitlan removed her gown, and phased. Anita just stared at her, and then, jumped back several feet pressing herself against the wall when she saw her. She was flabbergasted. No! It couldn't be true! How? Was she seeing things?

"The White Wolf!" She whispered in amazement. "Kaitlan, you are The White Wolf!!"

Kaitlan smirked beneath her snout, then turned her backside to Anita.

Anita slowly approached her friend, and bent down to examine her. She was totally proficient in both human and wolf anatomy. She moved her hands gently over Kaitlan. Again, she stared in disbelief! Kaitlan was the right size for a male werewolf! Holy shit!!

"Holy shit, Kaitlan! OK. You can phase back." Kaitlan phased, then retrieved her gown.

She turned to grin at the stunned Anita. Anita had just seen the ancient prophecy come to life in her dearest friend!

"Kaitlan! How the hell?" Then, whispering, "I never really believed in the prophecy! But, Kaitlan, you are The White Wolf!"

Kaitlan nodded. Still reeling with the revelation, Anita told her it would take about three hours to get the results. Anita would call Kaitlan with them. She grinned. Anita already knew the results - or at least she thought she was pretty damned sure.

"Kaitlan, you do show symptoms of pregnancy already. Your period will cease immediately if you are. When is your next cycle?"

"Anita, I am already a day late, and I'm feeling a bit nauseous."

Anita's eyebrows rose.

"Really? Well, like I said, that's another symptom of pregnancy."

Kaitlan, now as The White Wolf, the implications would reverberate throughout the werewolf world!

~ 19 ~

SURPRISE is NOT the Word for It!

Kaitlan had spent the next three hours at her apartment packing for the trip for the burial. When she had asked to be excuse from the rest of the council claiming she felt sick, Cordone asked her if she were OK, and she said she'd just go check with Anita. He nodded his head, and sent Dan with her. Now, Dan was outside her apartment door. He had given her a strange, knowing look, but how could he know?

She was in the bathroom, again, when her phone rang. She had been running to the bathroom a bit more often through the afternoon. If she was pregnant, that was just another symptom. She ran to pick it up.

"Hi, Kaitlan!" Anita said cheerfully.

"Oh, come on, Anita! Stop with the hi's." She felt awful at talking to her this way. "I'm sorry. I'm just on edge."

"Are you ready for the amazing news, and even amazingly greater news?"

Anita sounded so excited, and Kaitlan rolled her eyes seeing her bouncing up and down in her office chair. Every time she had discovered something new, she always bounced up and down in her chair, or she ran around doing a victory dance.

"Give, Anita." She was shaking like a leaf.

"First, I found a discrepancy in your DNA."

OK. That was not what she expected. Kaitlan's legs buckled underneath her as she fell to the sofa. She was too surprised to say anything.

"Let me give you a bit of background."

Kaitlan rolled her eyes. She so did not want Anita to beat around the bush. "I know you don't want to hear it, but it's important you know, first."

"OK, Anita. I'm listening." Not! She thought. She was only concerned with one thing right now.

"We have many supernatural species, I'm sure you have already guessed by now. A couple of thousand years ago, the female of the species began to die, and procreation for them came to a dead halt. They are the Elves."

OK. That got her attention. Now, Kaitlan was listening.

Anita continued. "I was working with, and head of, a group that was specifically designed to deal with medical problems of the entire supernatural world. My job was to find out why the female elves were dying out. By the time I found the answer, they were all gone."

Kaitlan gasped. "All the female elves were dead?" How horrible.

"Yes. To make along story short…"

"Yeah. Sure," Kaitlan thought. Anita's short stories were always long ones.

"What, Kaitlan? What was that? I didn't get it."

Cordone asked when he heard his mate.

Damn! Kaitlan was going to have to learn to control her thoughts better.

"Nothing. Just Anita with another of her long, explanation ridden stories." She told him.

"Poor little Kaitlan. Anita has always been like that! Love you."

"Love you, too!" Kaitlan saw a door in her mind, put it in front of her thoughts, shutting it tight.

"…cause after months of searching. They had been fed Wolfsbane. It's an anticoagulant for supers, and was given to them in pure form. The pure form causes any super to bleed out, but it's easy to find."

"They were poisoned??" Kaitlan said in horror.

"Yes. Someone tried to eliminate the Elven race - and they did one hell of job! I was also part of the 'invitro patrol'." Anita could just imagine Kaitlan saying, "No way!" So, she continued her story.

"Yes. Remember, our races have been around a very long time, and while we didn't have a lot of technology, we had advanced in many areas. Anyway, I accidentally spilled Elven sperm into a human egg petri dish, one night. I hadn't had much sleep, but I wanted so badly to find a way to save the elves. They were not compatible with any other species that I could discover. I had precious little sperm to work with, and I had just made that smaller. I picked it up to wash it out. Just before I put it under the water, my wolf eyes noticed something odd. The fluid was beginning to glow. Curious, I used a dropper, and put a specimen on a slide, and looked through an invention I had been working on at the time. The forerunner of the microscope, of course. But, with the aid of our sharp, wolf eyes, we could see through my device as well as a human can see through one today. Anyway, the cells were dividing! I was couldn't belief what I had discovered! I contacted the King of the Elves at the time who was Durond, and asked him to come into the office for a fresh sample. He would do anything to keep his race alive, whatever it took. One of my human friends, Zelah, had not been able to become pregnant. Her husband had died in a battle the year before. I had an idea, and the only way to test it was with two live guinea pigs, Durond and Zelah.

I told her I had an idea for her to have a child. She jumped at the chance when I asked her if she would be willing to let me experiment with her. The King of the Elves, Durond, also agreed separately.

So, I extracted eight eggs from Zelah, and Durond provided me with semen samples."

Kaitlan was breathless with anticipation.

"I mixed his sperm and her eggs together. To my amazement, all eight eggs were fertilized!

"All of them? Isn't that odd?"

"Not so much today, but back then, absolutely! I called both of them in to talk to them immediately. And, I introduced them, despite my own rules of never allowing donors to meet the receivers.

"She didn't notice that he was different?"

"He was dressed as a human with a cap over his ears, Kaitlan! Geez! Anyway, they agreed to let me try. I prepared Zelah while Durond was getting me the freshest sperm sample possible. Then, he paced around like an expectant father waiting on the results."She shook her head as she remembered it.

"I did the procedure quickly, and Zelah had to lay still for awhile in order for pregnancy to take place. At this point, I saw no reason for the hopefully soon to be parents to meet. So, I sent Durond into see her, and keep her company. Hope has a wild way of making things come true, sometimes."

"She was pregnant?" Kaitlan asked.

"She was pregnant, and because he was a super, the pregnancy took place within an hour. Ah, but it was what happened next which startled all of us. The second the cells began to divide, something happened. Durond found his mate, and she fell for him like a ton of bricks!"

"How?"

"With us, it is by sight; with Elves, it is by smell. With humans? Who the heck knows. Combination of things more than likely. But humans do seem to have an affinity toward sight, first. Anyway, their recognition as mates was instantaneous. It is my belief that when Durond smelled her pregnancy, he found his mate, and she did as well. Long before I delivered their baby eleven months later, they had Blood Bonded, and married."

"Wow! Surely he had to tell her about himself?"

"Well, of course! Instead of them living in the human world, they retreated to the Elven. They were happily mated until she died four hundred years later." Anita waited for Kaitlan's response. She didn't have to wait long.

"Four hundred YEARS? What about the child? How does a HUMAN live that long?"

Anita laughed out loud!

"Child? You mean sixteen children! You forget, Kaitlan. A human mate takes the lifespan of their mate just as we do."

Humph! Kaitlan forgot about that one. Wait!

"Did you say SIXTEEN?"

Seeing Kaitlan's astonishment, she continued. "Yep. Sixteen. Their first six were delivered over their first seventy years as mates. Her last child I delivered upon a car crash in the human world. She was pregnant, and the baby was early."

Kaitlan was stunned. "Wait. How long can supers have children?"

"Depends on how long you live. Werewolves, in the past, lived so long, there were usually at least five children born within their lives, but that ceased. Just one is a miracle! But, in the past, we could have children until we die. The White Wolf has appeared, and there should be more babies, now!"

Kaitlan's eyes opened in astonishment. Even though Cordone had told her, hearing it from Anita was making it far too real. Then, she softened a bit. She and Cordone might be able to conceive children, in effect, forever, as long as they were alive! She had a hard time wrapping her head around that one. Anita was still talking.

"...Zelah died in that accident cutting her

lifespan short. Most mates die when their link is severed, and the other mate dies within days. Dying mates can give an order to their surviving spouse when they are dying, and it must be obeyed. It severs their bond link, and effectively stops their mate from dying afterward. It killed Durond not to follow Zelah, but he knew he had to raise their youngest children. So he lived until that was completed. Then, finally, he followed her in death about twenty-five years later. He never truly recovered from the severed link between them. Other elves mated after my success in proving that they could mate with humans. It saved the Elven race."

Kaitlan considered the story she had heard. Then, a thought occurred to her.

"My Father? That explains why he did not die after my Mother, doesn't it? She gave him an order to raise me."

"Yes, Kaitlan. She did."

A tear slid down her cheek. Her Mother had made him promise to raise her, and keep her safe forever. She did not want him following her. It was purely love for Tara, and for his daughter.

"That was such a beautiful story, Anita, but what has that to do with me?"

"Because, and this is the amazing part, somewhere within your DNA exists a small part of an elf, Kaitlan."

Nothing could have prepared Kaitlan for that in any way.

"But, my Mother? If she was part elf, then

wouldn't she have taken my Father's longevity?"

"Yes. And, she could have lived for thousands of years, except murder took her. We are not immune to being killed, and even humans more so. We are long-lived, and just a lot harder to kill. She was given Wolfsbane, Kaitlan. She was highly protected, and yet, somehow, someone breached our defenses, and was able to give it to her through her IV. Before Cordone left, he and Sam investigated everything, but found nothing."

Shit! Seriously? Her Mother was given the same thing that killed out the female elves? The more she thought about it, the more another thought came through loud and clear. And, it almost made her double over in sickness. Her Mother wasn't just murdered. If what Anita said was true, it meant someone INSIDE their Clan - HER Clan - had killed her Mother.

"Anita, is it possible that the same thing is happening now, and it began with my Mother? How many more were females have been killed with Wolfsbane?"

"Canaan knew, but Cordone doesn't, yet. Yes. Canaan was on the verge of finding out who murdered Tara, but he was murdered by an assassin known as the Viper. No less than thirty-two females have been poisoned like Lynne, and only one, just recently, has died in the same way Tara died."

Another thought. If it happened with the Elves and now, is being done to the weres, could there be a connection? From that long ago? No. That made no sense.

"Anita. Have any of the other supers had this same problem?"

Anita was startled. Was it possible? It had never occurred to her that other supers might be killed as well.

"No. I never even thought about that, Kaitlan!"

Was someone, systematically, trying to make the supernatural world extinct by poisoning the females of all the races? That needed to be looked into, and Kaitlan made a mental note to discuss this with Cordone later.

"And, the other news?"   She held her breath.

Grinning from ear to ear, and Kaitlan could see it even through the phone. She knew she was pregnant. She just knew it!

Anita   said,   "CONGRATULATIONS, MOMMY!"

"I-I-I AM pregnant?"

She was right! Cordone had given her his child! Incredible peace and love poured over her. She was having his child! THEIR child! Her entire body went warm with the knowledge. She looked down at her belly, and placed a hand on it. She knew Cordone was going to thrilled, and began to make plans on how she would tell him. She allowed herself to lapse into a dreamy mode when Anita interrupted it.

"Yep! You should feel movements at any time, now. They develop very fast. Now, are you ready for the best, and most amazing news ever to have happened in the werewolf world?"

Kaitlan gulped, and her hand gripped the phone. What could be better than being told she was pregnant with Cordone's child? There was more?

"O…K?"

"You are having twin pups, Kaitlan! TWINS! I still can't believe it! And, they were conceived in both forms! It's never happened in werewolf history!" Anita squealed.

Twins? She was having twins? She and Cordone had made two babies? She carried TWINS within her womb? TWO BABIES? Fathered by both forms?

"Oh, my God! You can't be serious, Anita? Twins?" She squeaked. "How? Why?"

"Well, number one, if you want to know how, ask your mate. I'm pretty sure he'll be very happy to show you! If I had to give a clinical response, I'd say Cordone gotcha knocked up in both human and wolf form!" Anita laughed. "Number two, if you want to know why, ask the Creator! Only He could have had his hand in this! The White Wolf Prophecy is coming true!" And, Anita was off in fits of laughter at her own joke.

"Anita!" Kaitlan feigned outrage. Then, started laughing herself. Twins. She was carrying two little babies in her womb! Uh, oh. Realization hit her! Oh, crap! Was she going to give birth to…what?

"Anita, focus! This is serious! How, I mean, what will they look like? I mean conceived both ways? I mean both of them?"

That just started Anita off in fits of laughter again. Oh, she is SO going to pay for this, Kaitlan thought!

"Relax, Kaitlan. They are both healthy, and you will give birth to normal werewolf babies - with a bit of elf and a lot of human in them. In just under four months, you will have two little wigglers that came from Cordone's own, little wiggler!"

Another joke Anita had made, and she grabbed her sides with another bout of laugher. "OMG!!! Cordone…," she gasped between laughs, "with…one wolfy baby is hilarious. But two…….?"

Anita's giggle box really was turned over this time! The idea that Kaitlan's gorgeous hunk of a mate, holding a baby let alone two in his arms was suddenly hilarious the way Anita described it, and Kaitlan's giggle box turned over, too. Kaitlan couldn't wait to tell him that his gorgeous "little wiggler" helped create two little wigglers!

The two girls laughed until their sides were hurting.

After they calmed down, Kaitlan asked her to go with them for her Father's burial. This, apparently, was an immense honor to be present, and Anita gasped.

"I would be most honored that you chose me to go, my Alpha. I most humbly accept." She had gone into formality upon her Alpha asking her. Kaitlan was so going to have to change all that. She wasn't used to all the formality, but knew that some had to be maintained in public. However, when she was speaking alone with her friends, that definitely would stop as of right now!

~ 20 ~

Two New Mates Prove the Prophecy is Real.

After the simple burial, everyone was exhausted from the last several days, especially Kaitlan. So, Cordone invited everyone back to the house to stay the night, and they would return to Missouri the next day. Well, that was the plan, anyway.

After being shown their rooms, it was definitely time for girl talk. Kaitlan had enough of men over the last few days, and now, she was ready for some girl time.

The girls gathered in the main room on the first floor, and they went wacko over the house. Anita and Lynne had seen it before, but they hadn't been there in a very long time. So long, that there had been many changes.

The council members met in Cordone's study for the day's reports. Sam and Dan were watching over the girls with Cordone's approval. Dan was trying his best not to laugh at the girls, while Sam just stood silently, glaring at them. Dan looked over at Sam. He sure was acting angry the last couple of days. He wondered why. Then, he noticed that Sam's eyes were almost constantly on Sarah. Uh-oh.

Kaitlan had noticed, too, and she took a moment to look over at Sam. He had her worried. She had noticed when they were on the plane, his silent and brooding face watching Sarah under his lashes, glaring in anger. Sarah had always been an innocent flirt, and she had been flirting with Dan. The two had been laughing and carrying on since they were on the jet. Kaitlan knew that Sarah and Dan were great friends, but Kaitlan knew he wasn't her type for a love affair. But, Sam very easily could be. Sarah had called him "Hunkalicious" more times than not. Like Sarah, he would sit for hours on end in silence, and yet, he had no problem discussing all kinds of subjects. He loved deep thinkers with thoughts and beliefs. Sarah was a deep thinker. Another thing she wanted, she had told Kaitlan, was great "sex-a-robics". Most men just thought she was a bouncy, flighty girl without depth. A real airhead. Her antics entirely were for show to mask her true past. The man who won her heart was going to be more lucky than he would ever know. While everyone talked, Kaitlan glanced every so often to watch Sam frowning at Sarah. Sarah had turned twenty-seven five months before. This was the first time they'd seen each other since then. Hmmm. Had Sam been ignoring Sarah? Why? Again, Kaitlan frowned. Sarah was human, and she had no idea she was surrounded by werewolves.

But, Sam was starting to worry Kaitlan. What WAS his problem with Sarah? Frustration? Hatred? She didn't know what, but she had a really strange feeling about that stare. Now, he was glaring even more angrily at Sarah. This was making Kaitlan very protective. She was going to lay down the law to him as Alpha as soon as she had the chance when - NO! Dammit! His eyes were glowing dimly. She darted her head back at Sarah, and then at Sam again. She realized what was in his eyes. Oh, shit! Sam had just tagged Sarah as his mate! Damn! Sarah was all human! The dangers of this were explosive! Kaitlan was shaking her head at yet, another coincidence, when she heard Sarah's little musical voice chiming. She was gawking at the entire room.

"What the fuck? There is a SWIMMING POOL inside the house fed by a three-story, natural, rock waterfall? And, an open fire pit in the middle of the room? Where's the pendulum? No, friggin' way! Well, first things first! Anyone up for s'mores? Let's fire up the fire pit, eat, and go skinny dipping! Hey, you guys can join us! I call first DIBS! I'm not opposed to it!" She glanced at Dan who was waggling his eyebrows at them in amusement. Sarah was just hilarious to him!

That brought a huge burst of laughter from the girls who all yelled, "I'm in!".

Sam's eyes glowed brighter at the words "skinny dipping". No other male is allowed to see his, or her, mate's nakedness. No wonder he looked more angry than ever. This was getting dangerous. If Sam lost his cool? Oh MAN! Kaitlan was going to have to tell Cordone fast. Sam was much, much older than Cordone, and had never found a mate. She had no idea what she was going to do if she was right, and he lost it trying to claim his mate! Kaitlan didn't know how Sarah might take it if she knew that she was standing the middle of a supernatural world. And, now, one of them had chosen her as his mate! Crap! Crap! Crap!

While the girls were lighting the fire pit, and scrounging around to make the treats, Kaitlan took a moment to look at her best friend, Sarah. Trying to see what Sam might be seeing.

The day Kaitlan had arrived at Cordone's house, Sarah had been meeting with her fiancé. What she had not known was that Sarah was breaking their engagement. Sarah had told Kaitlan that she just couldn't marry him. She didn't love him enough. At their meeting, though, she found out he had felt the same way, except that he had met another woman, and had fallen deeply in love with her at first sight. They parted happily friends.

Kaitlan had chosen her description of Sarah when they were little girls. Sarah was a "pixie". She was about five foot tall, ice-blue eyes, and slim with shockingly natural bright red hair that was shoulder length, and always curled around her face riotously. Even as an adult, Sarah still couldn't tame it! Her skin was very fair with lots of freckles. Her eyelashes were naturally long, and many women envied her for this point alone. She didn't walk. She "flitted" around. Her breasts were perfect for her size, and her waist very small. She loved wearing blues and reds, but pink was her favorite color! She knew nothing about the fact that she was surrounded by no less than eleven werewolves, but then, she had always had some sort of feeling that there was something odd about Kaitlan's family! She was bubbly, and happy all the time making people think she was adorable, but shallow. And, Sarah liked it that way, given her past. She always made Kaitlan forget her troubles, and made everything better. Her life until five had been horrendous with lasting scars, but with Kaitlan always there to let Sarah talk about it, it had been the best therapy of all. Sarah and Kaitlan were like sisters, only closer. They always had each other's backs. Sarah would march into hell to defend Kaitlan to the death. She would truly sacrifice herself for her friend. Kaitlan had always told her that one of these days, Sarah was really going to get into trouble with her flirty attitude. And, it appeared today may very well be the day given Sam's face!

She saw, in an instant, why Sam had claimed her. She was the polar opposite from him, but had some similar traits as well. That made his claim even stronger than mates who had little in common with each other. She had to do something, now.

"Hey, kiddoes! I have to go. I'll be back in a few!"

The other girls nodded, every one of them knowing when a girl had to go, well, she had to go. They continued giggling, gawking, and laughing while she went to the elevator. No one questioned why she didn't just use the bathroom on the main floor. It was a bit awkward, and silly now, that she had to use it when she could have just simply leaped up.

"Sorry to interrupt, my sex god, but could I speak with you a moment?"

"YES!   These guys are driving me insane! Meet me in our bedroom!"

Cordone joined her in their room at the same time she arrived.

"God, he's so sexy," thought Kaitlan.

"Really, mate? You want…some…thing?" He laughed in her mind to which she whacked him on the arm.

"I'll take your 'stick' later, but at the moment? 'Houston, we have a problem.'"

"What kind of problem?"

"It's Sam. Look at his eyes, Cordone."

She turned her head to look down at the main floor where Sam was in the shadows, eyes glowing as he glared at Sarah. Cordone followed her look. He took another look, then stared at Kaitlan in total disbelief.

"What the hell?"

Kaitlan nodded. *"Sarah. He's claimed her as his mate, Cordone."*

DAMN IT! Sam was just barely holding it together. Cordone knew Sam was about to lose it, and shot down the platform.

Before he started to leave, Kaitlan grabbed his arm.

"Cordone, if this is happening to them, I need to speak to Sam, first. It's about Sarah. I'll tell you later about it, but it's imperative I speak with him, before he proceeds to say anything to her."

He frowned at Kaitlan, but nodded. He checked to see that Sarah wasn't looking, and leaped down to the main floor. He jerked his head at Dan who looked at Sam. He had not even noticed? Dan frowned, and grabbed Sam in a vise. Sam didn't struggle. He knew what had happened to him, but didn't want to admit it.

"Sam, come with me," Cordone ordered quietly while Sam turned his glowing, angry eyes onto him. Cordone knew he had no intention of leaving Sarah. "Now!" Cordone used his Alpha to corral Sam.

What was wrong with him? Sam had never felt so strongly about a woman in his entire life. He had been angry when he had seen Dan and Sarah flirting with each other, and that only exacerbated his feelings more. The night in the shower, he knew Sarah was his mate, but he ignored it for years. Now, it caught up with him. He should have claimed her then. Looking back on it, he was a fool. His wolf was angry with him, and now, it was trying to take over.

He nodded to his Alpha, and followed Cordone who took him to the garage.

"Sam?" Cordone asked without asking.

"I don't know what's wrong with me, Alpha."

"You can call me Cordone, Sam."

Sam nodded. "Cordone, I don't understand what's happening," he lied.

Sarah's face was still in his mind. He knew the truth, but refused to acknowledge it. Knew he needed to stop it. But, honestly, he didn't think he could.

His jealousy since the plane had grown ten-fold. He thought that his feelings for her since that night in his bathroom when she was seventeen, were a fluke. But, when she announced she wanted to skinny dip, that was when he drew the line in the sand. He was about to claim her in front of everyone!   He didn't care that she was human. He was truly glad Cordone and Sam had stopped him.

Cordone put his hand on Sam in total sympathy. He knew exactly what his Second was feeling. It only happened when one found their mate. But, this? A human mate had been extremely rare. Canaan had been mated to Tara, but Kaitlan had told them all, just before they had left for the funeral, that Tara had some minute Elven blood in her. Knowing the circumstances that meant Kaitlan was a tiny part elf, but more human. It was the elf that had recognized Cordone as her mate.   But, was it really more?

But, Sarah was all human. Well, there was always a slim chance she was part supernatural, but that seemed highly unlikely.

"I'm so sorry, my friend.Sarah is your mate," Cordone explained to Sam.

Sam's head jerked up in alarm. His eyes automatically stopped glowing, and stared into Cordone's eyes as if his friend had lost his ever loving mind. It was one thing to know it; another thing for it to be spoken aloud! Still he resisted.   He had never found his mate. He'd come to grips he never would.

"What are you smoking, Cordone? Seriously?

My mate? That tiny, little 'minx' with the red hair whose very giggles drive me up the fucking wall? Fuck that!"

Cordone smiled with tolerance. "I never said who it was, Sam."

More distress registered on Sam's face. No. Cordone had NOT told him who it was.

"Damn!" Sam said vehemently. "Why the hell did the Creator do this to me? Three damn, fucking thousand years I wait for a mate, and she turns out to be a tiny, giggling, red-headed, annoying – since - I've – known - her, airheaded vixen." He muttered.

Cordone and Dan both burst out laughing.

"I think your description is a bit off, Sam. Look. You're about to lose it, and we all know it. But, don't make rash assumptions about Sarah. Kaitlan has asked that you meet her in the library so she can tell you about Sarah's sad life. Then, if you claim her, you will have to talk to Sarah. Sarah is all the bubbly person you see, but she is an amazing young woman with more brains than anyone ever gives her credit. You WILL reign in your surface description, and feelings until you speak to Kaitlan. If I have to, I'll order it."

Sam stared at Cordone. That small, little vixen in there had a bad life? It was almost impossible to believe, and he didn't.

Sam nodded, and Cordone let him go. Sam went back into the house heading to the library desperately trying not to look at Sarah. His mate.

He knocked on the library door, then opened it.

He looked at Kaitlan with all the guilt he held in his eyes. His mate was human; she was gorgeous; and worse, she was his female Alpha's best friend. This so couldn't be a good thing. Shutting the door, he sat down in the matching wingback chair next to Kaitlan's. He noticed her hand was laying on her belly almost lovingly. Her eyes were brighter green than ever, and she glowed with a beauty he had never seen in her. Realization struck him, and he hung his head to keep her from seeing his excitement for them both.

"Look at me." Kaitlan ordered.

Sam's eyes slowly slid up to the beautiful woman who was his Alpha.

Kaitlan looked him over. If this man was going to be her best friend's mate, she wanted to make sure he understood Sarah a lot more. She looked him over thoroughly. His hair was sandy, and cropped quite short in military style. Maybe six-foot three or four. His chest was very large, toned, and well defined. He sported a very dark tan. Sarah's pale skin, and height next to him would make anyone turn twice to look at them. What a pair! His hips were perfect proportion to his size, and his legs just kept on going. His eyes were a rich hazel, and his deeply tanned face perfect. She almost laughed as she thought about Sarah and her description of sex with her ideal man! Sam would really give her a run for her money! Then, she smiled at him.

"Cordone told me that you wanted to talk to me

about Sarah." Sam told her.

He was almost was pleading with Kaitlan with his next words, and he was ashamed.

"I'm sorry, Kaitlan. I never meant this to happen! I-I don't know how it happened. Oh, hell! This is such a mess! For God's sake! I watched her grow up with you! Am I just a pervert?"

Kaitlan laughed at that. Sam, the stoic, impeccable Sam. Brought to his knees by her little pixie friend! This was almost too good to be believed! Sarah would have to move fast on her feet to keep up with him!

Sam looked even more miserable as she laughed.

Her laughter had her crying so hard, tears were streaking down her cheeks. What the hell was she laughing about? Didn't she know how miserable he was?

Kaitlan wiped her tears away, and suddenly felt a flutter inside her. She closed her eyes feeling the first movement of her children. The girls were going to have to help her prepare their bedroom so she could tell her mate he was to be a Daddy. How she would explain her rapid gestation to Sarah, though, was another matter, but she didn't think it would be long before it wasn't a problem. Looking at Sam? Oh, maybe by tonight! She didn't know how Sarah would react, but secretly, Sarah had always joked about how she thought the O'Hara Clan were some supernatural group. Kaitlan had always laughed at her, but maybe Sarah had an intuition she didn't know about?

"I did. I want to tell you about Sarah. Before you may, or may not, do something that will effect all of us forever. It's not really my story, but you need to know if you have chosen her as your mate."

She folded her hands in her lap. Sam looked directly at her. A breach in protocol, but Kaitlan didn't seem to mind at all. He waited.

"This is awfully hard for me. It brings back terrible memories of when I first met her. I know you remember when I met her, right?"

Sam nodded. He did. And, she had annoyed him ever since. Well, except that one night in his shower that only the two of them knew about, and neither had any intention of telling anyone else. He had avoided her since.

"Sarah was a very shy, sad, lonely little girl, Sam. Her Father," and Sam heard disgust and horror in her voice, "beat her Mother to death, and took Sarah to his bed, raping her before she even turned three." She looked at Sam somberly. "We met when we entered pre-school. We were five."

Sam's mind was reeling. Sarah? Raped by her own Father? Before three years-old? How could she ever accept any man after that had happened? Then, he remembered the shower! Oh, GOD, NO! What had he done?

Kaitlan's looked at him with understanding. What she didn't know was that not only was he angry against Sarah's father, but himself!

"One day at school, I went to the bathroom, and

heard Sarah crying in one of the stalls. Her crying was so quiet, it scared the hell out of me. I asked if she was OK, and she just told me to go away. I almost did, and I thank the Creator I didn't. I sat down out in the floor in front of the stall, and asked her what was wrong. Even at five, I knew something bad when I heard it."

Kaitlan's voice broke up with the next part, and she spoke through broken sobs as she remembered. She didn't want to remember. But, Sam needed to know what was behind the bravado and talk.

"Sarah's voice was soft, but it was in pain."

Then, she told Sam the conversation held between two little girls from their point of view having never spoken before.

"'What's your name? Can I help?'

'Sarah. N-n-no.'

'Are you hurt, Sarah?'

'Yes.'

'Did you get a cut? Are you bleeding? I can get the nurse.'

'Y-yes. N-no.'

'Are you sure? Where are you bleeding?'

'Where I pee.'

'Does it hurt?'

'Yes. Oh, NO!   I'm not supposed to tell! Daddy told me not to, or he'd hurt me worse! Please don't tell? Please?' Sarah begged me. I remember Sarah opening the stall door, and seeing blood all inside the commode. Her legs were running with blood. So much, I was terrified!'"

The horror on Sam's face was indescribable. His fingers were drawing blood from his claws digging into his hands as he tried to keep his temper.

"I didn't listen to her. Daddy had always told me that if someone was in trouble, and asked me to keep silent, it was the worse thing I could do. So, I told the nurse. But, no one else. I'd never seen so much blood in my life! I was so scared, Sam!" She tried to calm herself so she could finish. It was still hard after so many years.

"The next day, our teacher told us that she was in the hospital. We were little, of course, so she didn't go into detail. She asked the class to all write get well cards for her."

She looked at Sam with all the pain of that five year-old little girl turned woman, and sobbed again.

"I broke down, and told Daddy it had been me who had called the nurse, and what Sarah had told me. He was furious beyond belief, only stopping long enough to tell me he wasn't mad at me. I remember him petting me on my head, and told me he would take care of Sarah and her Father. And, I knew Daddy would do what he said. I just wanted to see Sarah. To make sure she was OK.

Daddy didn't tell me till I was much older, but the cops had told him about how her father had murdered her mother, and took Sarah to bed raping her until she almost bled out in that stall. And, that by telling the nurse, I had saved her life that day. Sarah would have bled to death if I had left her!" She gulped as the tears flowed harder. "There isn't a day that goes by that I don't think of the fact I could have left her alone to die in a damn toilet stall! Daddy finally told me that Sarah was safe, and that her Father could never hurt her again. I was just so happy about that, it never occurred to me to ask why. And, quite frankly, I really didn't care as long as he was gone. No one ever saw him again. Daddy paid for all her medical bills, then she came to live with us for a couple of years with Daddy as her guardian. It took her a long time, and lots of therapy for her. And, we became fast friends. She was always thanking me for saving her life. She still does. She still has some nightmares, but they are lessening with time. I know, now, that Daddy was behind his disappearance, and if he had him killed, that is good enough for me!"

Sam nodded. He remembered when Sarah came to stay with them, but never knew why. His eyes closed, and he let the first tear he had ever shed in his life slide down his cheek. Then, he remembered. Around that time, Canaan had ordered him to take care of a matter for him. He didn't tell him anything except he wanted a murderer dead. Sam had arranged it through his contacts in prison. That must have been Sarah's Father! He was glad he was the one to send him to hell!

"Daddy said she needed a family. I really wanted her to stay and be my sister. But, he finally found a lovely couple, the Collins, who wanted a child, but could not have a baby. He had them checked out over and over, and when he was satisfied, he arranged for her to be adopted. I was angry with him for not adopting her and let us be sisters, but, he was right. Especially knowing what I know, now."

She raised her head to Sam unheeded, or embarrassed by her tears.

"We all have regrets, Sam. We all have bad things in our lives. But, Sarah had more than her share in just under five years of life. I am the only one who talks with her about it, now. She really doesn't remember much about it, though, and I thank the Creator every day that she doesn't. She only remembers hurting. She knows everything, of course. Under the Collins love and care, she blossomed into the pixie you see today. Daddy and her parents helped her, made sure she got the finest help, and while she will never get over it, she lives with it, now. For the one person on Earth I knew who had gone through the worst kind of hell, she is also the one person who brings me down to Earth when I am upset, and cheers me up when I'm down. I have no right to ever be upset, and she does. But, she cares for others more than herself. You see her as she is, now. She truly is that beautiful soul who would hurt no one, but desires above all to help. That's why she became a child advocate, and works helping other little children who went through what she did. She's one of the smartest people I know, Sam. I'm telling you this only because you see her as a flighty little girl. That, alone, is going to cause you hurdles - a lot of them. Perhaps even intimately. If you ask if I think she could handle even more weirdness in her life, being mated to a were, I will tell you that it would be nothing in the face of what she has endured. And, quite frankly, I would be tickled to death if I could finally have her in the O'Hara Clan! But, you have to go slowly with her, Sam. She has never been able to be intimate with a man. She still feels dirty and not a virgin. I hoped maybe she might fall for someone who she would not be afraid of, but I don't know. She has never been really in love."

She grinned at him through her tears.

"But, I guarantee, you will NEVER be bored with her. But, if there is another thing? Your babies would be AWESOME looking!" She teased him.

Sam shook his head. What would Kaitlan say if she knew the truth? Obviously, Sarah had never told her anything. For that, he was grateful. For himself, his heart was broken. What kind of damage had he done to her at seventeen?

"Do you think she might feel the same about me sometime in the future? I mean, humans don't have mates."

Kaitlan shrugged, trying to muffle a laugh, remembering that Sarah had whispered to her on the plane what a gorgeous "Hunkalicious" was sitting watching her. Oh, yes. Sarah had noticed. But, she wasn't going to tell Sam that. He was just going to have to do this himself.

"You never know if you don't try. It worked beautifully with my parents. But, kill the glowing eyes, Sam. She'll know something's odd if you don't. If it works out, THEN you can tell her."

Sam nodded, and started to leave. He turned back.

"By the way…congratulations." He nodded toward her hand still placed over her belly. "Cordone really doesn't know what he's in for!" Kaitlan grinned.

Sam never missed a thing, and he walked out the door.

Standing on the landing, he peered over the railing. The girls had been kidding about skinny dipping. They were all dressed in bathing suits - Sarah's revealing way more than he liked. Suddenly, Sarah looked up straight at him with those blue eyes which gave him an immediate erection. As if she heard his thoughts, she deliberately waved at him, and he saw a wicked, knowing grin spread over her face before she turned back to the girls.

"Oh, shit! I am in terrible, terrible trouble!"

~ 21 ~

One Plus One does not Equal Four?   Take a Math Refresher Course!

The girls swam all afternoon, and Kaitlan joined them.   But, Sarah wasn't stupid. She had noticed Kaitlan's tummy was a bit larger. Not even enough to show, but she knew her friend's body, and knew it was always slender.

Sarah jumped out of the pool next to Kaitlan.

"OK, friend. Give. Whassup?" Kaitlan looked at her innocently. "Oh, and don't give me your 'I'm innocent' look, Kaitlan! You know it doesn't work on me."

Kaitlan laughed, and waved the other girls in around her.   She looked back and forth. Anita just grinned at her, and at the other two girls knowingly.

Lynne hit her arm. "You KNOW what's up, don't you?"

Anita just looked at her with as innocent a look as she could garner, earning another whack from Lynne on the same arm.

"Ouch, Lynne!" Anita complained rubbing her arm.

"OK. Girls. I need your help," Kaitlan whispered.

"Ooooh. I LOVE sneaky," said Lynne. "What

do you need?"

"I need you to help me prepare Cordone's room for us."

Warily, Sarah asked, "Why?"

"Because I want it beautiful and perfect. You know, candles, sexy food? Why? To tell him he's going to be a Daddy!"

Sarah's mouth dropped open. She had been so happy for her friend when she had found Cordone. She had been told they had eloped.

"A bit early?" She asked a bit puzzled. Nah! This was AWESOME! She was going to be an Auntie! "Auntie Sarah! I like it!"

"Nope, Sarah. Not these days. What can I say? Cordone just had to look at me, and I was pregnant!"

The girls squealed so loudly it brought all the men to the landing looking down at them in irritation.

The girls just grinned up at them, and then got down to designing the room for Kaitlan's amazing news!

Sarah, in the back of her mind, puzzled over why Kaitlan would be showing even a little bit this fast, but she was too excited for her friend to ask, or care.

Kaitlan didn't want it known, yet, that she carried two babies.

The girls went all over the house looking for just the right things to use for ambiance.

They ran in and out of Cordone's room making preparations. They took their time, and made sure everything was in total detail.

As they finished, Sarah deliberately missed the

elevator when she felt eyes on her, and turned. Sam was standing, glaring at her from the shadows at the other end of the landing. Glaring daggers, she might add.

Sarah had never been bold to any man before, but she and Sam weren't total strangers. She slowly walked up to him swinging her hips still dressed in her bathing suit. She looked straight into his eyes, and then backed up a step. Were they - glowing? She shook her head, and looked again. Of course, they weren't! She was imagining things.

She put her hands on her hips.

"And, just WHAT are you staring at, Hunkalicious?" She asked with a wide grin.

Sam's eyes looked her over from top to bottom. Her nipples were hard pushing through the thin bathing suit, and the apex at her thighs was just barely covered by the low thong bikini she was wearing.

He stopped glaring, and his eyes were replaced by a stunned "Did she just call me Hunkalicious?" look.

Sarah looked at him. His hair was the color of sand, while his eyes were gold. Sarah strolled closer to him, and poked him in the chest with her finger resisting the drawing urge to splay her hands all over his tight chest, and beg him to take her right then and there. She was awed by her own behavior. This man had known her all her life. Was there something wrong with this? She was so much younger, but she didn't care. WTH? Why would she feel like this? She could drown in his eyes. She couldn't stop herself. She had to goad him. It didn't help that she remembered that night in his shower, either. It was a good thing that Kaitlan had not known.

"You heard me, buddy!"

Sam was stunned silent while this tiny little creature he had chosen as his mate poked his chest yet again.

Without thought, Sam grabbed her hand holding it to his heart where she could feel it beating hard, his chest tight with nothing but muscle. Her heart was beating so hard, she wondered if he could hear it. He grinned, and leaned down to her ear.

"Don't say things like that if you aren't prepared for me to take you right here, and now, little girl." He whispered to her.

Sarah's mouth dropped, and her legs turned to jelly. Other men had wanted her, but she never could allow them to do so. She had to literally hang on to his arm to keep upright. This Hunkalicious man? Did he just…just…tell her he wanted to hump her? HER? And, was prepared to do it right here and now to her? She was wet just with his words! And, if he had done something about it, she would have let him take her right now! Sam took his finger, traced her lips, and shut her mouth. Again, he leaned down to her ear with a huge wolfy grin. because that's the only way she could describe it.

"That was only one time, little girl. The next time that sexy and luscious mouth opens in front of me, my tongue will be down your throat so fast, you won't know what hit you!"

Then, his left eyebrow raised as the left lip curled up into that same, wolfy grin. Sarah had an orgasm right then! Oh, shit! She had an orgasm! She desperately tried to gather her wits about her, feeling the wetness between her legs as she had come. Well, two could play that game, and Sarah wiggled her finger for him to lean down toward her.

As he leaned down, she grabbed his head with her hand, kissed his mouth, then warned him, "Not if my tongue gets in yours first, Hunkalicious!"

She thrilled watching his own mouth drop open, her right finger traced his open mouth, then stuck her finger inside, petting his tongue. She looked down at his pants, and saw she had succeeded in what she was wanting. He was hard! Oh, man! How she wanted it in her!

And, while Sam stood there frozen with surprise, Sarah turned, and walked away from him to the elevator. More than that, he saw her ass wiggle from side to side while he watched. His eyes narrowed with desire. Before she entered the elevator, she turned, and gave him a sexy grin. Then, wickedly sucked the finger she'd stuck in his mouth. A wink followed with the promise of so much more than he ever could have realized. His eyes began to glow again, and he saw her eyes look puzzled again. Then he grinned another wolfy grin as his eyes told her, "Little girl, you have no idea what you have unleashed."

In the elevator, Sarah collapsed against the wall. Did what happen actually happen? She was breathless with desire, and need for this man. He had given her an orgasm with only two sentences? OH, yes! He DEFINITELY was all man! Her man! Her man? What was that all about? Her teasing had gotten out of hand, and her face reddened remembering her actions and words!

"Oh, shit! I am in terrible, terrible trouble!" she moaned under her breath. "I'm in way over my head!"   She stood back up as the doors opened, gathering her wits as she had always done, and her mouth curved into a wild, and sexy grin.

"OK, Mr. Sam. I'll jump into trouble with my entire body, since I'm already in over my head! Hunkalicious, you have no idea what you are getting yourself into, but you WILL know it by the time I'm through with you! And, believe me, you will be so far in over YOUR head, you won't be able to stop it!!"

The mood was set, thanks to Kaitlan's friends. They had done an amazing job! She glanced around the room.   Flames danced away on the multiple candles. The girls had even decorated the tub, and filled it already! Laying beside the tub was a can of whipped cream and a large bowl of bananas and strawberries! She saw Sarah's touch in that, and laughed.   She had a very dirty minded girlfriend. And loved it! When it was their time, she'd be doing the same to them!

But, this was a bit naughty, and a lot romantic. She had just one last touch, and then, she'd be ready to tell the man of her dreams that his seed had taken root inside her, and she would be presenting him with two children in just a little under four months. Outside her mind, she wondered if Sarah would be a part of her world before her babies were born? Sarah will make the perfect godmother for them! No one would fight more fiercely for her children if she was not here to protect them. That eased her mind. And, she also believed that Sam would make the perfect godfather. Yes. She was going to have to help them fan the flames of mating if needed. Later.

Kaitlan undressed, and slipped into bed naked. They had not worn clothes to bed since that first night together. But, her body was showing a slight change today. She wanted him to notice it. The slight bulge was apparent to her. The flutter she felt just then confirmed her babies were growing quickly. Pushing the sheet down, even in the firelight, her belly undulated as the two moved around inside of her. If she could feel them, so could he.

Cordone stepped into their room silently, and shut the door. The even breathing of his mate told him that she was asleep. He hardened for her immediately, but she had been through so much lately, he would just take a cold shower.

He turned around, and saw candles - everywhere. He was surprised at this. But, at the same time, it excited him. OK. So. Apparently she had wanted him, but had fallen asleep waiting. That was OK with him. He went into the bathroom, and stared. A bath had been drawn complete with whipped cream, bananas and strawberries on the side.

He turned to look at the woman in his bed who was smiling back at him. Cordone stepped to the bed, and slowly undressed in front of his mate who was raking her eyes over his body as he did. When he stepped out of his pants and briefs, her eyes went straight to his hardness, then she looked up at him, and threw back the sheets for his eyes to view her in all her naked glory.

He slipped down beside her, pulling her into his arms. Kaitlan grinned, because she was ready to give him his surprise that he would feel the moment he entered her heat. She was wet for her mate, and wanted him inside her.

Cordone started to caress her breasts slowly, noticing that they seemed much fuller than usual. Her nipples were larger, but hard for his mouth as he reached his mouth down and suckled one of them gently. Suddenly, something leaked into his mouth from the nipple. It was very sweet, and quite tasty! He suckled some more, but nothing else came out. Then, he changed nipples only to find that one also leaked out that same sweetness.

Kaitlan was unaware of the sweetness that her body had given to her mate until he looked up into her eyes, licking his lips.

"Wow!" He exclaimed licking his lips.

"What, Cordone?"

"I don't know what that was, but your nipples taste so amazingly sweet tonight."

Kaitlan started. She was already lactating? And,

her breasts had given him a taste? Oh, boy! She'd better distract him right now, or her surprise would be too late.

"I need you inside me, now, Cordone. Please? Make love to me!"

Cordone reached down, and he felt her heavy wetness waiting for him. He moved over her, denying her nothing. She spread her legs wide for her mate to allow him entrance into her body as she felt her babies moving inside her. She wanted to feel them, and him, inside her. It was infinitely more sexy than anything she had ever felt before as he slid into her tightness, only it wasn't as tight as before. She could feel his surprise that she was more open for him.

He began to slowly move inside her at her request, not hard or fast. Her wetness became more pronounced than ever before making it easier for him to slide in and out of her. He was thrusting deep, and retracted entirely from her heat. And, then, his wolf came out in his eyes. His eyes glowed with the lust and passion he felt for his mate who looked back at him with equal passion and glowing eyes. He began to move harder and harder inside of her until he felt he was close to his release. He wanted to take her with him, but her cries into his mind told him she was not ready quite yet. He slowed down a bit.

She grasped his shoulders feeling the movements of her babies and her mate inside her at the same time. It was the sexiest thing ever, but she wasn't ready for him quite yet.

"Cordone," she gasped.

"Yes, mate?" He groaned against her lips as his hips pushed his hardness even deeper inside of her, but still slowly.

"Would you stop for a minute, and look at me?"

Cordone stopped moving inside her, and looked at her in confusion. That was a first. Just before he was going to ask her why, he felt something hit his lower abdomen. He looked down at where their bodies were locked together. There it was again! What the hell?

His eyes shot back to Kaitlan who had the biggest smile on her face he had ever seen. Then…there it was again. What was that? He not only felt it on his stomach, but inside her as well where he lay still.

Suddenly, Kaitlan gasped, and her head came up startled. She had felt a harder kick than before. Cordone's scared look made her pet his face with a smile as she leaned back against the pillows with a satisfied smile on her face. His puzzlement told her all she needed to know. He had felt their children inside her.

She took his head, turned it, her fangs descended. She bit into her mate's neck, sucking his blood, then wiping her tongue across it healing the marks immediately.

Cordone's head came up in an instant. As her fangs had descended, he had felt something in her body move harder against him.

Kaitlan grinned her sexy grin. If he didn't know by now, she just guessed she'd have to tell him.

"Like my new moves?" She grinned wickedly.

"What the hell, Kaitlan! What was that? Why did you bite my neck?"

"Well, I had to ask Anita what the procedures were when telling a mate that he was going to be a Father in four months! She was pretty clear that the rabbit died, and I thought you'd be happy about it?"

"Father? You're pregnant, Kaitlan?" He honestly had never expected that it could happen, but he had hoped. He couldn't believe it! His mouth came down on hers hard.

Kaitlan laughed at Cordone as his face expressed all kinds of emotions after feeling his child move inside his mate, against his belly, and hardness at the same time. That was the single sexiest thing he had ever felt in his life, and he hardened even longer inside her.

"As pregnant as a wolf can be, mate! Your seeds worked!"

She shook her finger at him as she silenced him again.   He got back at her by jamming himself harder into her.

Wait! "Seeds? What do you mean seeds?"

"It appears your seed worked twice - in both wolf and human forms. We are having twins!"

Cordone looked at her, howled loudly, and the entire house rumbled because of it as he pushed down into her fast and hard in triumph! He had never felt so proud in his life!   He was going to be a Father. They had been able to conceive in their Blood Bond! And, not just one! But he had impregnated her as a wolf and a man! Two babies grew within his mate's womb! He pulled out of her, and slipped down, kissing the tiny kicks of his children inside her body.

He rose over her, and entered her again. Holding her to him, feeling him pound inside of her, and feeling their children kick at the same time gave Kaitlan a feeling of power she had never known in her life, then, she felt Cordone's fangs bite her neck, suck a small amount of blood, then wipe his tongue across them. When he had done that, she, too, let out a howl to equal his as he released into her, and her orgasm burst forth stronger than ever before.

Their howls woke up everyone in the house. The werewolves knew that howl. It was the elated howl of a were who had just found out he was going to be a father. No other howl sounded like that. They all grinned, and settled back down to sleep - all except Sam. He laid listening to his Alphas howl their happiness. It gave him chills. It was so rare to hear, it was amazing to hear once again after so many years. The last time he had heard that howl was with Canaan and Tara upon the conception of Kaitlan.

Sarah had jerked awake at the howls. She looked over at Anita and Lynne who just grinned, and settled back down to sleep. That was really weird. Either there were wolves inside this house, or she was going nuts.

~ 22 ~

Werewolves are Real? I want One of Them!

Sarah lay awake, listening. Whatever it was, it was an extremely happy sound. It made her smile even though she didn't know why.

Sam put his hands behind his head as he listened. His body suddenly wanted that same feeling in him. To howl with pride as his mate tells him they are to have a child. He'd never wanted this in his life. He had just finally concluded that he was left on the outside of such happiness.

A vision of Sarah appeared before his eyes. His mate was more beautiful than he would ever see her, still wet with sweat, cradling their newborn baby in her arms immediately after birth, still a bit bloody, but with strawberry blonde hair, and beautiful fair skin. She smiled at him, and reached out to hand his little girl to him with a huge exhausted smile. He took the baby in his arms…the baby that had her beautiful pixie face, while her golden eyes stared up at him twinkling.

The vision faded. He knew that Cordone had told him that a vision was verification that Kaitlan really was his true mate more than the pull toward her. Sam never expected it to happen to him. Even though he wore loose fitting lounge pants wearing no shirt at all, he hardened at the vision. And thirsty for some very strange reason. He needed a scotch, yet he never drank it. The urge for one was so strong, he decided to go downstairs.

He got up, and made sure no one was on the main floor to see him before he stepped off the fourth floor landing, and barely made a sound as his feet touched the floor. He headed straight for the bar.

Sarah envied Lynne and Anita's ability to go right back to sleep with all that loud howling. She couldn't. It scared her to know wolves were in the area, and she still didn't understand everyone's reaction to the noise. A vision appeared to her. She had just given birth to a baby daughter, and was holding her while Sam looked down on them. She turned and handed her to him with a very tired smile. The two of them were a priceless picture she would never forget. The vision faded. Damn! She needed a scotch. It wasn't her favorite drink, but she needed something to put her back to sleep fast.

Silently, she left the bedroom on the main floor. Just as she reached the pool, she heard a light whooshing sound, and looking up, saw a figure falling from the fourth platform landing on the floor right in front of her without a sound. She stepped back in alarm! She was seeing things! She had to be! Without noticing she was about to fall, she backed up to the pool behind her, tripped, and fell into it, mouth open, and barely a squeal.

Sam whirled around just in time to see Sarah fall backward into the pool! He shut his eyes, and berated himself. He shouldn't have jumped. Cordone was going to kill him for this. There was no way that they could keep it from Sarah, now.

OK. He had to rectify this. He heard Sarah sputtering. He saw her head bob up and down twice, and he went into action. She was drowning! Without a thought except his mate was in danger, he pulled off his pants, and dove, buck naked, into the pool. Sarah was struggling to get to the surface, but she sunk the final time. He grabbed her around the waist, and swam with her under the waterfall to the pool room. They surfaced, and he held her as she coughed and choked on the water. When she caught her breath, he found her shocked and terrified face staring at him. Still holding her with one arm, Sam shut his eyes so she couldn't see their glow, and ran his hand through his wet hair.

She could have drowned, and it would have been all his fault! He started to shake with reaction to the fear he was feeling, when he felt a gentle hand stroking his face. Kaitlan had been right. This tiny pixie of a girl who was his mate, and with whom he was deeply in love, sought to comfort him even in the face of her terror. He was so ashamed of himself.

He opened his eyes making sure she did not see them. They were glowing with fear, shame, and love. He could not let her see him this way.

He easily bounded out of the water in one jump pulling her with him, and laid her on one of the long chairs holding her head while she coughed up the water she had swallowed. He sat down beside her after she had stopped, and buried his head in his hands breathing hard with the fear he still bore thinking she could have died, and it would have been because of his stupidity. There was no going back, now, and she deserved to know the truth.

"Sam?" She finally asked. He didn't raise his eyes. He couldn't. Not with them glowing. He had to reign it in, but he knew he wouldn't be able to do it. Not this time. Luckily no one had heard her while Cordone and Kaitlan were howling their happiness. Cordone was going to kill him. And, Kaitlan? Oh, man! He was going to be killed twice over! What had he done?

"Sam, look at me!" Sarah ordered, still coughing a bit.

He had no choice. His mate had ordered him to look at her. He could not deny her order.

He turned his head toward her, but did not look into her eyes. She would draw back in horror if she saw them. He couldn't bear it! This, with everything she had gone through, would send her over the edge!

"I'm not going to ask how you jumped from four floors, and not get hurt. I'm not going to ask that. You startled me, that's all. I fell in because I'm clumsy, sometimes. You scared me."

She placed her gentle fingers under his chin, and pulled his face up to hers.

"I don't know what you are, but I do know that you saved my life, Hunkalicious," she teased tenderly. "Please, Sam. Look at me. Don't be ashamed to show me what, or who, you are."

He caved, and opened his eyes. Her eyes widened at the golden glow that came from them. She drew back just a bit in surprise. He pushed her hand away trying to turn his head. Sarah wouldn't have that, and she forced his eyes back to hers. He was helpless. She was his. She was his mate. She was the love of his life. And, she was comforting him!

Sarah studied the man. He was glorious. Huge muscles, six-pack abs, and sandy hair. He looked the very epitome of a god. His golden eyes were very unusual, but they fit him, and she wanted to drown in them forever. His skin tight with a golden tan, that resembled the sun. His arms were huge and very strong. The muscles standing out easily. He could break her with a flick of his finger. Yet, his hands were gentle.

She looked deeply into his golden, glowing eyes with her blue ones, and something happened to her in that instant. He was hers. She didn't understand it, and she didn't want

to understand. It was as if her entire life had been nothing until this moment. Their last meeting took place in his shower when she was only seventeen. But, she had never been afraid of him. Ever. Every horror disappeared from her. Hunkalicious was hers - forever. And, for the first time in her entire life, she was home, and truly felt safe. After everything she had been through, she was safe, and he loved her.

Sam saw the dawning in her eyes. The dawning that she was his. Without a word, they looked at each other, and he reached around to her head drawing her lips to his in a kiss so gentle, tears came from Sarah's eyes. She opened her mouth inviting that wonderful tongue he told her he'd stick down her throat. In answer, his tongue slipped into her mouth as he tasted her fragrance. Oh, what was he going to do? He loved this woman with ever fiber of his being. How could a human want a werewolf? Canaan had done so, but it was finally discovered Tara was part of the supernatural world in her genes. But, Sarah was human. All human.

He was totally helpless. His tongue and mouth pushed harder against hers, and she wrapped her arms around his neck as he pulled her into his lap. He couldn't stop. He didn't want to stop. He wanted to bury himself in her body, claim her as his for all the world to see, and then spill his seed inside of her. She kissed him, kiss for kiss, tongue for tongue, and lips for lips. Suddenly, he loosed his inner wolf into his eyes as he pulled back from her. Sarah gasped at the eyes, and then she pulled his lips onto hers harder, and more desperate than before. She wanted him like she needed to breathe! He kissed her lips, her eyes, her mouth again. Then, his lips trailed down her neck to kiss the tops of her breasts.

Sarah moaned. OMG! She wanted him. Now. She didn't want to wait, and she would not. No. This man was hers, and she was going to mark her territory, now. Not later. She felt an animal instinct she never knew she had invade her being.

He cupped one of her breasts, and squeezed it gently. She gasped in pleasure as his hand began to stroke it. Just like he had done in his shower ten years before. Then, he stopped and pulled back. His glowing eyes told her that he was losing it, and he would take her. With that look, she realized that she was sitting on something very hard in his lap. Her bare bottom was on it, and it was - OMG! It was his cock! He was naked, she never wore panties to bed, she was in his lap, and her ass was sitting on his hard-on! Her eyes widened as she moved her bottom against it. He jerked realizing he had saved her naked, and she was rubbing his cock with her luscious ass! He actually blushed a bit. Then, he noticed Sarah's clothing - or lack thereof.

Then, Sarah decided there should be no embarrassment with them. She never slept with panties on at all, and what covered her body, well, Sam didn't really need to use his imagination. It was soaked through, and being snow white, it bared everything she had to his eyes.

"I don't sleep with panties on, Sam. I haven't since I was seventeen."

He jerked her to him when she said this. Sarah stood up, straddled him, and lifted up until she felt his tip at her flooded entrance.

Sam was a little shy, she realized, but she wasn't. This man, or whatever he was, well, she intended to take right there; right now.

Sam had been a bit reluctant after everything Kaitlan had told her, but that ended when his little vixen sitting on his hardness with her bare bottom stood up, straddled his legs, and sat back down on him about to take him inside of her. His eyes closed in desire.

No! He couldn't do this. Not without her knowing what he was. He stood up, and plopped her down on the chair stunning her!

Sarah looked at him hurt. He couldn't stand it. He turned to let her see his glorious nakedness, and his manhood standing hard against his belly. He wanted her to be in no doubt he wanted her. They had to talk first. He never knew he had so much strength.

Her description of him as some type of god was truly appropriate! Oh, GOD! She wanted him!

~ 23 ~

"I can't make love to you until you know everything."

"Look, Sarah. You need to know everything before anything may, I mean, will happen between us. It's going to happen between us."

Sarah was silent. It was hard for her to think looking at the maleness saluting her in all its glory. She shook her head trying to listen. Somehow, she knew this was important to both of them.

"Kaitlan gave me permission to tell you if something happened between us. I told her my feelings for you, but I can't make love to you until you know everything."

Sarah nodded, listening. She had suspected for years that Kaitlan's family was more than human. She had always joked with Kaitlan, but never seriously. She just never said anything to anyone else. Sometimes, she almost was jealous she had no coolness about her.

"I am a werewolf, Sarah, and I was born three thousand years ago."

He looked straight at her watching her eyes widen in surprise. Well, THAT was soooo not what she was expecting! She still said nothing. She always listened before speaking.

"Kaitlan's Mother was human, mostly. She was part Elf, but no one knew it until Anita did tests on Kaitlan. Kaitlan was born against all odds. She was a miracle in itself. Sarah, we take mates, and we do marry as human customs, but mating is personal and private, and considered our marriage ceremony. Unlike marriage, it's forever." He looked at her. "And, Sarah, that can be an extremely long, long time."

Pushing his hands through his hair he sat down on the chair beside hers. His testicles were horribly full, in terrible pain, and he was about to burst open if he didn't get release soon. Preferably into Sarah's body.

He jerked when he felt Sarah's warm hand wrap around his hard-on. His eyes opened widely as he looked down at her hand holding him. His eyes shot back to hers.

"Sam, I've known for years something was different about Kaitlan's family. I suspected something supernatural, but didn't know what. And, I never pried. I waited. I knew someone would tell me when it was needed. Do you think, for one second, that I give a rat's ass what you are? What any of you are? I don't think Kaitlan knew until recently, did she?"

"No. She didn't." He told her.

"I don't give a shit that you turn into a wolf, or that you become human again. Do you think I would really care about any of it?"

She raised her voice slightly, then lowered it so

no one would hear them in the quiet of the house. The waterfall hid them, and their words from others. They were totally alone.

Her hand stroked his shaft gently as she spoke to him. He hardened even more. He hadn't even noticed that she had removed her clothing while he had been talking, and was naked. She grabbed his shoulder with one hand while gently stroking his erection with her other, Sam trying to stop her. He was filled with such guilt he couldn't believe she would want him after all that let alone after what Kaitlan had told him. She grabbed the hand that was trying to stop her, and placed it upon one of her bare breasts. His hand began to move of its own accord as he looked her beautiful body over.

"Listen to me, Hunkalicious! You are mine! Do you even understand that? I don't know what has brought us together, nor do I really care. It's there. I feel it between us; you feel it. Since that night in the shower, no other man was allowed to touch me. I've waited for years for the right man to come along, and he did - ten years ago. I've just been waiting for you to realize it. I'm no virgin, Sam," she whispered as she dropped her head in shame. He knew she was thinking back.

He caressed her face with his glowing eyes that were filled with tenderness. She looked into his eyes, and realized he knew about her! She turned her eyes away from him, again. Her shame had never left her, and he knew it. She wanted him! So much right now it was almost killing her with the need. How could he want her? Her stomach was throbbing, and her soft, silky folds were wet with wanting.

"You will never, Sarah…I repeat NEVER look away from me again that way. None of that matters to me. You are mine, and if you agree to it, will you become my mate?   Again, I warn you. It's a lifetime with me, and that could be incredibly long. I've lived three thousand years waiting for my mate." He stroked her hair, and continued. "I waited three thousand years for YOU!   Werewolves are like real wolves - we mate for life, but it's instantly. There are no waiting periods, or courtships. Once done, the mating must be immediate. But, you need to know, once mated, you will take on my longevity. You also need to know that I do not know if we can ever have children. Humans and weres are not compatible.   It's another miracle that Cordone and Kaitlan conceived even with her one, Elven gene. I want you to realize this before you commit to anything. There is a ritual called the Blood Bond. We claim one another, ask if the other will accept us as mate, and then, we bite each other's neck, take a small amount of blood from each other, and finally, consummating our mating. What is left, one time, are the scars showing all that we are mated."

Sarah smiled at him with a wicked look. His eyes glowed more than ever before.

"Well, don't know about the biting. I guess we'll

figure that out since I have no fangs. The eyes could take a bit of getting used to, but I bet they make a great nightlight!"   Sarah stood up, and straddled him. She dropped her heavily, swollen entrance, flooded with her wetness down over his hard tip partly taking his shaft inside of her. She held it there.

Sam throbbed as he felt her tightness around him. Wait! Did she just agree to mating with him?

"I don't know what all will happen with us, Sam. But, I can promise you this. I don't care about any of it. To be with you, forever, is the most wonderful thing I can imagine! If we can never have a child, I can live with that." She sat down allowing him to penetrate her a little more.

He groaned as he felt her pushing over him taking him deeper.

"I can't take much more of this, Sarah! I'm in a hell of a lot of pain!" He growled. He grabbed her breasts with both hands.

He licked his lips in anticipation, and she shuddered with desire, as his mouth licked her hardened tips. With another wicked grin, she took more of him inside of her.

"Does it have to be bite then consummate, or can we do both at the same time, Hunkalicious?"

He lost his breath right then as she took his entire shaft into her. He felt it throb inside of her at the same time she felt it. She was so damn wet! His lap was covered in her creamy wetness, and it was still flowing from her as if it were rapids. God! She felt good hugging his cock! She wiggled that gorgeous ass of hers. He grabbed her hips as he began to move in her. She arched her back jutting her breasts at him. He grabbed a nipple in his mouth, and suckled hard listening to her - growl?

Sarah growled as he began to move inside of her. She wanted him to fill her body full of his own brand of cream! Sink it deep into her!

Sam moved slowly, and looking into her eyes sent him over the edge. It was time. He stopped moving in her.

"I claim you as my mate, Sarah Collins. I think we can mate, and consummate at the same time. It's always been done bite first, consummation after, as our ancestors did. Seriously, we should go about this the other way around, Sarah, with you taking my blood, and then I yours. But I have a feeling we need to do it the opposite way. Why I don't know."

He gasped as he felt her tighten around him sending him into waves of desire, and lust for this woman only.

"But, there is nothing in our laws that says it has to be done that way. So, Sarah, will you accept me as your mate?"

"OK, big boy. And, I mean BIG boy!" She giggled tightening around him more than ever. He grew bigger inside her, if that was even possible? This time, he loved that giggle!

"I accept you as my mate, Sam Knight! Now, tonight. I won't wait a Second longer."

With that, she sat still on him. A bit scared, she turned her neck to him. He turned her head back to him. She needed to see his fangs. He allowed them to descend in front of her. Instead of being scared like a normal human being, she took her fingers, and caressed both fangs. He jerked hard! That felt so incredibly sexy! He never knew fangs were an erogenous zone! He kissed her lips, then turned her neck back to him, kissed her pulse, and then bit into her skin releasing a small amount of blood which he took into his mouth, then licked her wounds sealing them permanently on her neck.

Sarah moaned in ecstasy. It didn't hurt. It was sexy beyond belief! She tightened around him so tight, she though she'd orgasm right then.

"Did I hurt you?" Sam asked after gently taking his final kiss of mating.

"No! Sam! That was so beautiful - and damn sexy! Do you know how I do this?"

"I have no idea. I never asked Canaan, but now that I think of it, Canaan's neck did have fang bites! How the hell would that have happened?"

"OK. Then, we're in new territory, so here goes!"

"I claim you as my mate, Samuel Knight. If it had been time, I would have mated with you ten years ago. I fell for you like a ton of bricks. I had such a crush on you since I was about nine. By the time you found me in your bathroom, I was more than ready to be yours. But, now is just fine, too. Will you accept me as your mate?"

"I accept you as my mate for all time, Sarah Knight. I have never been in love until I saw you as a my mate ten years ago. I just refused to accept it. But, I love you with every fiber of my being - forever! I will never make that mistake, again. We could have both saved ourselves a lot of misery if I had mated you that night. But, now, you are my mate!"

Sarah tightened her core as she felt him thicken, and enlarge even more inside of her. Sarah copied what Sam had done, and took her kiss of mating. Sam turned his head. She kissed his pulse as he had done, then bared her teeth. Her human teeth did something amazing. Fangs suddenly descended from her mouth. She drew back in shock bringing Sam's head back around fast.

"Sam?" She asked.

She had fangs? How the hell? But there they were! He took his finger, stroking her fangs, and she jerked.

"OMG! That is so exciting!" She took his head before he realized it, turned his neck to her, and her fangs sank into his neck. He held her tightly feeling her breasts fill and harden against his chest. She took just a little blood, swallowing it. It tasted so sweet! Like chocolate covered strawberries! Yum! She licked his wound, and watched them heal leaving only the scars. Her fangs retracted, Sarah took her final kiss of mating.

Sam grabbed his mate, and began to move in her again.

"I'm really hurting, Sarah. I've been hurting

since I found you in my shower years ago, but even more so since the plane!" She smiled at that. She knew what that meant.

"Then, let's just finish this fast, Sam! I'm so wound up right now! Take me!"

With a smile that would light up the entire room, Sam slipped out of her, and flipped her on her back and onto the rug by the pool. He covered her with his body, and slid between her legs sliding right back into her hot, flowing, wet, creamy channel, and took her forever as his mate. Her legs came up, and she clutched them around his waist.

"You are so damn wet, Sarah!" He panted at her.

"And, you, Sam Knight, my mate, are so damn huge!"

"Did you know that I can enter your womb?" He asked her before his cock grew to the length needed to enter through her cervix, and she felt it.

"Really?" Gasping, she tightened her legs around him. "How?"

"Would you like me to do it?"

Entering her womb? Would she like it?

"Sam, if I could take you any deeper than my womb, I would!"

"My cock will lengthen, and my the wetness from my tip's wetness will caress your cervix, opening it to me. I will slide through it easily, and my cock will enter your womb. There will be no pain, only a pleasure you cannot imagine. When I come, I will thoroughly coat it with my seed."

Sarah just nodded. The sound of what he said

had sent her excitement over the edge. His words caused her channel to flood even heavier, and it opened larger.

"You can do it with a human?"

"Any female, Sara. It's one of our biggest powers. Oh, GOD, Sara! I need to give you my seed!"

"And, I need you to give it to me!"

Sarah felt Sam's tip nudging her cervix. His wet tip coated her, and it opened fully to him. She felt his cock slide through it without any pain, and into her womb. She even felt the tip of his cock at the top of her womb! She needed his semen like she needed to breathe! No. She needed it more than breathing. She arched her back at the feeling! How it excited her to know he was able to be that deep within her body! He was right! It WAS an incredible pleasure! She doubted any other human female would get to feel anything like this!

Sam would suffer Cordone's wrath tomorrow, but for tonight, he would love his mate to erase all the evil that had ever been done to her. In moments, he spilled all the contents of his balls that had been causing him so much pain for so long. His semen filled her womb completely, as he pushed over and over again until he was completely empty. He felt her shudder, and shake with her orgasm as well.

They laid locked together in a state of ecstasy that neither had ever known could exist. He remained hard, but stranger than that, he was already full again. What the hell is going on with him?

"Oh, Sam! That was…I don't know how to describe it!" Sarah said to him.

"Sarah, your channel is so wet and creamy, I can't believe I didn't slide out of you!" He laughed at her.

"That's because you're studliness is so humongous, Hunkalicious!" She laughed back at him.

He pulled her tightly to him, and he began to move inside of her again. She gave him thrust for thrust until their release hit them hard, yet again. He filled her womb full of his seed. Still, he was huge, and hard. The smell of them drowned his sense of smell. It was incredible!

"We smell so good together, Sarah!" He told her.

"Yep. Let's see how much more we can make, Sam! I need you desperately!"

"Whatever you want, mate, I will give to you!"

"A baby, maybe? You never know, Sam. It could happen! Anything can happen if two people love each other enough."

"Then, let's just put that as our goal."

Sarah bucked under him for more. He smiled an obliged her as much as she wanted till dawn broke. They would finish their mating bond after they received the wrath of Cordone and Kaitlan. They were in so much damn trouble! Sam grinned anyway. It was worth it!

~ 24 ~

"Wolfalicious" and The Red Wolf!

Sarah was invigorated! No sleep at all, but she didn't need rest right now! She wanted to stretch like a cat who'd been well satisfied, but knew it would be short-lived, and she would want her mate inside her again. What would Kaitlan say when she saw her neck and Sam's? Sam had explained that now she was part of the Clan, she would have to follow their Alphas' instructions. That was OK with her, she had told him. Finally, Sarah was a part of Kaitlan's family as she had always dreamed of being having to admit she never thought it would be this way.

Sarah put her discarded gown back on, and making sure no one was looking, darted to her room to change, then hopped out to do some cooking!

She was an awesome cook. Her friends knew it. So, she went into the kitchen to start breakfast having so much energy, she had to DO something. Sam had left her earlier to go into the garage, and, now, she heard him come behind her burying his face into her neck snuffling it.

"I have no idea what Kaitlan is going to say, Hunkalicious!" Sarah teased, turning to throw her arms around his neck standing on her tippy toes to kiss him.

"We are both going to be in the doghouse, Sarah. I don't know what is going to happen either, but we will stand as mates, and receive their decision. Cordone will probably kill me."

"Not on your life, Hunkalicious! He'll have to go through me, first!"

"Gotta go to work, Tink! See you later, lover." He thought to her, kissing her soundly on the mouth, then skirting away as she tried to slap his ass!

"Watch it, Tink!"

"No.   YOU watch it, Hunkalicious!"

Talking privately like this! It was a surprise to her when it first happened, but just so damned, well, cool!   She sent him a thought with a picture of them later. He sent her one right back, and she had an orgasm in front of the stove! Sam had explained, after the fact, once mated, they could hear each other's thoughts. Damn! Did he have to do that to her? Now, she had to change her underwear, and she heard him chuckle at her thought. She sent him another picture of her walking around downstairs without underwear. She heard him growl, and laughed.

Sarah had a-hankerin' for sausage, bacon, eggs, muffins, and hash browns. Kind of strange for her. She always ate healthy foods. Oh, well, probably had to do with their sex-a-robics all night long! She'd burned up more than enough calories!

Kaitlan snuck up on Sarah, and poked her in the back causing Sarah to jump, and squeal.

"WTH, Kaitlan! Are you trying to give me a

heart attack?" Sarah growled at Kaitlan.

Kaitlan looked over her shoulder.

"That smells so good! I'm so darned hungry! Eating for three!" She grinned as she took the first piece of bacon off the plate getting her hand slapped in the process.

"Three? TWINS? YES! Oh, and stay out of the food, preggers! You can eat when everyone else does!"

As she turned, Kaitlan saw her neck, and her smile widened as she sneaked up to whisper to her. But, something was weird about it. She couldn't put her finger on it. Kaitlan was still a bit sleepy being up half the night with her mate's attention to details!

"Isn't it amazing, Sarah?" Kaitlan poked her again.

"I have no idea what you mean!" Sarah said innocently.

"No?" Kaitlan reached for her head, and turned her neck to face her. "Really? Nothing to say?"

Sarah frowned. "Wait! You knew, didn't you?? How?"

Kaitlan sort of hummed and hawed a minute not sure how to tell Sarah how she and Cordone found out. Best to just say it like it is!

"Well, you see, uh, after I told Cordone…"

"Yeah. We ALL heard you!" Sarah laughed.

"Shutup, Pixie! Anyway, I was extremely hungry, and Cordone, darling that he is, traipsed down to the kitchen to see if he had some chocolate ice cream. I told him to get used to it, because I was going to want a LOT of it over the next four months!"

Both girls giggled.

"Problem was, he didn't have any in the main freezer, and, um, well, you see? The big freezer is in a storage room off of the, um, uh, pool," Kaitlan stuttered.

Sarah's eyes widened as she realized what her best friend was saying. She reddened all the way up into her hair. Kaitlan continued, loving to embarrass the little pixie who had embarrassed her all her life!

"Honestly, though. He wasn't spying, Sarah. He was half-way into the room when he realized he heard talking. He came in just as Sam leaned down to bite you. He turned faster than possible, and ran out of the room, and leaped all the way up to our room." Kaitlan laughed aloud. "I've never seen him so embarrassed in his entire life. I petted him, and told him he did good to leave."

Sarah looked everywhere but Kaitlan. The mating bond was sacred, and private. Kaitlan reached out and touched her pulling her into a bear hug. So, Sarah told her what had happened to her, and Kaitlan's face was one of horror.

"Both of us couldn't go back to sleep when you guys were howling, so I decided to go get a scotch."

"A scotch? You don't drink scotch." Kaitlan reminded her.

"Well, duh! I needed a drink after all the howls thinking there were wolves outside. I never dreamed they were inside! You two were so damned noisy, no one heard us at all! Anyway, I had just gotten to the pool, when I heard something, and I saw a figure falling from the fourth floor landing in front of me! I just remember making some kind of noise with my mouth open. I tripped on the stones, and fell back into the pool. Water filled my mouth, Kaitlan, and I began to choke on it."

Kaitlan's hand went to her mouth in terror.

"The next thing I remember is bobbing twice, sinking, and then two strong arms swept me through the waterfall into the pool room. I was coughing and throwing up water when 'it' jumped out of the pool holding me in one leap! And, I was on the long chair throwing up more water. I felt him stroke my back until I finished. Then, his arms left me, and I found him holding his head in fear.

He told me he was never so scared as he was in his entire life. One thing led to another, and he pulled me onto his lap. And, well, I… uh… noticed he was…um…naked," Sarah finished in a whisper.

Kaitlan dropped her chin on her hands that she had plastered on the bar as she listened smiling. Then, suddenly, Kaitlan sat up as she remembered!

"OMG! You don't wear panties to bed, Sarah!"

Sarah grinned at that. "Before you ask, yes. He noticed, too! After he explained who, and what, he was, the tension was too much for either of us."

Kaitlan nodded knowingly.

"We did things a bit backward. Anyhow, he asked me to be his mate, and I agreed. That's probably when Cordone came in. He bit me, and I bit him back, and well….." She trailed off as she saw the other two girls.

"Hail, hail the gang's all here! "Yelled Anita and Lynne together. They saw the bite on Sarah's neck, and squealed loudly. They hugged her, and welcomed her to their Clan and family.

"I'll help you, Sarah. I'm a damn good cook." Lynne offered.

The two girls continued to whip up breakfast. Anita took this time to tell them that Kaitlan was The White Wolf of the Prophecy. This brought all of them to a halt staring at Kaitlan.

"NO! Really?" Squealed Lynne.

Kaitlan grinned, phased for them, and turned back.

"Apparently, I am The White Wolf. But, only Cordone and Anita knew it until now. So let's keep it on the down low, OK?"

"What's this about a White Wolf Prophecy?" Sarah asked.

Well, now that she was a part of their world, the three girls told her about it in relays.

"That is awesome!" Sarah said after hearing the story. "And, now that you are, then other changes are going to happen, too? Well, I guess that's a BIG YES after Sam and I became mates, right?"

Kaitlan nodded. "Probably, Sarah. I was never supposed to be born. I was. Cordone and I were never supposed to be able to get pregnant, but I am. nd, we were never supposed to mate in wolf form, but we can. So, I think we can safely say that other changes will happen."

Lynne and Sarah returned to making breakfast, and Lynne answered other questions that Sarah had while Kaitlan pulled Anita aside.

"Did you notice?" Anita just nodded.

"Hey, Sarah!" Anita began.

"Yep?" Sarah replied turning out pancakes onto a plate.

"Is there something you need to tell us?"

Sarah turned with a puzzled look. "What?"

"Something odd happened last night, didn't it?"

Sarah had no idea what they were talking about.

"Sarah, I'm the Clan doctor. Do you mind if I examine you? Just to make sure you are OK. Matings between weres and humans are rare, and our males are usually a bit larger than human males. I just want to make sure you are OK."

"They sure are!" Sarah whispered to herself. "Sure. After breakfast, I guess." Sarah shrugged.

After everyone had eaten breakfast, the men adjourned back to Cordone's office. All were very happy for the newest mating in their Clan! It was a surprise, but the joy was there, nevertheless.

After eating, Anita beckoned Sarah to come see her in about an hour while she got set up for her.

Sam was curious.

"Why does Anita want to exam you? Are you OK?"

Worry came through his thoughts. After Sarah explained, he breathed a sigh of relief. He hadn't thought of it that way. Made sense, actually. He got her coat, and took her outside to the deck.

"Do you know how much I love you, Sarah? I couldn't bear to have anything happen to you when I just found you!"

He pulled her tightly into his bare chest. Werewolves never felt the cold. She wrapped her arms around him.

"Ditto. I love you to distraction, and I will never get enough of you!"

Sam kissed her passionately not caring who saw them. He didn't have to worry, because everyone had left the new lovebirds alone - just in case things got a bit out of hand.

They stood together for the longest time, until Sarah started feeling extremely hot. It come on slowly, but now, she was almost hot to the point of feeling scorched. She broke off from Sam as he stared at her in question.

Her coat was too hot. She shrugged out of it, throwing it across the railing. That was so much better! The cool air blew across her heated body as she stood in a sleeveless blue top. She sniffed. How did she not know there were so many wonderful smells before?

Sam was becoming a bit concerned about her. He saw that her skin was covered in sweat, cooling and drying in the air. He watched her sniff the air. WTF? Then, she turned her eyes to his. They were full of desire looking at her mate. Not that Sam didn't like it, but she was starting to act strange. Even her eyes looked a bit strange.

"Sarah, put your coat back on before you freeze

out here!" He ordered.

She turned to reach for her coat, then sank to her knees. The heat! The pain in her stomach was excruciating. Sam picked her up whirling as he darted inside screaming at Anita. Kaitlan jumped down from the platform as did Cordone. Anita ran out of the guest room. All of them saw Sarah doubled over in horrible pain. She was hunched over, sweating so heavy it was dripping on the floor, and she was holding her stomach.

"H-hot! So h-hot!" Sarah barely could get out as she yelled in pain. She started to claw at her neck as if trying to peel the skin off of her body.

Kaitlan was terrified for her best friend, and Cordone saw her about to break. He put his arms around her as she buried her tears of terror into his shoulder.

"Quick, Sam! Bring her in here, now! Lay her on the table, and get the hell out of here!"

"NO!!!" Sam almost screamed.

"P-p-please, Sam!" Begged Sarah. Whether it was for him to leave the room, or stay with her was unclear. He wouldn't let her go.

Anita yelled for Cordone to help her.

"SAM!!! I am ordering you out of that room, now!"

Sam had no choice. He had to obey his Alpha, but he didn't have to like it.

Anita slammed the door, and turned to the girl writhing in pain on the table. She gave Sarah a pain shot, and that seemed to dull it down for a short time.

Long enough for the exam.

"Sarah, look at me."

Sarah was sweating heavier than she had ever seen anyone sweat. She was scared, and she was worried. She took blood samples. That shot should have knocked a human out cold, but while Sarah's eyes were drowsy, they were wild. She barely focused on Anita's face. As if she were turning. Impossible! No human who had been bitten had turned in known history - at least not since ancient times!

"S-s-so hot!!! Why am I so hot?" She started clawing at her skin as if that would help.

Sarah screamed so loudly, Cordone banged on the door.

Opening the door, Anita said irritably, "What? Cordone! I don't have time for this!"

Cordone and Kaitlan had seen something that had them puzzled. Sam was staring into space as if he was in a catatonic state.

"This is important, Anita! Look at Sam's neck."

Anita was grouchy. She had a sick young woman on the table in the next room, she was tired, and she did not like being torn from the side of one of her patients - especially a friend!

"Seriously, Anita! LOOK!" Kaitlan cried.

Sam didn't resist as Anita walked over, and turned Sam's neck aside. Anita did a double take! What? Was she seeing things? Those were FANG marks on his neck! How in the hell did Sarah bite him with fangs?

"Sam, how in the hell did she bi…. Oh, GOD! NO!!" Anita yelled.

And, as realization struck her, she was already in motion.

A growl came from the room, and a howl broke loose. A beautiful, red wolf with ice-blue glowing eyes slammed through the door shattering it to pieces. Cordone had already opened the glass door, and the beautiful red wolf streaked through it at top speed.

Stunned beyond belief, Sam phased into his sandy colored wolf form, and bounded after Sarah as she ran out into the cool, morning air.

Cordone and Kaitlan just stood staring from the deck. How the hell had she turned into a wolf? She was human!

Anita followed the wolves out onto the deck. She knew exactly what had happened! Turning to look at Cordone and Kaitlan, she explained with saddened eyes.

"The White Wolf Prophecy happened. When the curse - that's what I'm calling it lately - hit us, biting humans stopped turning them into werewolves. It appears that has also been reversed."

Kaitlan and Cordone became distressed as they realized what she was saying.

Anita nodded. "I'm not sure, yet, but I highly suspect that when Sam took her as his mate, his bite turned her into a werewolf."

~ 25 ~

"Before Him, a Red Werewolf ran."

Sam let his mate run it out for almost three hours. He had no idea whatsoever was happening, but the one thing he did know. Before him, a new werewolf ran. He could not let her hurt herself.

Finally, the red wolf in front of him stumbled as she collapsed. Even in her wolf form, Sam could see that Sarah was terrified. He approached her slowly, and saw a tear fall from her beautiful blue eyes - her beautiful, and GLOWING blue eyes.

"Sarah?" He ventured, scared he would scare her more.

"Hunkalicious? Is that you?" Her voice shook.

"Yes, Tink. I'm here." He gave her a slight wolfy, but worried grin.

"What happened? I'm a wolf? How? Why?"

"I don't know, Sarah. Everyone was too much in shock with worry to think - including me."

Sam dropped in front of her laying his head on his paws.

"How are you feeling, now?"

"It's really funny. I mean. I feel more free than I have ever felt in my life! The run was so amazing! It's a high I never experienced before! Should I be scared of this, because I don't feel scared at all!"

For the life of him, Sam had never seen anything like this in three thousand years.

"Never? As in your entire long life?" She answered his thought.

Sam hadn't even realized he'd thought it.

"Never. It's obvious that something has turned you into a werewolf." Sam saw her shake in surprise. *"Look, are you willing to go back with me, and let Anita find out why?"*

They still had not completed the twenty-four hour mating, but he didn't want to take a chance that something else might be wrong.

His mate whined, and nodded her beautiful head. Sam stood observing her. He was stunned by her beauty in wolf form. He had accepted that his human mate would never be with him as he ran, but this? Never, in his entire life, had he ever seen a wolf with such red fur.

"You are so beautiful as a wolf, Sarah!"

"Really?"

"Oh, God yes! I have never seen a bright red wolf before! Honestly? Your red fur is just so sexy!" He told her, feeling himself harden for his mate, and in his wolf form. Damn!

Sarah stood, and pranced around with her tail up. He had just made her day! Was it really that important that they know why she was a werewolf?

"Yes, it is, my love."

Truly, like Kaitlan, Sarah was one of a kind, and she was his! But, the mating needed to be put aside until they knew why.

"Not on your life, Wolfallicious!" She grinned.
Hell!   He really needed to reign in his thoughts!
"What did you just call me?"
"There is no way I will put our mating off. Forget about it! Wolfalicious, you are so handsome as a wolf! And, I'm horny! "
Her wolf suddenly felt herself wet for her mate, and let him know it in no uncertain terms by presenting herself to him. Sarah wiggled at him.
"Come and get it, BIG boy!" She grinned under her muzzle.
Whatever was happening to her, it made her more horny for her mate than before. The run seemed to have cleared her mind.
"Whatever is going on, I love it! You won't get off that easy with me!"
His eyes rolled at her. *Wolfalicious* she called him. His desire won out instantly. Knowing it was impossible, he would play her game. Sam circled her stalking her as if she was prey. She wiggled her butt at him as he did. He rounded her three times, then stopped behind her. He was hard and ready. He knew he should stop, but he couldn't. Even knowing it impossible, he could at least give her release in some form. Just not the way he wanted.
He parked his paws on her back, and planned to tease her. Sam was astonished, and surprise flew through his body when he found himself inside her! He was completely dazed as he felt her tighten around his extremely, large wolf's cock! Her snout came around looking at him in irritation.

"Uh...waiting, mate! You just can't plunge inside me, and leave me this way!" She complained.

"Sarah! We are not supposed to be able to mate in wolf form! This is not possible!"

"Well, Sam, apparently we can, or you wouldn't be inside me now! Kaitlan and Cordone did, you know."

That was an even bigger shock to his system. He forgot he was even inside his mate!

"What?"

"Sam...she's The White Wolf of your prophecy! She is carrying twins inside her.   She conceived both in human form and wolf form! Didn't you know that? She has made this possible somehow. I'm a wolf, now. That can't be coincidence. You are inside of me. I feel you! Again, that can't be coincidence!"

Sam was till stunned at this. Kaitlan? The White Wolf?

She nodded her head. *"She showed us this morning, and that's why we were all squealing! She has brought about a new world to the werewolves, and the rest of the supernatural world!"*

Kaitlan had finally told the other two girls that she was having twins. That set all of them off jumping, squealing, and crying as they hugged her.

Sam breathed hard. His mate was a wolf. He was inside of her in wolf form. Kaitlan was The White Wolf of Prophecy. Twins. It was too much for him. His musings had been so intense, he'd forgotten what he was doing. Then, he thought of something, and his heart sank.

"Sarah?"

"Yes."

"I think I know why you're a wolf."

She turned her muzzle to him with a question in her eye.

"Thousands of years ago, a bite from a werewolf would turn a human into one. Whatever happened, that was completely ended. Since then, we have not been able to turn any human to a wolf."

Her eyebrow area went up.

"I bit you, Sarah!"

She started at his words. He had turned her into a werewolf? She stopped for a moment thinking about it. Suddenly, her muzzle went up in a devilish grin at him.

"Thank you, Sam! I have never been so happy as I am right now! I love you, and now, I can be your equal."

He looked at her, and saw in her eyes she wasn't lying. She was glad he had turned her! If she was glad, then he was happier than he had ever been in his life!

"Uh, Wolfalicious?"

His dazed eyes looked at her turned head.

"Do you want to finish this before nightfall? I mean, I don't mind being like this forever, but the least you can do is take care of your horny mate!"

That knocked him out of his reverie! He laughed.

"Well, Tink, I guess we are definitely going to find out if we can mate as wolves!"

And, he proceeded to find out that not only did it work, it was a turn on like he had never experienced in his life as he spilled his seed into her, and they howled together for the first time.

It was then, he discovered that like other animals, he was locked inside her for a period of time. Strangely enough, his mate was the one who told him why.

Sarah had never felt such pleasure as she did when she felt his hot liquid pour into her. She felt it as it slid into her womb. Kaitlan must have felt the same thing. She also knew that this is what caused pregnancy in animals in the wild. The thought gave her a small bit of hope, but she thought she'd not tell Sam - yet. It was a week before her time of the month. She would wait to see if her period came. She desperately hoped it didn't. She wiggled again, and he accommodated her immediately. He softened, finally, and was able to leave her body - not that he wanted to - but they both collapsed on the ground cuddling next to each other.

Sarah fell into a most needed sleep, and just before he joined her, his eyes looked upon her. Never had he desired anything more than if she could have his child, and if it came in this form, better still. Then, he, too, fell asleep.

Like Kaitlan and Cordone, when they awoke, they were human and naked. They made slow love to each other followed by twelve more hours of sex-a-robics While laying in each other's arms, Sarah was tracing his chest with her finger, she had long wanted to know the answer to something.

"Sam?"

"Hmmm?" He said stroking her body gently.

"You remember that night, right?"

He stopped, yanking her to him tightly.

"How could I not remember it, Sarah. I'm still ashamed of myself. I'm so sorry for what I did." He wouldn't look at her.

"Why did you not take me as your mate, then? After everything that happened between us?"

He lifted his head leaning on his elbow looking down at Sarah as both remembered that incredible night.

Sam had come home early in a bad mood, because of a bad business deal. He'd finally won, but all he wanted was a shower, and bed.

Sarah had a part-time, secretarial job at the Publishing House, and she was running late for the movie Kaitlan, and she, had so wanted to see. She had no time to run home. Kaitlan had told her that Sam was out of town, and could use his shower to get ready. So, Sarah did. She always had extra clothes just in case.

Stripping, Sam had gone into the bathroom not noticing his shower was running. Sam started to step into the shower, and a vision of beauty walked out of it. Sarah.

Sarah had frozen to the floor. The man she'd had

a crush on forever stood naked in front of her. She had her towel in her hand, and quickly covered herself.

Sam and Sarah stared at each other. Then, without a word, he moved to Sarah, and stood looking down into her pixie face. He had gently reached out to take the towel from her, and yet, she didn't stop him. His eyes drank in the sight of her naked body. Her breasts, her flat stomach, and the red curls at the apex of her thighs.

Sarah's breath caught in her throat as she gazed upon his body. His muscled chest had her licking her lips, and his cock was growing quickly. Sam wasn't ashamed of his body.

Sarah had been accosted by so many guys who wanted to get in her pants, this was the total opposite. She wanted to get into Sam's! Well, if he had been wearing them!

Sam touched her breast teasing her hardened peak causing her to moan in pleasure. Then, he had pulled her to him in a gentle kiss which morphed quickly into a mind blowing sensuality she had never felt before. She had never let a boy touch her. But, this was different. She wanted Sam. The fact she let him touch her, and kiss her like this proved it to her heated body, and it was confirmed with the massive flow of wetness from her entrance.

Sam's hand had gently lowered to her red curls, and without hesitation, she had spread her legs to let him touch her. She had arched at his touch.

He had been in heaven when he felt her

readiness for him.

"Sarah, you are so beautiful, and so wet." Sam had told her.

Sara had melted right then. She wanted him to be the one who took away all of the ugliness that had racked her young life. She had reached to stroke his steel and velvet shaft, closing her hand around it. His breath had sucked in at her touch.

"Sam, please?" Sarah had begged him.

He needed her. Wanted her. She was his. His mate. He slipped his hardness between her legs rubbing her entrance. She was very wet.

Sarah had gasped at his size against her, then closed her eyes. She let a moan come through her lips. She had never felt anything like this except in her fantasies about him! She NEEDED Sam inside of her.

"I'll be gentle with you." He had whispered to her.

He had led her into the shower, and turned on the water, making sure it did not run over them - yet. He laid the towel on a very soft mat that covered the bottom of the shower, and she laid down on it. Then, he dropped down, and spread her legs gently, lifting them so he could see her beauty. He gently stroked her wet folds and clit, then placed three fingers inside of her wet heat. Sarah panted with desire and need.

"God, you are so beautiful, Sarah! I'm going to give you an orgasm this way, first."

"Why?" She gasped.

"Because of my size. Your channel needs to

soften in order to take my size into you." He had explained. He was big! Really big!

Sarah nodded her head, and let him do what he wanted to her. She felt his tongue dive into her, and lick her nub gently and continuously. She bucked hard as she felt his fingers inside her moving in and out, and his tongue tickling her clit. She finally had felt her very first orgasm just with his fingers and mouth.

Sam had slid back up over her, and gently slid his tip into her wet entrance. Sarah had grabbed his head to kiss him hard as she felt him slide completely into her.

"I don't want gentle, please, Sam?" She had whispered to him.

Sam's cock had grown at her words, and he had felt her tighten around him. Her thrusts matched his. Their rapid breathing and passion flared as they reached their climax, and he had spilled his seed into her.

Sam had buried his head in her neck, and her head leaned against his chest. What had he done? She was seventeen years old, for God's Sake! He had made love to his mate who was seventeen! Technically, she would be eighteen in two weeks, but still, he felt horrible for taking her virginity. His mate? Did he just say she was his mate? No. Not possible. A werewolf and human couldn't conceive, and he was sad about it. Sam knew he should have removed himself from her wetness, but he was powerless. He needed Sarah badly. And, he could feel she needed him just as much.

Sarah had never felt so alive! She wanted them to be like this forever.

"Sarah?" He didn't know what he was asking, but she did.

"Make love to me, Sam. Let me stay with you tonight? I need you."

He was lost, and he knew it. Sam pulled out of her, and carried his naked beauty to his bed. He had given her cell phone to her so she could send a text to Kaitlan that she was ill, and begged off for the movie. She hated lying, but a movie with Kaitlan, or a night with Sam? There was no contest.

Then, they had made love all night long, and in the early morning, she had dressed, and left Sam sleeping soundly. From that point forward, he did everything he could to avoid her.

"I thought you didn't want me." Sarah told him.

"Not want you? Not want you, Sarah? My GOD I wanted you so much I couldn't stand it! I was trying to protect you!" He kissed her soundly on the mouth. "I was a damn fool, Sarah. I thought I was protecting you by letting you leave me."

"I wish I had known, but yes, you were a fool, my love. It will always be our secret. I never told anyone about that night."

"Me, either. Sarah, you were my mate then, too. I just refused to admit it. I should have mated you when you turned eighteen. I'm sorry I didn't."

"Well, that's water under the bridge. We are

together, now. Forever."

Sarah reached up, and kissed her mate. And, Sam showed Sarah how much he really wanted her.

After twenty four hours of sheer bliss, Sam taught her how to phase at will. She did so before he finished explaining.

"You're a natural at this, Tink!"

"Are you kidding? I'm a natural at EVERYTHING since mating with you!"

Sam phased, and the two took off at a run next to each other, stopping at least once for another "sex-er-cise" as his mate called it. Yes! He was going to love having her with him in any form forever. Kaitlan had been right. He would never be bored with her.

The two lovers made it back to the house, and Anita took Sarah inside to do some more tests. They were both told that Sam's bite had turned Sarah. Sam still felt guilty, but Sarah wouldn't let him continue. She had NEVER been so happy in her life!

So, Sam left her there while he and Dan drove to get the jet ready. Dan didn't say anything at all, but grinned for his buddy. He was very happy for him. Dan wondered what it might be like to have a mate, then sighed. Probably never know. Not with his history. He already had his first, and only, shot.

Anita pulled off her examining gloves.

"How are you really feeling about this, Sarah? You can be honest with me."

"Oh, come on, Anita! Are you friggin' kidding me? I have never been so alive and so very, very happy in my entire life! It should be clear that mating in wolf form is going to be the norm, now. Not a bad way to go, either!" She grinned.

Anita laughed. "Well, then you'd better be prepared for my checking you out in a week if your period doesn't come, little pixie! To have two werewolf females pregnant at the same time would send excited ripples throughout the werewolf Clans all over the world!"

Silently, she thought that what had been slowly killing their females off the way the elves had been might be reversed if several wolf females were to be highly fertile. The prophecy had already changed several things. Replenishing the Clan would put a stop to losing others, before what happened to the elves happened to the werewolves. And, they had to find out who was poisoning them with the Wolfsbane. Fast. When they returned, she planned to have a word with the council. Someone inside the Clan was deliberately trying to kill the female weres. Had to be. Anita was exhausted. She was tired, and her brain wasn't working right. But, she was determined. And, that's the only thing that pushed her forward despite being so tired.

~ 26 ~

Insufferable! That's what they are!

"They are just so damned insufferable!" Dan grumbled to himself.

Cordone was strutting around like a stud flaunting his prowess while his mate grew larger every day as a beautiful, bouncy, pregnant woman carrying twins. Kaitlan was glowing. No one had ever seen a more beautiful, pregnant wolf.

Sarah was taking to the supernatural world as if she was born to it. Sam was standing taller, because of his new, pipsqueak of a mate. Dan just smiled. He was happy, but these guys were just way too happy! It was just irritating!

Sarah had been disappointed three days after her mating when she had told Anita that she wasn't pregnant. But, Sam had told her that is was OK. He was willing to keep trying much to Sarah's delight as she drug Sam, grinning, all the way into his office locking his door behind her. A "nooner" was just fine with him! Ah, yes! There were definitely perks that came with finding your mate!

Anita sat at her desk, playing with her dark brown ponytail. Rarely did anyone see her hair down, and everyone thought she was a Tomboy - which she was. Sarah's tests were confounding the hell out of her. None of it made any sense. What she hadn't told anyone was that they showed that Sarah was still as human as ever. Not a wolf gene in her, yet they had all seen her. There was no doubt about it. Sarah was a werewolf, but why was still the question. Sarah's red coat was like none the Clan had ever seen.

"Damn!"

She pushed her chair back, and realized she was supposed to meet with the council in ten minutes. She'd been so engrossed with Sarah's results, she'd almost forgotten she was supposed to present her findings about the poisoning of the females.

Shoving her cell phone in her pocket and grabbing her laptop, Anita ran to the elevator. The door opened, and she took off running, again, saying a quick "Hi' to Lynne before darting around the corner to the council room - and flat into Dan almost knocking him over. Dan grabbed her laptop as she dropped it before it slammed into the floor.

"In a hurry are we?" He laughed at her handing her laptop back to her.

"Back off, Third! I'm late!" Anita growled.

"Come, come, Anita. You look like you had just run a race in a hurricane." Dan was amused at her blustering.

He reached out, and tucked that same lock of hair that had fallen out of her ponytail, behind her right ear. He had always done that since they were cubs, because it was always happening. Being her best friend since they were kids just made it too easy for him to tease her. Damn! She was as cute as a button when she was like this, Dan thought. One of these days, the male who mated her would be damned lucky!

"Yeah. Thanks," her tone was dry. "Dan, open the damn door! I don't have time for this, and Cordone will be angry with me for being late." Anita looked at the time. "Shit," she muttered. "I'm already ten minutes late! Open the damn door, Dan!" She ordered, again.

Dan just gave her a taunting grin, and it aggravated

her that he turned the handle very slowly before letting her proceed. He lost the grin immediately when he saw the somber faces around the table. This was a very serious meeting. This was about the poisoning and murders.

Anita looked at Cordone's thunderous face as she entered, and walked to the table almost slamming her computer down on it. Kaitlan looked up at her mate, and put her hand on his arm, calming him immediately.

"I really am sorry, Cordone. I know I'm late, but I was checking out Sarah's tests."

Kaitlan spoke before Cordone.

"What did you find?" She enquired.

She was as eager as everyone to find out what had happened to Sarah when she changed to a wolf after she had mated with Sam.

Richard Morton O'Malley drug a chair to the table for Anita.

She murmured, "Thanks," to him, and plopped down as if she had run a marathon.

"Nothing. Nada. Not a damn thing! She is still as human as ever, but she is, most definitely, a werewolf!"

She looked up at Kaitlan who was totally confused.

"Nothing? How can than be, Anita? I thought you said it was Sam's bite."

"How the hell should I know? I've run every test I could think of for both wolf and human. Nothing indicates anything but that she is completely human! In fact, nothing

is making sense to me! Every time I think I have a break-through, the tests prove negative! I'm finding this very frustrating! It's as if I'm only getting half of the results!"

Anita was horribly wound up, and tired, and irritated, and…and…and…ANGRY!

Kaitlan's eyes narrowed. What was wrong with Anita?   She'd never seen her be so rude.

"Then, how could she change?" Asked Wayne O'Kelley. "How is that possible?"

"I don't know! Will you stop asking me stupid questions I can't answer?" Anita was really about to lose it. Dan stepped over to put his hands on her shoulders hoping to calm her.

"I'm just so damned frustrated!"

Sam was sitting at Cordone's right running his hands through his sandy hair. What was going on with Sarah?   Sarah was the only one not questioning it, because she was adamant that since Kaitlan was The White Wolf of prophecy, the explanation was clear.

"Well," Cordone began, "We'll let the problem of Sarah slide at the moment, and let's get to the matter at hand. Anita, what have you found about the murders?"

Anita looked around the table. What a mix of characters. Richard O'Malley who had pulled up a chair for her was the most interesting. Like Sarah, he had red hair that bordered on the strawberry blonde side. Definitely had to be a Viking descendant. His shoulders were broad, his torso tight, and many women in the Clan were dying to see his abs which he never revealed to anyone. They all giggled about how they must be great to touch! About six-foot 4, he was all muscle, and built like a bloody tank!

Sam, was a Greek god without question. Sarah was very lucky. If they ever did have a child, that child was going to be absolutely, hands down, the most beautiful ever in Clan history. And, Anita hoped to deliver it!

The other council members were very handsome, and had the same muscular stature. There wasn't one Clan woman who wouldn't mind being their mates.

Only McClain was missing. Frankly, the guy gave her the heebie geebies, using an old-time phrase, and she sure as hell didn't miss him!

Standing up, Anita began. She had to control herself! She'd never felt so out of control. She just didn't know what was wrong. Had to be exhaustion.

"As you know, there have been sporadic poisonings of our females. Tara O'Hara the first death, of course. The culprit is a poison, as you know, made from Wolfsbane."

She stopped as the council began to stir a bit. No one wanted to believe it.

"Wolfsbane? Really? That can be completely poisonous to us. What makes anyone think that our females are targeted? There is no way that could happen."

Roland Tanner was the most skeptical of the bunch.   Like McClain, he made Anita's skin crawl.

"Yes, Tanner. That's right. That is the culprit. It was delivered through a saline bag to Tara. It is colorless, odorless to all within the supernatural world, and deadly as hell if it is refined into a clear liquid. To be totally effective in killing, it must be delivered through the veins. Drinking it will make a wolf sick, put them into a coma, and if not given the antidote I have developed for the oral version within thirty minutes after ingestion, death might occur. This accounts for the recent illnesses to some of the women who are all exhibiting the same symptoms. The only way to do this is if someone in the Clan is trying to kill the females wolves."

She gazed around the table, and continued.   She had their attention. These poisonings, were not coincidental, or accidental.

"It can be given in anything.   Cola, water,

coffee, tea, and so on. You get the idea. As long as it is a liquid, it could be easily placed in a drink, or injected into an IV. Since we have had extra security within the clinic, we have only had two other cases of female deaths. But, that's not good at all. Now, I have here," she continued as she lifted her laptop making sure everyone could see, "the results of eighteen year-old Anna Quinn who died recently. As you can see, the blood sample on the left is normal; the sample on the right was after the autopsy."

The council drew back in horror. Her blood was interspersed with a green substance that seemed to disintegrate blood cells. They watched it actually happen through the video.

"Wolfsbane, as I have said, is colorless and odorless. After injection into the blood stream it turns this thick, green substance. I've studied the effects of Wolfsbane for many years. It can be used to heal, or to kill. But, this new, liquefied version prevents coagulation that is necessary to stop bleeding in the event of injury, or in Tara's case, childbirth followed by death."

Cordone didn't like where this was going, and looked at his mate who didn't take her eyes off of Anita.

"Now, this photo will show you that we found another problem with Wolfsbane. It also semi-paralyzes the body as well. I've spent all this time working on it since Tara's death, and it has taken me all this time to even begin to put it together. Of course, technology has advanced greatly allowing me do this. As I have also said, I have developed an antidote for the oral poisoning of the wolves, but, as I said before, only if it is given within the first thirty minutes of drinking the deadly drug, and the results have been positive so far. But, the faster, the better. Even ten minutes might be the difference between life and death. Now, I have print outs of my findings, and am giving each of you a copy. It's a lot of information, I know, but you ne…"

WHAM! CRASH! A horrible noise in the outer office interrupted the meeting. Dan was out the door in a flash with Richard at his heels followed by everyone else. Anita saw Lynne on the floor with Richard hovering over her, and shot to her side.

"Oh, God!" Her face was set in worry. She looked at Cordone. "She has been given Wolfsbane! I have to get her to the clinic NOW!"

Everyone burst into action at the same time, but it was Richard who grabbed her, and was off to the clinic with Anita right behind him on his heels shouting for someone to bring her Anita's coffee mug, but not to touch the cup itself. Lynne loved her coffee, and everyone knew it. She drank it as if it was water. Apparently, the killer knew it as well. The very fact that he did, proved that he had access to even the council! A traitor was in their midst, but no one wanted to admit it, yet.

Anita ran into an exam room. "Put her on the table, Richard!"

She ran to her office, and was back again in

seconds with the syringe containing the antidote. Anita had not had the time to tell them how she had to administer the antidote for the oral version of Wolfsbane, and it looked like they were going to find out first hand.

Kaitlan had arrived along with Cordone, Sam, Dan, and Sam had called Sarah who was there within mere minutes. The girls were frightened. But, what grabbed their attention most was Richard O'Malley. He looked as if he'd been hit by a truck. He would not let go of Lynne's hand, and nothing anyone could say would make him drop it. He just glared at all of them with glowing hazel eyes to back off. He had no idea his eyes were glowing.

Kaitlan and Sarah looked at each other. No one had any idea that Richard had chosen Lynne as his mate. Even Lynne. That just added to the sadness and horror of everything.

Anita started to inject Lynne with the antidote when Richard grabbed her arm to stop her.

"Richard! I understand how you feel, but if I don't

get this inside her, now, she WILL die! DO YOU UNDERSTAND?"

Richard's face was almost wild, but Cordone took over. He always hated to force his Alpha will onto anyone, but sometimes, it was necessary.

"Richard. I am ordering you to remove yourself from Lynne's bedside, now."

Richard slumped. He had no choice. He backed away to let Anita inject the antidote into Lynne's stomach, and a massive flow of blood erupted from the needle entry. They all cringed when they saw how it had to be delivered.

In moments, Lynne went into convulsions. Anita yelled at her nurse, Teri, to get everyone out.

"Shit!" Muttered Sarah.

Sam grabbed her, and pushed her out of the way while the men forced Richard out into the hallway.

Richard leaned against the wall, his face a mask of terror, and slumped against it, dropping to his knees and covering his face. He should have claimed her. She was his mate, but his pride and stubbornness kept him from doing so. He was a damn fool! And, now? Oh, CREATOR, NO! He may have lost his true mate!!!

Cordone placed his hand on Richard's shoulder. Cordone didn't know. No one knew. Or so he thought.

Kaitlan and Sarah held each other in a hug as they cried for their friend.

All kinds of horrible howls, screams, and growls came from inside the room after Teri had shut the door. Richard tried to stand up, to run to her, but Cordone kept him compliant on his knees.

But, amazingly, Richard found the strength, and against Cordone's order, stood up, grabbed Cordone's hand, and twisted it around his back pushing him away. Then, Richard tried to enter the room. Cordone yelled at Dan and Sam to help him use their own powers to force their mental and physical power to restrain him in addition to the Alpha's.

Everyone realized that Richard's strength and power was far beyond any one person to control. This was an astonishing revelation to all of them.

But, it worked, and Richard couldn't shake them off, now. He was forced to his knees, again.

The noise continued for an hour and a half. Everyone was crying by the time the sounds stopped - even the men. Richard had almost gone into a catatonic state.

And, then, silence. Absolute, dead silence. This was far worse than the screams. The door clicked, and out came a disheveled, sweating Teri with her head down. She pushed her hair out of her eyes, and just stopped. Anita, looking far worse, came out also with her head down.

Richard's gut clenched. Was his mate dead? He couldn't stand it.

Kaitlan whispered, "Anita?"

Anita ran her wet, and bloody hands through her hair, and looked straight at Richard.

"She made it. She will be alright."

Those first three words had everyone hugging, laughing, and crying at the same time.

Dan's eyes widened as he saw Anita start to collapse. He caught her as she fell.

"Anita?" He whispered to his best friend.

"She's just fine, Dan. She's so tired, she just passed out. We almost lost Lynne. But, she's going to be OK," Teri said, but was looking at Richard. "It's OK, Richard. You may go in now."

Richard was already at Lynne's bedside in a

heartbeat, holding her hand. The look that Richard had on his face when Richard broke down almost made Sarah break down, too. She knew that look. Pure terror.

"Dan, bring Anita with me. She has been under a lot of stress, lately. She used her last bit of strength in order to save Lynne. She is exhausted, and needs to sleep. I'll take care of her ."

"That's fine, Teri, but I will take care of her, and stay with her until I know she is awake." He was not about to let his best friend down. He never had; he never would. Teri nodded, and helped Dan get her to the bed in her office.

"Everyone needs to get a bit of rest. The crisis is over." She turned, and followed Dan down the hallway.

The rest of the council members looked at each other. For the first time, they realized that there was no more denying it. Lynne's poisoning meant only one thing. They had a traitor, and that traitor had easy access everywhere within the Clan. If he could get to Lynne, he could get to anyone on the council. Fear grabbed them all as they realized that the traitor had to be a Clan member.

~ 27 ~

Can There be a Second chance for Love?

That night, Kaitlan and Cordone lay together sweating and panting heavily after their vigorous love making. Cordone reached out, and pulled her to his side as Kaitlan laid her head on his very damp chest, his hand stroking her blossoming belly feeling their children do flips inside of her. He wondered why all that movement didn't hurt her. It was still amazing to him that they had conceived two babies, but even more impossible, in both wolf and human form. Their love was growing every moment of every day. The love he had for her, and their two little babies, was infinite. He heard Kaitlan sigh as he stroked her stomach, and reached down covering his hand as he did.

"Cordone?"

"Hmmmm?" He answered absently.

"Can I ask you something?"

Turning to look at his beautiful, green-eyed blonde, he smiled. "Anything, love."

"I've been thinking."

He snorted.

"I know. It's always dangerous when I start thinking." She laughed. "You told me that the Elven females were killed out long ago, right?"

"Well, yes." He was not sure where she was going with this.

Kaitlan propped up on her elbow looking at him, and stopped his stroking. His eyebrows went up in question.

"Stop that a minute. I have to be able to think, and I can't while you're doing that." She grinned up at him. "Let's see… they were killed out with Wolfsbane."

Cordone nodded, still puzzled.

She continued. "My Mother was killed with it, and, now, someone is targeting our females with Wolfsbane. Is it possible that someone is copying the person who killed out the Elven females?"

Her words jerked him upright! Why hadn't he thought of that? Perhaps it was because they were so long lived, their memories had dimmed, and the reason why no one else had ever thought of it. Shit! He bounded out of bed, and started pacing the room. Kaitlan watched for a while until it was making her a bit sick, and she stopped looking at him. And, for her, watching her mate pace naked with everything swinging around, that was saying something. He stopped, and walked to the bed looking down at her.

"I never saw it before, Kaitlan. And, yet, in a few weeks, you come up with what the rest of us missed!" He rubbed the back of his neck. "But, why? I mean, what possible thing could the person gain? That doesn't make sense."

This time it was Kaitlan who bounded out of bed and paced.

Cordone looked at his naked mate's body as she paced. Her breasts were beautiful. They were getting heavier as they prepared the milk for feeding his children which caused them to hang lower on her body. God, she was beautiful! And, she still let him make love to her! Refusing to lie to himself, making love to her while his children kicked him in his stomach was a real turn on!

Kaitlan stopped, and turned fast, her eyes dawning with realization. Her breasts swung from side to side gently.

"How long did it take before the Elves died out?"

Geez! Did she have to ask a question that was taught to them in school? As if he could remember! He closed his eyes, wrinkled his brow as he tried to remember what he had learned. His eyes opened, and he snapped his fingers.

"If I remember right, it took only about two hundred years. Why?"

"Cordone!" Kaitlan grabbed him with excitement. "Of course! The reason why the Elf succeeded is crystal clear! Only an Elf could get close enough to poison the females! It had to be someone with access even at their highest level. Someone they trusted." Cordone frowned. She continued. "Think about it! A wolf could not get close to the Elves, nor a vampire! It had to be an Elf who destroyed his own species. But, again, why would someone want to destroy their own?"

"Kaitlan, you've lost me."

"Just listen!" She started impatiently pacing again. He wished she'd stop. It was really causing him to want her again, and it was hard to concentrate with that beautiful body walking and bouncing in front of him.

"It's obvious that what happened to the Elves is happening here and now. But, nothing until my Mother, right?"

"You are saying that the same person who poisoned the Elves is doing so again?"

"Of course not! Geez! I'm saying it may be a copycat. We've established, as we know, it's someone inside the Clan. But, I'm saying that the traitor in our midst is someone high up, or someone who has clearance, and total access to us. He has to be in order to even make it as far as poisoning Lynne. His use of the name, Zanack, was deliberately chosen after what you told me you had killed the original one and everyone's fear of the name. The person who poisoned the Elves is not the same person, obviously. That elf was probably someone who had a terrible grudge, and wanted revenge. More than likely it was jealousy over a woman, or perhaps someone who wanted to take over. I don't think anyone knows, or ever will, as long as it has been. Another clue is that nothing has happened between the time the Elven women died out, and my Mother." She thought another minute. "But, Cordone, could this be bigger? Who is to say that this Zanack is just trying to kill werewolf females? Have any of the others in our supernatural world had these same poisonings?"

Kaitlan grabbed her mate yanking him to look at her.

"You told me you had killed Zanack, right?" Cordone nodded. "And, yet Zanack is at the heart of these poisonings which just can't be, because he's dead. Again, it's obvious that a werewolf has taken his name, and is using it! Of course, he would be trying to hide his identity from all of us, especially if he has access to the council. Is he killing the other females? What if he is wanting to erase the supernatural worlds altogether? And, if so, is it possible that Zanack is doing so to deflect his real intentions? Perhaps he is really only after the werewolves? Or, maybe revenge of some kind? He may have more than one goal, or only one goal."

Kaitlan was desperate, finally relaxing when she saw Cordone's understanding taking the place of confusion.

"HELL AND DAMNATION!"

Cordone streaked for his cell phone, and called Sam and Dan on conference. They, like him, had never considered that someone might be out to destroy the entire supernatural species. And, even if that proved not the case, it would have even more dire connotations. If Kaitlan were right, Zanack could be targeting the supernatural females only. They needed to know.

"Dan…get on the phone with Stefan and Ali'on. Tell them what we suspect, and ask them if they have had any poisonings using Wolfsbane. If so, then call the rest of the leaders of our world. Dan, also ask if their females have been poisoned, or killed within the last thirty years, or so! If the answer is yes, tell them I'm calling the Master Council to convene immediately!!"

He slammed his phone down in anger. Damn! He broke another one.

Kaitlan shook her head. Her mate went through more damn phones that way!

"What is a Master Council, Cordone?"

Cordone turned. He kept forgetting she hadn't known about all this before.

"The Master Council consists of all the leaders of the supernatural world. This includes us, the Elves and the Vampires. It has not been called but twice before. And, it's only when it directly threatens our supernatural world, and this definitely qualifies!"

"No! Seriously? Vampires are real?" Kaitlan asked.

"That's all you got from that?" His eyebrows went up in disbelief.

"Calm down, mate. For goodness sakes! Breathe!"

She put her arms around his neck, and landed a giant kiss on his lips, her naked body feeling his hardness against her.

"We will discover everything, and make sure this monster is put down for eternity. Right now, though, what I do know is that that watching that gorgeous naked body of yours pace back and forth with your cock moving side to side, is driving me nuts! I am crazy in love with you, and you gave me your miracle children. We are a family, and no matter what, we will do what it takes to keep them safe." Then, her face turned serious.

"I won't let this filth hurt my family, and certainly, not my Clan. I will make sure he is ripped to pieces, and never found again, even if it means I have to do it!"

It worked. Cordone grinned.

"A little blood-thirsty are we?"

Kaitlan pulled his lips to her, and looked in his eyes.

"I am The White Wolf, and it's my destiny to take care of my Clan if not the supernatural world. As daunting as that is, I'm not a fragile flower, Cordone. But, I can promise I will never let these monsters - ever - take my Clan away from me! I'll do what it takes, and if that means killing them myself, then that is exactly what I will do! When our children are born, I want you to teach me to fight."

Cordone looked at his mate with a whole new expression of respect. He looked for her eyes to back off of what she just said. He didn't want her to become a killer like her Father, Sam, Dan, or himself. But, he couldn't argue. It was there in her eyes. She really was her Father's daughter, and she meant every damn word. And, worse? She was right. It was her responsibility as the heir. It was his, too. That didn't mean he liked the idea of her getting involved in a fight if it came down to it.

Dipping his mouth to her nose, he lightly kissed it.

"Remind me to never get on your bad side, will

you? OK. When our children arrive, I will teach you to fight."

She smiled as she brought his mouth to hers, closing the gap between her body and his. She felt her children move inside her again, kicking Cordone who laughed when he felt them. It felt like heaven to feel them, and her mate next to her belly so he, too, could feel them.

"Oh, my gorgeous mate! You don't want to be on it! But, making up might be a whole lot of fun!"

And, she slammed her mouth into his as he lifted her in his arms carrying her back to their bed. She had been even more in heat since she had become pregnant, and every day, needed more from her mate. Cordone's last thought as he pulled her on top of him was that Kaitlan was insatiable. He didn't know why. She had even been coming to his office for sex on a daily basis at noon, or when she wasn't editing. He loved making love to her as often as possible, and who was he to stop her? At the rate they were going, they would have a great many children!

~ 28 ~

Humans Really Don't want a Rogue Wolf Around!   Trust Me!

Anita was angry, and frustrated, and furious, and…and…fucking, damn tired! She looked at the clock on her desk. It was 2:46 in the morning!

Why couldn't she get this right? Why? She ran her hands through her ponytail again. She jumped up, took her chair, and slammed it against the far wall. Her wolf was demanding to be released, but she wouldn't. No. She had no time to let her take over!

Lynne had been released for light duty this morning, and was taken back to her apartment by Richard. Anita was jealous. Richard knew Lynne was his mate, but Lynne had no clue! How the hell did Lynne not feel, or know it? For the first time in, forever, she wished she had a mate, too, just to keep her settled and on an even keel. Sex would keep her wolf calm, and maybe she could concentrate! Even if he was just to hold her at times like this. She was so damned tired! Too tired to think any longer, but she couldn't stop. She had to find the answer. She felt she was so very close!   Yet, every time she felt close, the results were negative on everything lately!

She had been working for what? Three days without a break? She had passed out from using her strength to help heal Lynne's poisoning. But, that was two weeks ago. Ever since she had awakened, she'd felt she was walking a tightrope, and about to fall off!! Oh, hell! She had to admit her mind wasn't functioning well. She didn't know why.

She walked back and forth in her small office. She'd tried everything! She had Kaitlan's tests, Sarah's tests, and Lynne's tests. And…not even Wolfsbane showed up even in Lynne's tests! Nothing was making one bit of fucking sense!

She was missing something, she knew it, but what? When Kaitlan had explained her theory a week ago about the Elves, the Wolfsbane, and the connection, it had given her a whole new perspective. Her Alpha was brilliant!

But, now? STILL nothing! She grabbed her chair, and threw it against the wall so hard, it left a huge dent in the wall. Trying to continue thinking, all she saw was a blur. She stood, and threw her laptop against the wall followed by her chair again! Then, she found herself picking up anything and everything, and throwing it at the wall. She'd never been so upset and angry!

She picked up a cut glass award she had won for a breakthrough in vampire anatomy allowing them to live as humans, eat human food, and go out in the sun again. They still needed blood, but not as often, and it was made available by human, volunteer donors. She had changed everything for them. She was revered, and honored for doing it.

It crashed against the door just as it opened, Dan

jerked back just missing it by inches.

"Angry much?" He asked coming in and shutting the door behind him.

Anita threw her hand over her mouth! Oh, God! She could have hurt Dan with her recklessness!

She fell to the floor, and horror grabbed her as she burst into tears. Dan shook his head, knelt down, and put his arms around her. He just sat there, and held her. It felt kind of nice, actually. It had been a very, very long time since he had held a woman in his arms. Only Cordone knew that Dan had a mate, once, and that his mate had died because of himself and her Father. The guilt was still with him, now, and every time he thought of it, it made him sick. His mate had been an Elf.

He rocked her back and forth just like a baby, and just let her cry. Her tears soaked all the way through his t-shirt. Their friendship went all the way back to when they were children.

She finally looked up at him, tears streaming from her eyes that were tortured.

Dan studied her in a way he had never done. Anita Carol Moore was very tall. Maybe about, oh, say, five-foot nine, maybe ten. Anita never wore makeup. She never primped, or tried to lure any man to her with wiles. She was beautiful without makeup on her oval shaped face, her coal black hair was sleek, and smooth, but she always wore it in a ponytail, never down. In fact, he didn't remember her having it down in her entire, adult life. Her eyes were a beautiful hazel with tiny flecks of navy. He bet they'd have a very unusual glow if she ever found her mate. She was Italian in heritage, and her light olive skin was beautiful. She never went out in the sun that he knew. Her body was the envy of all the female wolves, and she never realized how the men raked her body over with their eyes. She was focused, entirely, on her work.

Dan turned his head sideways. Her breasts were extremely voluptuous. He figured she was at least a D cup. Her waist was very tiny in contrast, but her hips were full and rounded. She reminded him of the beauties in the 1940's and 1950's like Marilyn Monroe and Rita Hayworth. And, half of her body were her gorgeous, long legs. Yep. Pin-up girl. She had real, womanly curves. The man who mated her was going to be one extremely lucky bastard! He almost envied who that man would be.

Always in her office, she was the kindest, most caring Doctor, let alone wolf, whoever lived. She had even braved the vampires against Canaan's orders just to help them live as normally as they could. She had earned their respect, and she was honored among them. There wasn't one supernatural species that did not have respect for her. She had helped every single one of them live better lives. Dan was proud to be her best friend since childhood, but this was far, and away, the worst state he'd ever seen her in as long as he had known her.

And, she was losing control. This was not good. Not good at all. It wouldn't be long before she lost her mind in this state. He'd seen it before. Most never returned when they went rogue. For once, it appeared that she was going to need Dan's special skill of forcing a wolf to the surface when the human form refused to let his wolf free. Anita was the first female he'd ever encountered who suffered from this syndrome. And, Anita was desperately close to losing it. He stroked her cheek, and had to ask.

"Anita, how long since you let your wolf run?"

Dan knew the answer, but he was willing to bet Anita didn't realize it.

Whatever she had expected, it wasn't that. It just felt so good to finally have someone hold her for a change.

"What?"

"You heard me. How long?"

"Well, it was just last, uh, I mean it was a few, um...." Just when HAD she let her wolf out to run in the woods?

"I, uh, I don't remember, Dan," she admitted to him.

"I thought so. I know when it was."

Her eyes shot up to his. He knew, and she didn't?

"I remember. It's been twenty-seven years, Anita. The last time your wolf ran free was twenty-seven years ago. You and the council had gone to Cordone's to stay after burying Tara."

She blinked at him! Twenty-seven years? Surely not. But, her eyes showed her trying to remember, and she found Dan was right! It had been that long ago!

"Ah, you do remember. That's a good sign, but not good enough." He stood up, and held out his hand to her.

"Come," was all he said.

Anita was too tired to resist, and taking Dan's hand, he led her out of her office quickly, and down to the SUV. Without halting, he drove them directly to the airport, and dragged her onto the jet. She started resisting.

"I can't leave, Dan! I HAVE to continue my research! For everyone's sake! Get your DAMN HANDS OFF OF ME!"

Without missing a beat, he picked Anita up by force, and carried her onto the jet. Just after take-off, Dan flipped his phone out calling Cordone. Kaitlan answered.

"Kaitlan, I must talk to Cordone immediately." Kaitlan handed the phone to Cordone mouthing "Dan" when she heard Dan sounding jittery. She had heard the strangest, guttural sound she had ever heard in her life. It was scary!

"Cordone, here, Dan. What's wrong?"

He listened, growing more worried by the minute.

"HOW long did you say it's been, Dan?" Cordone's surprise was apparent. "Did you really just say it's been twenty-seven years since Anita let her wolf run? Holy cow!!! No wonder she's not holding it together."

"What's happening?"Kaitlan was pulling on his sleeve.

Dan answered him. "No. Cordone, she's extremely close to going rogue very soon if I don't do something about it, now. She's the first woman I've ever seen suffering this syndrome. We both have seen men, but never in a woman. I have no idea how this will turn out."

"Dan, I don't know of anyone as good as you are for helping wolves about to go rogue. I know the two of you have been friends since you were kids, so I know you want to make sure she is safe. You get that woman up to my place right now, Dan, and make sure her wolf runs her to exhaustion. Hear me? Use everything if you have to, but get her sanity back!"

"We're already on the plane, Cordone, and we'll be landing in ten minutes. I couldn't call you until we were on the way. I couldn't risk her going rogue around people. She would kill them! She threw her vampire award at my head! Slammed her chair into the wall several times, and even broke one of her laptops! She started shaking hard, crying, screaming, and hitting me. Pretty damn hard, too! This is, by far, the worst case I have ever encountered."

He looked over at Anita who was bouncing up and down in agitation. He had to tie her to her chair to keep from smashing up the plane.

"I just hope I'm not too late, Cordone!"

Cordone said two words, "Do it." Cordone hung up, and stared at Kaitlan who had heard it all.

Dan hung up his phone, and went to sit by Anita putting his arm around her hoping to calm her down. She tried desperately to shake him off. She lost.

Four hours later, they drove up to Cordone's house. Dan had floored it as soon as he reached Cordone's land, driving at least 100 miles per hour up the steep slopes. Anita was getting very close to rogue by now. He had her tied up in the backseat. If she went rogue, she could snap those bonds in a split second.

Dan dragged her, fighting, into the main room, opened the glass door, then turned her around to face him. Her hazel eyes were wild and darting everywhere. She was losing all reasoning. But, how could he shake her out of it temporarily? With guys, it was fighting with them, but he couldn't fight with Anita. Not in this state. She just might kill him. He thought about what might scare a woman the most. Ah! He had it! He extended his claws, and in just a few swipes, ripped her clothes from her body. ALL of her clothes. Anita stopped immediately!!

"What the hell do you think you're doing?" She yelled trying to cover herself, and not doing a good job. She really was as voluptuous as he had thought in surprise, not understanding why he would ever think that in the first place. But, hey! A beautiful naked woman is still a beautiful naked woman, and Anita was that in spades! Dan had never seen her in jeans, and he wondered if she had a tight pair of jeans to cover her luscious ass. He shook his head at the thought, and refocused. Anita was in trouble. Serious trouble, and she didn't know it. But, he had to calm her down long enough to force her wolf out.

"Anita, you are about to go rogue."

Anita's eyes bugged out. Rogue? Her? Was he serious? She was NOT about to go rogue, and her claws extended as she tried to attack him! He grabbed both her hands, and held them in only one of his. He had to think of another way to shock her system.

"You will phase, Anita. I am your Third, and you will do what I say. Now," he said as he ripped his own clothes off down to nothing.

He wasn't embarrassed at all with nudity, and the sudden surprise on Anita's face told him that his choice to strip for her was the right one. She regained some sanity.

"What the HELL are you doing, Dan!   Put your damn clothes back on!" She screamed at him.

She desperately wanted to avert her eyes from his hard body, but she couldn't. He stood there in all his glory. And everything was "hanging out"! This six-foot three, of solid muscle was gorgeous. His entire body belied the strength he held, while his hard body was perfectly formed with tanned skin. She continued to look, and he didn't flinch, once! He had nothing to be embarrassed about, and he definitely wasn't turned on by her. That was very clear. His hair was a rich, dark chocolate brown cut in a classic design. His abs very well defined, and his hips, lean. His body not an inch of fat, and built for protection. His left shoulder and top of his chest sported a black tattoo in an intricate, Norse design which also extended to his upper left arm.

She had seen him naked before - yeah, when

they were fifteen, and they loved skinny dipping together, much to their parents' displeasure. But, he was a gangly teenager then. Now, his body exuded pure strength. His very presence was designed for fighting. No wonder Cordone chose him as his bodyguard! Then, the part she had been trying to ignore she just couldn't. His testicles were twice the normal size of a were, and his penis was bigger even relaxed! That did surprise her. OMG! She would never get that out of her mind! Ever. How the hell would she EVER get the vision out of her head of her best friend in the world as a god standing naked in front of her? But, there, her musing stopped. She started to shake again, and began to lose focus.

He was Hunkalicious (using Sarah's term for her mate, Sam)! Not that she had designs on Sam, of course, but quite frankly, Dan had it over Sam in spades! If he ever mated, she was going to be one hell of a lucky woman!

Dan growled loudly as he grabbed her shoulders.

"You WILL do what I say Anita Moore!! I am Third in the O'Hara Clan, and you WILL obey me, now! Do you understand? You WILL PHASE NOW!"

She gulped and nodded. She had never seen calm and cool Dan pull rank on anyone. Her Third had spoken.

What if she had forgotten how to phase? She watched Dan open the glass door for her.

"I will follow you till you run out, Anita. I promise. You will not be alone. We've been best friends forever. I will never let anything happen to you."

And, Dan phased.

Anita's mouth dropped. It had been a long time since she had seen him in his wolf form, and he was beautiful! His fur was chocolate brown just like his hair, and matched his chocolate brown eyes. He was a large wolf. He swished his tail at her in warning.

She closed her eyes trying to remember how to phase. Good thing her wolf remembered, and she let her take over. Anita phased into a coal black wolf with those same hazel eyes dotted with navy. Dan looked at her in amazement. He had forgotten her beauty in wolf form.

She swished her tail, stomped her paws, then shot out the door with Dan right behind her.

Anita ran for so long, she lost count of the hours that flew by. It felt GOOD! She knew Dan was behind her giving her free reign, but she was still upset and pent up. She needed more than a run. She needed a fight! Now. With anyone. Dan would do.

She came to a dead stop whirling on Dan, growling. As if Dan knew what she was feeling, one side of his mouth drew up in a snarl. Anita was in worse shape than he had thought. She needed to fight. Good thing most werewolves could heal fast on their own. They used to fight as pups, but this would be entirely different.

"OK. You need a fight, let's do it!" He thought.

Actually, he needed one himself. He wasn't used to fighting a woman, and he was really, really angry with her, but he had no idea why. It had been a while for him, and he was absolutely willing.

She looked at him, turning her lip up, and started circling. Dan copied her movements watching; waiting.

They circled each other for several minutes, then Dan charged Anita. He knew she wouldn't initiate the attack. She was never good at that when they were in school. But, today, he was going to teach her how to really fight.

He jumped at her, and she jumped back sitting on her haunches. He growled at her, and nipped her left ear. That made Anita furious, and she met him with her paws slamming into his side. Dan jumped back up, and ran into her side with his head knocking Anita off balance. She fell on her side. She pushed back up, and charged Dan, yet again, barreling into his shoulder. It did nothing to Dan, but she bounced off of him onto her butt.

They fought. Dan was careful not to hurt her too badly. Dan taught her many things she didn't know, and she copied a lot of his moves as she learned.

Dan grinned. She was a great student! This just might work. At least he hoped so. He didn't want to lose her. He wouldn't lose her!

Fighting for another hour, or longer, their nipping had created small amounts of blood covering both of them.

Finally, Anita started to wear down, and she finally dropped in exhaustion. Dan ceased, too, but he stood tall over her. He had been counting on her losing her stamina. He wasn't even breathing hard.

That had felt so good! It was so good to FEEL something, again. She glanced up at Dan who looked at her with a wolfy grin. She stood up, stuck her tongue out at him, and turned to prance to a group of trees that looked a good spot to sleep. He grinned, and followed. The danger was over, thank the Creator!

Lightning and thunder suddenly raced across the sky, and Dan leaped to follow her to the trees. They would afford them some cover. Never good to hide under them in lightening, but they had no other choice.

Then, just behind the trees, Anita noticed a small outcropping, and headed for it.

Dan followed her prancing, sexy, swinging, little butt to the outcrop just as the torrent of rain broke loose. Both wolves stood in the heavy rain, letting it rinse off the blood on their fur, then took refuge under a rock to dry out. The lightning and thunder continued throughout the night, and was very loud.

Here, though, it was very comfortable and dry, and they both lay down to sleep. Anita passed out quickly, but Dan heard her moaning in her sleep. He laid down touching her back. He knew it was a bad idea, because they would be naked when they awoke, but she needed help. She needed him. He was the only one there, he reasoned with himself.

So, he parked his furry body next to her furry back, and Anita curled her back into him. He was suddenly very happy, and put his paw on her back stroking it. She stopped making the moans, and started to purr. He laid there listening to that purr, the thunder, and the rain falling asleep to the sounds.

~ 29 ~

Waking Naked Next to Your Best Friend, Who   is a Man, is Weird, Right?

Anita didn't hear anything. It was quiet except for the heavy rain still falling outside. She didn't want to wake up.   She was so comfortable. Yep. The rain sounded like a pouring waterfall as it ran off the ledge covering them. She stretched having had the best sleep and rest she could remember in almost three decades. As she stretched, her bottom hit something really hard. She froze, and looked down. She was naked, and remembered that Dan had torn her clothing off.   Red crept up to her heated face, as she realized his hand was cupping one of her breasts. Or, at least trying to cup her large size. She remembered he had looked at her up and down - at everything, before he stripped in front of her as well. She remembered seeing his cock hanging down, and had whipped her head away in embarrassment. No male had ever seen her naked let alone had ever been allowed to touch her. She had seen her fair share of naked bodies, of course, being a Doctor, but not like this!

She shut her eyes remembering it had been only a matter of minutes before she would have gone rogue giving her chills. She knew why Dan had shocked her into changing into her wolf. Her best friend had saved her sanity and her life. She knew he was the one to deal with rogues, but she had never seen it first hand. He was amazing! Definitely not that young, scrawny boy she used to go skinny dipping with all the time. They had never worried about it, because they were not mates. It was a bit unusual, so they made sure that very few knew they did it. Their parents weren't too happy about it, but that never stopped them. They would sneak out in the middle of the night, and went swimming under the moon. Their bodies were rather scrawny, but her breasts had already developed. They just never thought of naked as naked, so it never bothered them.

Anita wondered what time it was, and realized it was maybe noon the next day, and her need came to the forefront. She had been asleep for at least twelve hours, if not more. She was never embarrassed by it in her capacity as a Doctor, but she felt totally embarrassed as she realized what the hardness against her back was.

His hand was still holding her breast when she heard a chuckle behind her making his cock move against her butt. OH! He would never let her live this down!

Dan cleared his throat as he laughed out loud knowing she felt him against her smooth bottom.

"Uh, Anita. I think I really need to run to the left for a minute." He laughed even harder at her embarrassment.

Anita's face reddened deeper, but she nodded.

He stood up, and she heard him stretch.

"Me, too. Um, I'll go right." She said. "Uh…you go first?"

She heard him leave the outcropping, then jumped up and ran to the right looking for something. The rain was still pouring. She spotted a bush about thirty feet from the outcropping, and ducked under it.

By the time she got back, she was dripping wet, but she felt great. Dan wasn't yet back, so she scooted under the outcropping, sitting, and pulling her arms around her legs trying to hide as much as possible. She knew her wolf was sleeping within her. What would she say to Dan when he returned? What must he think about her after what had happened? He must think she was really stupid not letting her wolf out for twenty-seven years, and she wouldn't really blame him if he did. It had been a stupid thing to do!

A noise came from the left, and she kept her head turned away from him as he sat down beside her.

He turned to her, and grinned.

"OK, Anita. You can look, now! Geez! It's not like we haven't seen each other naked!" He joked.

She turned her head, and glared at him. He, too, had drawn up his legs holding them to hide "things". Not for him, but for her. He had no qualms about his body, and he didn't mind her seeing it in anyway. But, she had not seen him in the buff since they were fifteen, so he deferred to her shyness. Never thought he'd see her embarrassed to see him!

"Feeling better?"

At her nod, he told her, "I thought the fight

might be the best way to satisfy your wolf, and your mind after the run. Your wolf won't emerge again for a few more hours."

She turned to look at him, still lightly blushing. He thought she'd never been so beautiful.

"Yeah. I know. Dan, thank you for saving my life. I think I would have totally lost it if you hadn't brought me here."

He nodded. "With guys, I could have just taken them to the gym for several hours of fighting, but not you. I'm really glad I found you in time. I know how you're feeling. I'm sorry I stripped your clothes from you, but you needed a wake-up call fast, and I couldn't think of anything else. I've only dealt with men about to go rogue. You're the first woman."

She blushed again. "Well, it worked!"

"Actually it didn't. You were still in shock. So, I stripped for you. That's what really worked!"

He shot her a huge, devilish grin.

Oh, Anita! That wolfy grin will definitely be your undoing!

"Was something bothering you, too? I mean it seemed like you were upset about something."

He nodded. He'd never told her, but he decided he would, now. In fact, he felt like he needed to tell her. If he couldn't tell her, who else could he tell. He should have told her years earlier.

"My mate died, Anita." He stated simply.

Of all the things she had ever thought about that was definitely not it!

"You had a mate? I-I didn't know, Dan. I'm so

very sorry."

He turned to look at her with pained eyes.

"Yes. Her name was Miria, and an Elf. We tried to keep it secret, because it just wasn't done in those days - to mix the races. But, we were betrayed to her Father, Ali'on. I never found out who, and Ali'on still will never tell. He was very angry, and he attacked me. It was a very, very long fight. Bloody."

He leaned his head back against the rock, closing his eyes, and relaxed.

Ali'on? Dan was mate to Ali'on's daughter? Anita was stunned. Knowing Ali'on for as long as they did, she was not at all surprised that he would have gone after Dan!

"Our fighting upset Miria, and she took off running. We didn't notice until we heard a scream coming from the edge of the waterfall that was close by."

He looked at Anita whose eyes had sadness and compassion in them. He reached out, and took one of her hands as he finished. His face was pained, and she saw he was hurting. Anita saw tears gather in his eyes, and one slip down his face. She squeezed his hand.

"We dashed to the waterfall even though we were both maimed, and bloody. Miria was holding on to a monster of a rotten tree root that was sticking out of the cliff where she had fallen. She continued to scream for us to help her. Her Father, and I tried to grab her, but it was impossible from our vantage point. She was down too far. Ali'on helped me to climb down to reach her. Just as I reached her, she stretched her arm and hand up to me trying to grab mine, and…" Dan's voice almost broke. "…and the root snapped. We watched while she dropped onto the rocks below, breaking her back. The limb fell on her head, smashing it to a pulp."

Anita's hand flew to her mouth. Oh, God!   How horrible!

"We buried her with the other elves who had died in honor. From that time forward, her Father and I have been bound together as friends. We were both equally guilty."

"But, if she was your mate, how are you still alive?"

He looked at her sadly.

"We never completed the mating bond, Anita."

That was even worse! To find your mate, and lose her before mating with her was horrendous! She reached out her hand, and tilted his face up to look at her.

"I'm so very sorry, Dan."

She couldn't say anything else. Tears were falling from her eyes in a steady stream. Her heart broke in two for him. She wanted to comfort him in some way, and without thinking reached out to pull his head to her breast as if he were a child. Together they just sat there in complete silence for a very long time.

Finally, Dan raised his head. Anita's breast was covered with his tears. When she noticed, she blushed, again, and covered herself. Then, his eyes met hers. Time just - stopped. Dan was wondering what was happening when he heard Anita gasp in surprise. Was she seeing things? Dan's eyes had begun to glow.

"No! It can't be! It can't happen. It's not possible!!" Dan said as he saw Anita's eyes begin to glow.

He breathed hard as he realized what was happening. Anita? Anita had become his mate? That wasn't possible! It couldn't be! But, the truth couldn't be denied. Glowing eyes only happened when two were mates.

Like Dan, Anita's hazel eyes had also begun to glow, the navy flecks shining brighter than the hazel, and her mouth dropped. They could not take their eyes off of each other.

"It's not possible!" Agreed Anita. "No way!"

"I can't believe it! It can't be!" Dan exclaimed. Then, narrowing his eyes at her, "I claim you as my mate, Anita."

He couldn't even believe he'd even said the words, and Anita couldn't believe she even actually heard them!

Without shame, Dan unfolded his body to her, while delighting in seeing her flush of pink. He loved her blushing in shyness! He always had. It was beautiful. His mate! They had only been allowed one, right? How did this happen? They could figure it out later, though. There was something they had to do, and immediately. They must Blood Bond as soon as possible.

He wanted her to see him - all of him right now - so she could see what she was getting as a mate. It was natural and inevitable. She may as well get used to it, because she would be seeing it all the time from now on. He saw her looking at him - just as he wanted. But he wanted to see her body again, because it would appear different in his eyes as her mate.

Anita couldn't take her eyes away from his beauty! She vaguely remembered it when she was almost going rogue, but didn't care at that point. They had taken baths together as children, and skinny dipped all the time in a lake beyond the trees well away from their homes until she was fifteen. Neither had thought a thing about it! Somewhere, in the back of her mind, she wondered what Cordone would think about this. Sleeping next to his Third in wolf form, waking up naked against him, and now ready to let Dan see her body as she was about to enter into a mating bond with him. Without telling her Alpha. Or, Kaitlan. But, this was a private moment between them only, and did not require anyone's permission. Especially, Cordone's! No one else was allowed into the mating bed. Hell, she was more than old enough! That was enough thinking. It was time to act.

Her lifelong, best friend was now her mate. Her eyes traveled over his body - all the way down. He smiled at her with a raised eyebrow. His chest was toned, and strong with tightened abs, and she had an urgent desire to caress him with her fingers. She kept her eyes moving downward. When she reached what she had been seeking, it was impossible to tear her eyes away from his manhood increasing very quickly. How many times had she seen him naked? This Dan was no boy. He was all male, and his huge erection left her in no doubt about his desire for her. OMG! It was gorgeous! And, magnificent! She didn't have enough superlatives. She dipped her head trying to process what she had seen. Dan took her chin, raising her eyes to him. He dipped down, and kissed her lips. It began lightly, but he increased the pressure until they were both breathless with desire.

"Do not hide your body from me, Anita. You are my mate. There's no reason to be shy. It's not as if I haven't seen it before, you know?" He teased.

To make sure she knew that he wasn't laughing about it, he added, "I love you, and not as a boy of fifteen who loves a friend. That is over. You are the most beautiful woman I have ever seen, and you are my mate. I want to see you. I am totally, and unconditionally, yours."

His words brought her to tears. Her mate! She had thought to never find him! Without Anita resisting, he slowly took her hands that were crossed in front of her, and moved them away from her beautiful breasts. She was incredibly gorgeous! Her breasts were full with desire, and nipples hard.

Anita had always wanted to give them to her mate, only. The only man she would ever allow to see and touch them. And now, it was happening, and with her best friend growing up! She felt the swelling of desire begin to grow in her lower body, her nipples hardening under his gaze.

He placed her hands at her sides, looked her in the eyes, and reached out to cup her breast. She wanted him to touch her so badly, her breath came in spurts. Her heart had sped up, and she could hear his heart pounding in his chest hard. For her.

"You are so beautiful. You are an angel to me," he said simply.

He literally thought he had died, and gone to heaven looking at her.

Anita felt moisture immediately pool at her core. His thumb began a lazy circle around her nipple as she gasped in pleasure. No man had ever touched her, and it was an amazing feeling!

Shyly, she slid her legs down so he could see her full nakedness sitting beside his. She watched his eyes travel from her eyes to her breasts with her nipple hardening under his touch. He gazed at her beauty before his eyes lowered to her tiny waist, those gorgeous, luscious, black curls hiding her secrets from him, and finally to her rounded hips - just right to carry a baby - his baby.

He stood up, and helped her stand up as well. His erection was hard against his body. Anita was ecstatic that it was for her, and her alone.

The rain had let up to a nice gentle soaking rain.

"Come. Walk in the rain with me." He said.

The two mates walked out into the rain, naked, his arm around her shoulders. Dan stopped Anita several times during the long walk back, pulling her to him with kisses that burned in Anita's soul. She would never forget the moment when their eyes started to glow, and she became his mate. Reaching the perimeter of the yard, Dan swept her off her feet, and streaked inside.

Once inside, he set her down.

"I want this to be something we both remember for the rest of our lives. Will you give me an hour to prepare for our mating, Anita?"

Anita loved him, and she thought it was wonderful that he wanted it to be special. Then, she looked down. She was covered in mud. The rain had become light, and they had traipsed through mud as well.

"I will be ready, Dan. I guess it won't hurt if I take a shower first." She looked at his mud caked body. "You, too."

Laughing he nodded.

"Yep. Guess it won't hurt."

Anita wrapped her arms around his neck, and kissed him. His arms came around her pulling her to him.

"One hour," he told her.

Anita turned, and without glancing back, hurried into her room. She jumped into the shower, and bathed herself slowly. She wanted to be perfect for Dan, and their mating.

~ 30 ~

"We are Taught Never to Ask The Creator, "Why"."

We are taught never to ask The Creator, "why". Anita didn't ask, but she did a lot of wondering why two people who were such great friends who had been together for so long would suddenly find themselves mated. Everything she was trying to find the answer to didn't make sense. It was as if their lives were only partial lives. Sort of like an old record, there seemed to be skips in life. Perhaps Sarah was right when she told everyone she believed Kaitlan's White Wolf changed all. Is that what was happening? She still had no answer.

Well, that was beside the point now. Her body began to crave her mate. She dried off, and put on a bright blue silk robe she had bought it years ago, and used it only when she was out of town. Anita had accidentally left it there when they came for Canaan's funeral. It was very short - for her, but it brought out her hazel eyes changing them to a blue, and it was figure hugging. Her breasts were front and center in it, especially her hard nipples pushing through the thin material. If Sarah had it on, it would reach mid-thigh! That thought had Anita almost laughing.

Anita looked at the clock.

Opening the door, Anita walked out into the living area finding Dan standing in chocolate brown, silk boxers which did nothing to hide his erection at all. Anita felt more wetness pool. In fact, her body hadn't been without the wetness since they realized they were mates! Her breath came quickly, and she knew her nipples were hardening even more.

Dan held out his hand without a word, and she took it. He led them into the elevator which puzzled her, because his room was on the main floor.

"Where are we going?" Anita asked him.

"Wait and see, beautiful."

It was a short trip, of course, and the elevator rose above the fifth floor surprising her. She turned with a question in her eyes, and Dan just kissed her nose.

When the elevator came to a halt, the doors opened into a short hallway which led to another door.

Dan opened it, and Anita stepped out onto a massive deck. She stared in surprise. Even though the rain was still falling gently, the roof over the deck resembled a gigantic thatched roof found in the tropics. It was, quite literally, an outside room. Attached to the ceiling were no less than six fans, and the design allowed wind to flow through, but not the rain. A four-foot railing wrapped around the entire structure covered by white rope lights that softly lit up the inside. Large sofas surrounded the perimeter in natural colored fabrics of brown and sand. Covering them were brightly colored pillows in yellow, blue, and green. In the center was a large fur rug, or throw, piled high with lots of large, fluffy pillows. She blushed when she realized that this was what Dan had been doing for their mating.

"Let me show you something." Dan said, leading her to the railing.

Anita stood looking at the scenery around her. Her mouth dropped as she leaned over, and saw that it was suspended in mid-air! She turned to Dan with the "How?" look.

"Did Cordone never tell you that I designed these thatch structures for a living once?"

She just shook her head.

"I love the tropics. So, years ago, I built this on top of Cordone's house with his permission. This is where I come when I need solace and quiet. Cordone has never been here. He respects my privacy as much as I do his."

She was amazed that her mate could do this, and as his best friend, she never knew it!

"Anita? I need you." He said turning her around to face him.

"As I need you, Dan. Now."

Stepping onto the fur rug, she turned, and slid her robe off dropping it to the floor.

Dan sucked in his breath at her naked body. She was beautiful! Her body full and ripe with swollen breasts. He wondered if she was wet for him. He watched her lie down on the fur propping herself against the pillows. He slid his boxers off quickly.

Anita gasped at his size. She licked her lips in

anticipation of it being inside of her soon. He was glorious!   Really? Couldn't she find other descriptions for him?

"I won't make the mistake, again, of not Blood Bonding with my mate, and I will not wait."

Dan turned his back to her a moment so he could get two glasses of wine for them, and Anita froze. His back was a full tattoo! He turned back, and sat down next to her handing her a glass.

"Dan? Your tattoo? What is it?"

With a grin, he turned his back to her so she could see it well. Her fingers traced the unusual design, and he shuddered under her touch.

He turned back to her. "I am a guardian, Anita. I am a protector of the Clan. That is my designation, we just don't call it that. It is a Norse protection rune."

"When did you get it?"

"A very, very long time ago, Anita. When I was about thirty. I was secretly charged with the protection of Cordone, as I am now, openly, charged with the protection of Cordone and his family. And, now, my love, you."

"Well, it's very, very sexy, Dan!" She told him with her eyes glancing up through her eyelashes.

He propped himself next to her on his side, and she turned to him. They both drank the wine, and Dan took their glasses, and placed them to the side.

This was going to be the most beautiful thing to ever happen to her, and Anita reached over bringing his hand to hold her breast covering his hand with hers. She never knew what Kaitlan and Sarah had meant until now. It was overwhelming to her. How this happened, she didn't know, but really, did she care?

Dan stroked her breast, teasing her nipple with his fingertips. They both hardened as his mouth came down to claim one while his other hand stroked her other breast. He breathed in her scent.

"HAIL THE GODS!" He thought. He HAD been right! The man who mated her would be THE luckiest bastard in the world! And he WAS that bastard! He thanked the Creator for giving him a second chance at love.

She sighed with pleasure as he suckled her. The bonding was beginning. Her body began to shake when one of Dan's hands slid down to her curls. His fingers reached underneath her to find her swollen, hardened nub, and, further down, her wet folds, she jerked in pleasure as he entered her body with two of his fingers causing her to cry out loud.

Dan continued to caress her clit gently, then raised his head from her breast.

"Anita Moore. My best friend forever. My skinny dipping buddy! I, now, claim you as my mate. Even though neither of us knows how this happened except by The Creator's will, you are mine. My mate. My life. My love. Will you honor me, and accept me as your mate?" He asked, without removing his fingers from her channel. He held his breath, almost fearing this was all a dream.

There was a nice wind blowing through, and

over their heated bodies, which seemed to grow stronger as their desire for each other increased. Anita sighed in contentment cupping his hardness, reveling in the feel of his fingers inside of her.

"Dan Wheeler, my best friend always, even when we got in trouble for our escapades of old, I accept you as my mate forever. You, too, are my life, my love, and my fighter who brought me back from oblivion. I take you as my mate, now."

Dan sighed as he removed his fingers from her body to lay back. Without hesitation, Anita laid her breasts on his chest as she took her kiss of mating. Dan turned his neck to her for the Blood Bond. Anita kissed his pulse, and her fangs bit into his neck easily allowing her to drink from him. She raised her head, and Dan turned his head for her final kiss of mating.

"Dan Wheeler, I claim you as my mate forever. For whatever reason, The Creator has given us both an amazing gift. Even though we are best friends, we are now mates and lovers as well. Will you accept me as your mate?"

Dan leaned on his elbow facing her, and placed his head on her breast hearing her heart beat fast and furious for him.

"Anita Wheeler, I accept you as my mate, here, now, in your arms with my head at your breast where I wish to be, always."

Anita laid back, and Dan laid across her taking his kiss of mating. She turned her neck to him letting him kiss her pulse, and then she felt the ecstasy of his fangs as he bit her drinking her blood. He raised his head, and took his final kiss of mating.

Dan pulled her tightly against him, and moved her to lie on top of him. Her breasts, heavy with needing to be held and stroked, were crushed against his chest. He moaned as he felt his cock become harder than it had ever been. His balls were heavy with his seed, growing larger with every passing minute, and filling with even more liquid. He had no idea he could get this big, and this full. The pain he was in from them was almost excruciating! He needed to spill himself inside of Anita now! He had an urgent need to impregnate his mate.

A sudden, violent spasm erupted from Anita's womb, and she felt a very heavy, silky cream flow to her entrance, and down her legs. She desired him more than anything she had ever wanted. She straddled him as she sat up, and looked at his body. It unhinged her when she saw his hardness ready for her!

She lifted her hips, and taking her hand, she guided him to her wetness, and took his shaft deep within her in one movement. He grinned up at her as his hands grabbed her ass holding it as he began to move inside of her.

"You, mate, are wanton to the core!" He laughed, as his thrusts became harder and harder.

He was really enjoying watching her breasts bounce in front of his face with each movement. He grabbed one in his mouth, and sucked hard. Anita groaned with pleasure when she felt his mouth on her.

"Would you want me any different?" Anita

asked as she met his hips thrust against thrust.

"No. But, baby, my balls are about to bust! I need to spill my seed inside of you!"

Their movements were causing them to pant heavily. Her need was so great for his seed, she couldn't believe the urgency! Even with Kaitlan and Sarah telling her of the urgency, and need, it was still unbelievable how badly she wanted him to give her their child.

Dan flipped her onto her back so fast, she was temporarily surprised. She lifted her legs wrapping them around his waist to take him inside of her deeper and deeper.

"Anita!" He cried out as he felt her throbbing around him.

She was milking him hard, and their release exploded! He released the contents of his balls deep within Anita's womb. He continued to thrust into her until her channel had stopped squeezing his cock, and the hot semen, filled with his seed, had been completely emptied into his mate.

Anita felt his burning, hot semen flood into her body, coating, and filling her womb. She wondered if she would become pregnant with their child. She closed her eyes, and hoped so. They collapsed against each other panting hard.

~ 31 ~

Mate, Marry, or Bond with Your Best Friend!

The first twenty-four hours of mating is the most active of new mates' lives. The desire for sex is so strong, they need to be locked together almost constantly. Even food and drink take a back seat. They are unable to be around others, because this desire is extremely powerful, and they would not be inhibited by anyone around them. Quite literally? They wouldn't care who saw them! This is the reason for the privacy. No one is allowed to disturb them. Well, that doesn't always happen, such as in Sam and Sarah's case, but that was an entirely different thing.

Anita and Dan had just finished their "sex-a-robics", as Sarah always called it. Anita had lost count how many times, and let's face it, they weren't counting, anyway.

She sat up. The rain had stopped, and the stars had appeared bright and clear with a full moon outshining them. The entire landscape was bathed in daylight. It was magical.

"I need to find out if it's really true. Will you come outside with me?"

"OK. Why? Never mind. I'll follow you anywhere!" He grinned, and swatted his mate's adorable, bare ass.

The moonlight was bright enough that even wolves didn't need their eyes. Anyone could see everything, and that's what Anita wanted. Their human forms mated anywhere. Wolves only outside.

"Did you know that both Kaitlan and Sarah were able to mate in their wolf forms?"

Dan's eyes darted to hers. No. He didn't know that. He shook his head. What was she talking about?

"Shocked are you, huh? Me, too. But, I checked out both girls after their matings, and they had been able to mate as wolves. Kaitlan is pregnant with two different babies, Dan. One conceived in their human form, and one in their wolf form.

Dan's eyebrows flew up. He knew Kaitlan was pregnant before she announced it, but what's this about?

Anita grinned. "Kaitlan is The White Wolf, Dan!"

"What did you just say?" Dan's voice rose.

"You heard me. Kaitlan is The White Wolf of our prophecy!"

Dan quickly ran over the prophecy in his mind from his school days. When The White Wolf appears, the entire werewolf nation would be changed instantly. It would bring in things like being able to mate in wolf form, children would be plentiful, and several other things he couldn't remember, but those two things stood out front and center for most male weres - obviously. Realization hit him with her words, and turned to Anita finding her standing in front of him smiling - in her wolf form.

"Well, mate?   Would you like to find out if we can mate in wolf form? I mean, just for research, of course!"

Dan phased in an instant, and was already pushing inside her.

"Research be damned!"

And, they proceeded to find out that, indeed, like Cordone and Kaitlan, Sarah and Sam, they could mate in wolf form.

"You know," he thought at her as he moved, *"I could really get to love this!"*

Anita moaned in ecstasy of the wolves mating.

"Can I ask you something?" Anita thought breathlessly, feeling his thrusts pounding into her.

"Anything you want, Tits!"

Anita started at what he just called her!

"Did you just call me - Tits?" She pretended to be affronted.

"You bet I did, Tits! Don't worry. Only in our minds, or in total privacy, will I ever call you that!" He laughed.

"Well, as long as we are trading nicknames. I love it when you talk dirty! Let's see. What can I call you?" She tried hard to think of a good one. *"Ah! I have it...cock-adoodle!   Of course, it is with the emphasis on the co...."*

Dan slammed into her effectively shutting her off her words, and howled with his release. Anita totally forgot what she was going to say, and what she had planned to ask him. That ended their first, joint, research project! There was definitely going to be a lot more research, Dan promised!

They had moved into his bedroom, earlier, and Anita's head was laying on Dan's chest while one hand stroked her breast absently. She never wanted him to stop.

"OK, Tits. I'm going to fess up."

"Oh? And, what could that be?"

"When we used to skinny dip, I admit I did look at your body."

Her eyebrows went up in mock disgust.

"Really?"

"Yep."

"OK. I admit I did find my eyes lingering on your cock more than I should have."

Dan laughed out loud.

"One other admission?" He said.

"And, that would be.....?"

"When I "strip-shocked" you … I kind of like that description, by the way … I saw your luscious breasts as a man, and I thought the man who mated you would be the luckiest bastard on Earth to be able to touch, suck, and feel them up forever! And, honestly?   I was a bit jealous of that man."

Her eyes blinked. "Seriously?"

He caressed both of them. "Uh-huh." Then, he lowered his head to suck.

"THANK GOD, I am that lucky bastard!"

And, he suckled them while Anita laughed, and

held them for him to reach them easier.

A bit later, sweaty, panting, and exhausted, Dan told her to go make the call.

"I know you're dying to call Kaitlan, Lynne, and Sarah to tell them you have joined their ranks as a thoroughly satisfied, and mated, wolf!"

"What makes you think I'm satisfied, Cock-adoodle?" She laughed, jumping out of bed just as he made a grab for her.

Anita heard him laughing, but he had laid back with his arms folded underneath his head.

"I turned our phones off while we were mating. I'm going to call Cordone. What an amazing woman you are, Tits!"

"Back at you, Cock-adoodle!" She echoed.

Anita ran into the front room to dig her phone out of her purse, and turned it on.

What would have happened to them if she had gone rogue? She shook with horror at the thought. She swallowed the bile down that had crept up her throat as she even thought about it. Once turned, a wolf would become their namesakes of legend. They would kill indiscriminately, and the preference was human. They would go on a rampage that would devastate the human world, revealing that their presence was not myth. There hadn't been a rogue in over three hundred years, and that was because of her mate. He had discovered a way of keeping a rogue from turning. He had to put down several rogues himself in the past. Not all rogues could be helped. But, no woman had gone rogue in their history. She shivered just thinking about what would have happened if he hadn't "strip-shocked" her. Yep! She liked that term, too. Thank The Creator for Dan! She loved that man!

"I love you too, Anita. More than you will ever know. I'll always have your back. You are my life," Dan thought to her.

She could feel him shudder at the thought he might have lost her to rogue as well.

"I will be here to make sure it will never happen again, my love. And, will you please hurry up! I need you again!"

Anita was startled to find that she had an orgasm at those words. They weren't graphic, or anything else. Those tender words of love did it, and were more sexy than anything else he could have said.

"I love you, too, Dan. Thank you for giving me a life instead of having to end it. I love you more than my own life," she replied as tears ran down her cheeks.

"Anita?"

"Hmmm?"

"You gave me an orgasm, too, and right in the middle of talking to Cordone! He says you had better call Kaitlan and Sarah fast before he tells them about us! Oh, and he's thrilled!"

Anita smiled, and dialed the phone. The secret would be out soon, and she couldn't wait to hear them squeal when she told them.

Loud shouts of happiness shot out of the phone as soon as Anita told them that she and Dan had mated.

"Welcome to the club! WOOHOOOOO!!!" Yelled Sarah, then she started to gag.

"Well there's no need to get so choked up about it!"

She heard more gagging.

"Sarah? Are you OK?" Anita asked in alarm.

"It's OK," said Kaitlan. "She says she ate something last night, and has been sick ever since."

Anita pursed her lips, counting. "Kaitlan? Go ask her if she is late."

"Seriously? Hold on!"

Anita heard her sprint for the bathroom. Kaitlan put her phone on speaker for Anita.

As soon as the retching stopped, Anita asked, "How do you feel right now, Sarah?"

"Well, strange, really. I'm starving! I don't get it? I mean, I ate last night, and this morning, a lot, threw it up, and ran back to eat more only to throw it up again!"

Kaitlan let Anita ask the question.

"Sarah, are you late?"

Sarah, the mouth, was silent. Kaitlan spoke.

"Anita, you finally got her to shut up!" Kaitlan was laughing hard.

"Uh, let me think…. I don't know. Sam and I have been having way too much fun for me to have noticed!"

That sent Anita and Kaitlan into wails of laughter with tears running down their faces.

"Sarah, you came to me for that first checkup

three weeks ago. Have you had your period since then?"

Kaitlan laughed into the phone.

"You should see her face, Anita! It's a RIOT! She's in complete shock! I'm taking that it means she is late, by what?   About two weeks?"

Anita laughed with Kaitlan.

"Sarah, go with Kaitlan to my office, and get one of the pregnancy test kits. I don't think it's needed, really. I can almost guarantee you it will show positive. But, let's make sure, OK?"

"Anita," said Kaitlan. "We're on our way right, now.   And, by the way. I'm already HUGE!"

"Well, duh! You're having twin wigglers! Geez! Call me as soon as you have the results, will you? Oh, I just had a thought that I need to run by you, but right now, I have to go take care of a mate who is howling for me!"

"Right-o!" Kaitlan hung up, and laughed.

Dan came waltzing in, saw Anita deep in thought. He wrapped his arms around her waist. If it were his choice, he'd never let her dress! Clothes were way too much of a barrier. He liked to be able to do what he wanted to her whenever he wanted!

"What's up, hon?"

"Well, one…I think Sarah's pregnant. And, two, my head has cleared. And, finally, three I think I've just figured something out, but I have to question Kaitlan first."

Dan laughed.

"Knowing Sam, he's going to be the LAST one

to find out! And, what did you figure out?"

Anita turned with her eyebrow up at his booming laughter to poke his chest.

"Don't laugh, buster! That could be you in a week, you know."

She grinned when his mouth dropped.

"What? You didn't consider the possibility after our twenty-four hour sex-a-thon? We must have done EVERY way possible. After Kaitlan and Cordone? Don't you remember our history, or have you forgotten already? Remember? Kaitlan? White Wolf?"

Dan stopped. A pup? Anita might be pregnant already? Carrying his child? Warmth spread through him like lightning. He rarely thought about it before. But, the thought of it caused him to harden, and he nuzzled his mate's neck while pressing himself against her.

"Hey! I'm willing to help it along, if you want!" Anita saw him waggled his eyebrows. Anita actually blushed pink. He loved it!

"When is Kaitlan going to call you back?"

"Well, I guess when Sarah finishes the test. She really didn't say."

"And, that gives us what? Thirty minutes perhaps?"

Anita was already ahead of him, and raced him to the bed.

When they were in action, Dan stopped, making Anita turn her head to growl at him.

"Anita?"

"Hmmm?" She growled as she pushed her butt against him wanting him to move.

He leaned over her, and cupped her hanging breasts.

"Would you be sad if I gave you my child? Watching him, or her, feed on these will be a huge turn on!"

Anita jerked, and turned her head to look back at him, again. Was he asking what she thought he was asking?

"You want to….?" She partially asked.

He pulled out, and turned her to face him.

"Anita, do you know how long I've waited for you? Waited for my mate? The woman who would, one day, have my child? When I was young, I didn't care that much. But, I've lived a very long time as have you. I've waited long enough for you, and our baby."

Anita's eyes teared up. This admission of Dan's desire for their child went over the top at that question. To have his baby would be an amazing thing.

"Yes, Dan. You are right. We have both waited long enough," she replied.

Werewolf children were so rare, Anita had calculated that they would be extinct within no less than one hundred and fifty years dying out just like the Elven race did. With Kaitlan becoming The White Wolf, the prophecy of the werewolves had changed overnight. Mating in wolf form was, again, possible. Children from the first mating were also, again, possible. This was how it was supposed to be. Canaan and Tara had, somehow, overcome all odds, and produced The White Wolf for their people, but Kaitlan didn't come along for twenty-three years after Tara and Canaan had mated. It was a shock to all when Anita called them in to tell them they were going to be parents. She knew she was waiting to tell Kaitlan her idea, but while they were waiting, she was more than ready to do more research using herself and Dan. And, it sure would be fun research!

"Is that a yes?" Dan broke through her thoughts.

"No."

Dan was startled. She didn't want his baby? Anita wrapped her hand around his hardness, tugging just a little.

"I am ordering you to give me your child!"

And, grinning with that wicked growl she had grown to adore, Dan happily obeyed her.

"I have never been so happy to obey an order in my life. Well, Tits, get ready! One way, or another, I will give you my very best 'shot with my shooter!'"

"You think it has to do with the location of Cordone's land, Anita? Oh, and Sarah's test was negative. She isn't pregnant. Her calculations were off." Kaitlan told her, when she had called about forty minutes later. Anita was still a bit out of breath to Kaitlan's amusement.

"I'm sorry to hear about Sarah. I was just so sure, Kaitlan. Just another oddity that isn't making any sense! As for the land, well, it's all I can come up with. The three of us all changed after you became The White Wolf. But, all three of us did so here. There has yet to be a mating that has happened off this land in wolf form, and to cause pregnancy! There has to be something that counteracts whatever prevented us not being able to mate here. Until someone becomes pregnant off of Cordone's land, then we have to work with this theory. I keep saying that nothing is making a damn bit of sense scientifically."

"So, now what? How are you going to find out?

"Well, the three of us have already received whatever the *antidote* is, if that is what it is," Anita repeated, "so I can't use us. I need real-time subjects to test it out."

"What? You can't be serious!" Kaitlan was horrified at the idea.

"Don't worry. Their mating would be entirely private. Sensors under their skin might help me zero into where, and what might be causing it. If we can find out, not only new mates, but all might finally be treated!"

"Well, one thing I have discovered, Anita. Once you sink your teeth into something, you continue until you find the answer. So, exactly, who do you have in mind?" Kaitlan was wary about her answer.

Anita did not disappoint.

~ 32 ~

Memories of Home Long Forgotten.

For almost three months, the Clan, amazingly, was free from poisonings, and even fewer medical problems. Luckily, werewolves needed few medical needs which gave Anita the ability to do a lot of research, and why she had been able to discover many treatments for the various supers.

Anita and Dan had spent those months at Cordone's house while she had done more tests. As usual, she had found nothing. Not a damn thing. In fact, nothing had happened, and it had lured them all into a false sense of security.

Sadly, Sarah had not been pregnant. Sam had been keeping track of her cycle, and she wasn't late. What it had been, though, was that the night before Sarah began throwing up, Sarah and Sam had visited a local sushi restaurant. It was food poisoning. A few days later, the news stated that several people had become sick from the same restaurant. Sarah had been devastated.

But, two weeks ago, Sarah did take another test. She was late, and she was pregnant. But, Sam was away for a conference in Venice, Italy, with the vampire, Nico de Angelis, who was a great friend of Cordone and Sam. Sarah had been practically bouncing off the walls with happiness. She was planning the perfect way to tell him when he returned.

In the meantime, again, Anita told Kaitlan who she needed for her real time subjects. She'd been trying to convince both of them for the last three months! Kaitlan and Cordone were totally against it all the way. But, Anita was ready to FORCE them into admitting that they were mates, and had been for a very long time. She was wearing them down. She knew it!

"What the hell was Anita taking?" Kaitlan thought. Again, nothing made sense, and all her tests had come back negative. Yet, there was no doubt whatsoever that things had changed.

Had her brain been damaged by almost going rogue? Kaitlan would NEVER have picked Anita's choices. Cordone had to talk her out of her hairbrained scheme! She doubted he would be able to do it, but she knew he had to try at least one more time!

Opening his office door, Kaitlan realized that Cordone was already on the phone talking to Anita, and waved at her to sit down. So, Kaitlan sat down carefully in a chair in the front of Cordone's desk. Ugh! She was just so, damn big, and due any moment. There went that twinge in her back, again. She'd never make it to the delivery!

"What the fuck, Anita? Are you on crack? Has all that sex with your 'best friend' caused your senses to fly out the window? You have always been a damned pain in my ass!"

Kaitlan dropped her mouth! Why was he speaking like that to Anita? She was about to give Cordone a piece of her mind when he continued his insults, making her mouth drop even more.

"Watch your damn mouth, old woman! If Mother and Father were still here, so help me, Father would drag you by the hair, and whack you until you couldn't sit down for a year! Maybe even ten! Where in the hell did you learn those strings of expletives? And, don't tell me it's Dan's fault - again. Mating does NOT cause stupidity!"

He was quiet for a moment. Kaitlan could hear Anita yelling at Cordone on the other end of the phone. What the hell?

"WHAT! What do you mean I should 'watch my own language'? It's official! Your mind has left the planet!" Cordone yelled into the phone.

Kaitlan heard a slight "cracking" sound. Oh, great! She stood up, and opened the door to tell Lynne to get Cordone another one. She didn't even have to tell her what she meant! Lynne just nodded her head.

Kaitlan shut the door, again, and sat back down. Her eyes widened as she realized what she had just heard. It had slowly crept into her brain. Wait! Mother and Father? Was he saying…?

"I don't care if they aren't here! I put you over my damn knee enough after they died! You are not too old for me to do it again!"

Cordone had spanked Anita? A lot? What the hell? Dawn finally appeared over the horizon in her brain. Cordone and Anita both had coal, black hair despite the peppering in Cordone's. Cordone's eyes were black as night; Anita's were hazel with flecks of navy. They both had tanned, slightly olive complexions, and they were both of Italian heritage. She had been totally blind!   Her eyes narrowed. Damn them! They were both in so much trouble!

"Whatever! I'll do it, but I'm telling you right now, they WON'T do it!" He paused. "Why? Because, you idiot, he thinks of her as HIS DAUGHTER, that's why! How many damn times must I tell you?"

He turned to face Kaitlan. He'd forgotten she was there!   He also realized that he had totally forgotten to tell her about Anita and him! Kaitlan's face was livid with anger. He was in deep shit! Anita caught his attention, again.

"Anita, it IS official! Your mating with Dan has caused idiocy! You'd better get on the track for an antidote! Go to a shrink, too! Oh, hell!   I'll call you back later. I hear your mate growling for you. Go take care of him!"

He slammed down the phone, and the screen split!   Damn!

"Hey, Lynne! Get me another one!" He yelled so loud, Lynne could hear him through the door.

"Yeah. Kaitlan already told me. I bought them in bulk the last time!" Lynne yelled back.

He gulped, and turned to Kaitlan with guilt plastered all over his face.

Kaitlan didn't know how she was feeling. She

was between laughing about Cordone cracking another phone, and anger that he and Anita had never told her about their relationship.

"You. Anita. Brother and sister. She's my sister - in-law?" Kaitlan stated with narrowed eyes. Then, softer, "And, what if Lynne had heard you?"

"Calm down. I may have yelled, but not loud enough for her to hear me. And, yes. Anita is my sister."

"Why the HELL did you not tell me this before?" Kaitlan demanded. "Why didn't SHE? Answer me, Cordone! Why? And, why the last name difference?"

Cordone propped himself on his desk dangling one of his legs in the air, and looked at her.

"Will you PLEASE calm down, Kaitlan! I Just never got around to it, I guess. We don't talk about it that much."

He held up his hand as she opened her mouth.

"Let me explain. I was the only child in our family for about eight hundred years," he began.

Cordone almost laughed at her expression. Now, he had to explain, but he didn't know if she was ready to hear it. And, that just gave him a devilish sense of satisfaction.

"Oh, yes. As you know, babies are few and really far between, if they happen at all. Before whatever it was that happened…"

"Oh. Anita's, now, calling it a 'curse'. That's easier." Kaitlan interrupted.

"OK, curse, then." He huffed. "The first mating

after the Blood Bond usually produced the first child as you know. I'm very happy that seems to have been reversed with The White Wolf's appearance. The second and third came every several hundred years afterward - if it happened at all."

Kaitlan's mouth dropped. Her mind one-tracked for a minute.

"Wait! Rewind, and back it up. Are you KIDDING me? Holy cow! I thought Anita was exaggerating about having babies as long as we live?"

Cordone had a smug expression. "I guess Anita didn't tell you and Sarah all of it. But, yes. You and I could, quite literally, have a great many children as long as we are alive. Maybe thousands of years. And, if it is true, and you are the prophecy, it's going to be fun impregnating you over and over!"

Kaitlan's mouth dropped, again. She could conceive, and have children as long as they both actually lived? Holy shit! And, he WANTED them? With her? Hmmm. That thought wasn't all that upsetting for some reason.

Yes! Trying to make babies with her through the years to come was going to be a great joy for him!

"Remember, Kaitlan. I keep telling you. We are not humans. We aren't even wolves. We are werewolves, and are long-lived. You will live as long as I do. If we are both still alive two thousand years from now, you will still be able to have children - if you still want them with me, that is."

He reached over, and gently shut her mouth. It was rare she was speechless, but it was fun when she was. He kissed her lips gently, desire growing within him.

"Our story began after the Vampire Wars which were long and bloody. Many on all sides were killed, before it was over. Our parents fought, and they both died in that war." Cordone continued.

Kaitlan was still trying to cope with the fact she could get pregnant for thousands of years. Well, never mind at the moment. She'd deal with that fact later.

"Anita was barely fifteen years old when they died. She and Dan were the best of friends since almost birth. They did everything together, as I have said. Even skinny dipping which really freaked our folks out, and made me angry. Obviously, not angry enough, or I would have stopped them! Guess, now that they're mates, that's no longer a bone of contention with me. Anyway, after our parents were killed, I was charged with raising her, but she was a HELLION!"

His memories showed on his face. It wasn't hard for Kaitlan to imagine at all.

"She drove me nuts, Kaitlan! She disobeyed me over and over, and even your Father wouldn't have been able to handle her. Anyway, I did my best for the next two years, and, finally, one day, I almost lost it with her. I was so ready to beat the shit out of her, you just can't imagine!"

Kaitlan pressed her lips together to keep from laughing at him. Oh, yes, she could imagine Anita being a hellion! But, Cordone spanking her? Nope.

She couldn't picture that one.

"Our healer, that's what they were called then, was an older werewolf by the name of Billa. No one knew her real age, and she never told. Her mate had died many years before, but because she was needed in the Clan, he had ordered her, while on his deathbed, to continue her healing duties until she found a replacement. So, she was the natural person to ask how to contain Anita. I took Anita to her hoping that maybe she might help me find a way to stop Anita from her wild ways."

Kaitlan was fascinated, and crossed her arms, laying them on her rapidly expanding belly. But, that twinge was still there, a bit harder, now. She shifted in her chair.

"At Billa's request, I left Anita with her while I went to attend to Clan business. When I came back late that day, I couldn't find either Billa, or Anita.

Terrified, I called out their names. If anything had happened to my baby sister, I'd never have forgiven myself. No one answered, so I decided to look around for them. I finally found them in Billa's 'basement'. Her 'lab', I guess you'd call it. Anita was bent over a book that Billa had given to her. She raised her head to ask a question about something she had just read. I cleared my throat, and they saw me."

He closed his eyes with a smile at his memories. Kaitlan waited with baited breath.

"Anita jumped up, and brought the book over to

me. I'd never seen her so excited. She had just read about Wolfsbane, believe it or not."

Kaitlan's eyes widened. Was that a coincidence? Somehow, Kaitlan was convinced it had not been one. She did not believe in coincidence at all.

Cordone stood up, and walked around to stand at the window.

"I listened, but didn't understand a damn word she was saying. All I heard was babbling, and Billa was just laughing at her."

Remembering, he continued with that day.

"Anita has always been a mouth a minute. I had never seen her so excited about anything. Her attitude had totally changed. 'Cordone! Look! Billa gave me a book to read, and I found a wild weed known as Wolfsbane! Ever heard of it? Well, it's really interesting! Did you know it can be used for salves, and even a tonic if prepared right? It can heal, or even kill if it is used the wrong way! There are so many books around here! Look at them! Did you know that Billa has all kinds of medicines, and herbs, and rubs, and salves, and…and…and…well, she has just all kinds of fascinating things one can use to heal! And, it's all so won…'. At that point, I had to slip my hand over her mouth to shut her up for a minute so I could at least speak!"

Kaitlan laughed out loud.

He continued while narrowing his eyes at Kaitlan. He noticed she was wincing every so often.

"Billa got a word in by saying, 'I apologize for not answering, but I was in the middle of a potion that required my utmost attention. That's why I gave Anita a book to read while I attended to it.'"

Rubbing the back of his neck, "Anita had started mumbling into my hand, and I just kept it over her mouth, so Billa kept speaking. 'I've never found anyone so eager to learn about healing.'"

He laughed at his next memory.

"I remember Anita's head bobbing up and down so hard, I honestly thought her head would fall off!"

Kaitlan laughed even harder, then felt a twinge, grabbing her lower back. She had slept wrong last night.

"I couldn't believe she was interested in healing. Of all the things I could have thought of for Anita to be interested in, healing was not one of them! Billa, then explained her idea to me. 'Cordone, to answer the reason why you brought her to me, I have an idea. If you will permit me, I would like Anita to become my apprentice, and eventually, my replacement. I will teach her everything I know, and someday, she will take my place as Clan healer.'"

Anita had pushed Cordone's hand away.

"'Please, brother? Please? May I? I have never seen so much in my life to learn. Please? May I study to become the healer to the Clan? I promise you, I will not fail you, or our parents! Please?'"

Cordone looked at Kaitlan whose face was scrunched.

"You OK, beautiful?" He asked in a concerned voice.

"Yes, I'm fine. I woke up with a twinge this

morning. Pregnancy, you know. There are always aches. I'm fine. Please, go on! I'm excited to know that I have a sister, now!   And, it's cool to hear about her as a kid!"

He looked at Kaitlan, and after a minute, nodded.

"Over the next forty years, Anita was a glutton for punishment and knowledge. By the time Billa announced that her time as healer had ended, and Anita would become the new one, Anita had far surpassed Billa's expectations as well as she was far superior to even Billa's skills. Anita had grown up, and became not only a brilliant healer, but a researcher bar none."

"Billa was proud of her. 'Anita has a real purpose in her life, Cordone. This has always been her destiny. She was born to be a healer. As the years go by, I believe that she will be the answer to finding the cure for the affliction of mating and children that have plagued our species since the beginning. Perhaps, you both will live to see The White Wolf. Who knows? Cordone, I'm tired, and I want to go to my mate. I promised I would remain until I found one who would replace me, and teach her my knowledge. That has ended today. Anita has invented a device that allows her to see blood samples closely. She hasn't named it yet, but it's going to change everything some day. So, I take my leave of you both.' She hugged Anita tightly, and kissed her forehead. Then, Billa left, and we never saw her again. Anita turned out to be the most amazing healer in our histories, and she went on to study all of the other species on this world. That's why she is so knowledgeable about all races on the Earth, and why, when she can't figure out a problem, she can get a bit testy, and won't give up, and why she would not let her wolf out for so long."

Kaitlan saw the pride in her mate's face for his sister. She couldn't wait to give Anita a piece of her mind, and then hug her! She stood up with difficulty.

"That's such a great story, Cordone! Thank you for finally telling me. I can't wait to hug my new sister, then kill her! Oh! What about the last name thing?"

"Ah, yes! Well, actually, Carol Moore was our Mother's maiden name, and Anita's middle name. So, she dropped Valon, and chose Carol for her middle name, and Moore as her sir name to honor our Mother. I kept Valon to honor our Father. "

"Wow! Anita is an amazing woman, like I didn't know it!"

"I know. I'm very, very proud of her. I'm really sorry we didn't tell you, Kaitlan. We haven't talked about it in so long, we forgot you didn't know!"

He grinned at her as she stood up, and walked to his office door. There was not a more beautiful sight than her body heavy with their children. There was still about a week before delivery. He streaked over to her giving her a kiss, and patted her belly. She grinned at him, then left his office to go back to hers.

She had another, harder twinge, and felt something warm and wet. She looked down. The floor was wet with water.

"Shit! Oh, God!   My water broke!"

Lynne was out of her seat in an instant, yelling for Cordone. Werewolves deliver within minutes after their water broke. Kaitlan turned to look at him with surprise.

"I think I'm going to have our babies today."

"You are at that - in just minutes!"

~ 33 ~

Babies Wait for No One!

The elevator was maddeningly slow getting him to the infirmary floor. Teri had never gotten around to learning to deliver babies. She had been acting odd lately. When the doors opened, Kaitlan was already panting with very heavy contractions coming two minutes apart. He didn't have much time. Their children were coming, and no one was available who could deliver them - except himself.

He flew into the infirmary, laid Kaitlan on the table as she handled yet another painful contraction. For an instant, he remembered Tara's labor. It was much longer than the normal. But, he didn't think that would be the case with Kaitlan since she was half-were. His mate would be delivering their children in a matter of minutes, and he had no time for memories.

He gowned himself, ripped off her underwear, and placed her feet into the stirrups, covering her lower body with a sheet. Teri and Sarah came running into the room followed by Sam who had just gotten back from Italy.

"Sarah! Hold Kaitlan's hand. She will need you to help hold her up when she pushes! Teri, get everything ready for me, now! Sam, help Teri."

To let another male see his mate's private parts was unthinkable to any werewolf male. Even in the delivery room.

Kaitlan screamed out as the next contraction became harder. She squeezed Sarah's hand tightly until it subsided. Teri had brought a bowl of cold water and cloth for Sarah to

wipe off Kaitlan's face.

Kaitlan gasped arching her back as another contraction grabbed her. Sarah was excited to become an aunt, and happy for her best friend in the world.

Cordone checked how dilated Kaitlan was as he pushed the sheet back. She was already at eight centimeters! They delivered at twelve unlike human women. He was going to deliver his own children from the body of the woman he loved, and whom he had delivered from the body of her Mother. There was something really strange about that. Maybe a Karma thing? Coincidence?

"OK, Kaitlan. Do not push until I tell you," he ordered.

Kaitlan had another contraction, and let lose a long line of expletives directed directly at her mate. Sarah had a really hard time not laughing at Cordone's face

"Relax, Cordone," laughed Sarah. "She doesn't mean it, and it's normal for a woman in hard labor to say things she doesn't mean."

"Oh, yes the HELL I mean every fucking, damn word!" Yelled Kaitlan as the next contraction opened her to ten centimeters.

Cordone didn't have time to listen, as the next contraction came harder, and dilation was at eleven. One more to go.

Kaitlan started screaming, "I have to push! I have to push! I can't stand it!"

"Not yet, Kaitlan O'Hara Valon! Not until I tell you!" Yelled Cordone back at her exercising his Alpha command. He couldn't let her, not yet.

Sarah mopped Kaitlan's face with a cloth. Kaitlan looked at her, and gave her a weary smile. And, then!

"OH MY GOD! The baby is coming, now!" She screamed squeezing Sarah's hand so tight, it hurt - and cut off her circulation! Ouch!

Teri came running into the room, gowned, and gloved like Cordone, holding the clinic's disposable blue towels.

"OK, Kaitlan. It's time." Commanded Cordone. "PUSH NOW!"

Sarah held Kaitlan upward as she began to push her first baby out with the contraction. Then, she leaned back to rest, but not for long.

"OK, mate. PUSH!" His voice was loud.

Again, Sarah helped Kaitlan lift upward so she could push, again.

"I see the head, Kaitlan! You can do it! PUSH! PUSH!"

Cordone placed his hand under the baby's head to support it as it came out.

"I AM PUSHING, YOU JACKASS!" Screamed

Kaitlan.

"The next one should do it! Come on, Kaitlan! PUSH!!!" He commanded, ignoring her.

This contraction was harder, and Kaitlan screamed. The shoulders were out which allowed the baby to slide out the rest of the way into her Father's hands.

Kaitlan laid back. She was really thirsty, and Sarah gave her some ice Teri had brought.

Then, they all heard a loud wail from the baby. Cordone was mesmerized at the tiny being in his hands. It was a girl! They had a daughter! The eyes opened to look at her Father for the first time. Her hair, what little there was, was as black as his, but with her Mother's brilliant green eyes. Oh, crap! He was going to really have trouble with the boys! He lifted her while Terri cut the umbilical cord, then walked around to his mate who held out her arms for her daughter.

"It's a girl, Kaitlan! Tara," he said softly with tears in his eyes as he placed their tiny daughter in his mate's arms.

Kaitlan was having another contraction, hard, but not unbearable yet. She knew she had a few minutes before their second baby was born. She reached up, and wiped the bloody residue from her daughter's face. Tara's eyes opened seeing her Mother.

"Cordone...she's so beautiful! Hello, Tara," she said softly. Kaitlan lifted her face to her mate, and he kissed her. Then, she kissed her daughter, and smiled tenderly. Cordone thought she was so beautiful, holding their daughter in her arms! That's when the next contraction hit her.

"Cordone! The other baby is c-c-coming!" Cordone had the baby out of her arms in a split Second, handing it to Teri who rushed out of the room to clean up the baby with help from Sam.

Cordone rushed back to Kaitlan for their next child. She screamed again, and she grew to fourteen centimeters??? Cordone was very confused. It wasn't normal!

"PUSH, Kaitlan!"

Again Sarah helped Kaitlan raise up so she could push.

"The head's out! YOU HAVE TO GIVE ME JUST ONE MORE PUSH!"

"SHUT THE HELL UP, CORDONE!!!! I AM PUSHING, DAMN YOU!!"

And, with that, the second baby slid out, screaming bloody murder, into Cordone's hands. He smiled with pride. It was a boy, and bigger than Tara!

"Teri," he called gently.

Teri ran in, and prepared to clean Kaitlan up.

Cordone walked to the head of the table with his son in his arms, kissing him on the head, then giving him to his Mother.

"Canaan," he said softly.

The baby had a great lung system on him, and Kaitlan smiled. Like her daughter, she kissed him on the head, and his eyes opened. She gasped. He had blond hair like hers, but his black eyes were that of Cordone's wolf! They were so beautiful!   She and Cordone looked at each other not really understanding. Both babies were here. They were safe. They were beautiful. Cordone had never thought to have a mate let alone a child as well as delivering his own children. Yet here he was with his mate, whom he had delivered as well, and they were parents of twins!

Sarah came around so Cordone could hand him to her to clean while Teri continued to work on Kaitlan. Cordone had never been so moved, he leaned down to kiss his mate, and thank her for his life, for her, and for their children.

Sam saw Sarah come into the room with the Second baby. Sarah was so beautiful holding the child, he only wished that they could also have a child.

They bathed the baby boy together in silence, each reflecting on the beauty of the moment. The little girl lay in a clinic baby bed already asleep, and sucking on her thumb.

She handed the baby boy to Sam who looked down into the eyes of the wolf. He, too, was startled. But, they were gorgeous in his face! He looked at Sarah. They were left in no doubt which child had been fathered by Cordone's wolf.

This was all new. There were two of them. Custom demanded that Sam present the babies to his Alpha, but how to do it? Then, he looked at Sarah. Tradition be damned, and he gave her the baby boy.

"Sam?" She asked, knowing the traditions by now.

"Sarah. All our traditions flew out the window with The White Wolf. This is a special case, and you will stand at my side to present the babies with me - together."

Somehow, thought Sarah, that made sense. She wondered how Sam would feel when she delivered their baby in about three months. She hadn't had time to tell him, yet.

Sam picked up the baby girl, and they both walked into the room.Both Kaitlan and Cordone turned, and Cordone's eyebrow went up at the total disregard for protocol, until Kaitlan spoke.

"This is wonderful, Cordone! The Second and his mate presenting our children to us together!" Cordone looked at her, and realized he agreed. It WAS right!

He nodded his approval at Sam and Sarah, as they split up, and walked to both sides of the bed.

Sarah presented their son to Kaitlan laying him in his Mother's arms, while Sam presented, to his Alpha, their daughter placing her into her Father's arms.

There was something beautiful in all this, thought Sam as he and Sarah quietly walked out the door to guard the room together, since Dan wasn't around. Just as he and Cordone had done with Canaan and Tara, but this was a happy duty this time.

Sarah sighed.

"How amazing that the man who delivered his

own mate twenty-seven years ago just delivered his own children!   That's just so beautiful!"

"It is." Sam smiled down at his beautiful little Tink.

Werewolf females heal almost immediately after birth, apparently, because Kaitlan was able to leave within twelve hours, fully back to normal.

Sarah took Sam's hand in hers, and looked up at him with tears. Together, the two of them went to his old room. They had been parted for over two weeks. She was ready to tell him, but in her way. First, she needed her mate, now.

~ **EPILOGUE - Book 1** ~

It is not over…not by a long shot!

Sam undressed the both of them in his old room with werewolf speed, and he was inside her before they even made it to the bed! They loved sex in the afternoon, and in his office, especially! Sometimes, they snuck in a closet somewhere, or in his old room and shower, but mostly in his office with the door locked, of course. It was just so exciting! But, today, they needed more privacy without being disturbed having been away from each other.

His thrusts came faster and harder inside Sarah who was panting with excitement as she met his hips with hers with equal thrusts. Sam loved being inside of her! He so needed her after being apart from her for so long. He never got enough of her, and was ready for her all the time. And, she was just as ready for him.

The urgency of his thrusts matched those of Sarah's. Their release came at the same time as she milked him so tightly, his semen detonated inside of Sarah filling her womb to capacity, she was sure. Luckily, the baby was in its own cocoon.

"Uh…Sam?" She gasped, feeling her orgasm dial down.

"Hmmm?" He moaned as his cock, one last

time, spilled the rest of his semen into her womb, before he collapsed on top of her. He so wanted to keep it inside of her, and go to sleep, but work was waiting.

"Are you ready?"

"Always, Tink. Always!" He grinned, and sighed as he, reluctantly, pulled out of her wet channel. Damn! He was still hard for her, and he wanted so much more. He pulled her tightly to his chest slapping a kiss on her lips designed to excite her all over again.

"No. I mean are you ready to be a Father?" She asked looking him directly in the eye.

"Sure. No prob…" Sam started then stopped, and slowly looked at Sarah. "No. You're not…I mean…are you…I mean am I going to be a.…"

Sarah shut him up by quickly rolling on top of him. She kissed him thoroughly while her burning, wet channel devoured his cock. She knew he had to hear it from her own lips before he would believe it. She moved very slowly up and down his shaft, taking it all the way out, and back down again. Then, she answered him.

"Yes. Yes. Yes. And, yes, you are. I'm pregnant, Sam." She whispered into his ear.

Sam looked stunned, and then the entire building shook with a howl. Both of them howled together. Sarah silenced him as she held her breast to his lips urging him to suckle. He grabbed her nipple with his teeth as he proceeded to empty himself into his mate, again.

Everyone throughout the building, smiled widely as they heard the sound that gave all the werewolves joy and hope, now. Kaitlan was The White Wolf of Prophecy, and another baby was on its way.

Inside that rat infested basement, Alpha was furious!

Those bastards had thwarted him at every turn! He had someone on the inside of all the Werewolf Clans doing his bidding as well as in the Vampire Clans. The Elves meant nothing to him. Their females were not pure-blood.

Nothing made sense to him. His curse should never have been able to be reversed! He did something wrong. But, what? He had followed the spell to the letter. He would have to review it, again. He had to find a way to recast it to be permanent for good, this time! The answer HAD to be in The Hall of Records!

Thinking back, he had found a very ancient scroll that he found in The Hall of Records a while back. Only a few people knew the Hall even existed. He was one of the privileged few. The scroll had been written by an angry, jealous Elf in ancient times, and had been forgotten. He found it quite by accident, you understand, but nevertheless, a study of the scroll had discovered that an ancient Elf, in a fit of angry rage against the King who had chosen a mate not of Elven blood, had plotted to wipe out his own kind forever.

He had succeeded in wiping out all pure-blooded females. It was that Elf who had also discovered the mixture of Wolfsbane that he used to kill them, and was written on the scroll by hand - the mix Alpha had copied. Elves, now, had to mate with humans in order to save their species in some form. And, one of those included that bastard King of the Elves, Ali'on. His mate was human, although Alpha had never seen her.

Alpha had also discovered, through his own research and experiments, that Wolfsbane, refined different ways, could poison, heal, or kill. The most potent of all killed, but it had to be delivered intravenously for the werewolves. Of course, that made it much harder to administer. Luckily, he had a person inside Anita Moore's medical staff who had access to every patient. Alpha had delivered the poison to Lynne all by himself. He had brought her the coffee that day, and she had not even noticed who had brought it!

For vampires, simply adding it to their stash of blood would kill them. It acted differently on the different races.   For the Elves, well, wasn't necessary. Not enough of them to fool with anyway. A great deal of his goal was to redirect - to make sure that he distributed his refined mixture to the different races throwing off his real plan to destroy the werewolf hierarchy allowing him to take them over, first. Then, the rest of the world would follow afterward. It was brilliant, actually. As long as he could keep them chasing false trails, he would be in shadow.

Unfortunately, he had never found a mixture to kill off humans, which was OK with him, since he needed them as a food source. Humans filled the bill, and were his favorite anyway. When that whore of a bitch, Tara O'Hara, became pregnant through Canaan, he decided to eliminate females of his own species, using the ancient Elf's idea. He wasn't jealous. He hated Canaan with a hatred he could not quell. So, he had his "plant" give Tara O'Hara the poison, as a test, through her IV, and it had worked! He remembered how ecstatic he had been when he had heard that she had delivered a dead child, then bled out. He was after more than position.

Then, that damn, little bitch had lived! He tried to find out how, but could not. There was nothing to discover. Period. Nothing was making sense. His curse should have taken care of everything, and it seemed as if it was working perfectly . But, just recently, the fucking curse was no longer working. So, why didn't it?

It had taken him a very long time to find someone who would agree to kill for him. Almost twenty-seven years, and then he crashed his car, and it really set him back, He'd found the Viper who agreed, for a hefty price, to kill Canaan.

And, finally had luck when he found another who needed money, and he found the perfect person within Moore's Medical staff. Greed, and debts have an unbelievable ability to let someone be blackmailed.

The original plan was to kill Kaitlan as soon as

she went into labor like her Mother. He had to get rid of her, and her bastard offspring! His plans were falling to pieces.

He had used Lynne to warn them he was still here. His grin was devilish! She had actually almost died! That was not supposed to happen. He had more hope than ever at this point that he could accomplish his goals faster even orally. He started his experiments again. Nothing different. However, he would continue.

Suddenly, he started to smile, and a new plan was expanding with every minute as his next victim entered his mind. THIS time, he would not just poison any female werewolf. No. He would kill a specific werewolf. She was tiny, had red hair, and blue eyes. His "plant" had told him that she was pregnant. That was the best news he'd had. She would not get in his way, and he would get rid of Sam as well! Yes, they were his next target.

Turning to his fellow rats, his plot was unfolding.

"Contact my plant. Tell her to give a triple dose, orally, to that new werewolf bitch, Sarah. I want her dead, and most especially, that shitty kid growing in her filthy body!"

They nodded, and ran out of the basement. It stunk so badly they were always eager to leave!

Alpha didn't notice the stench. He was the stench. He waltzed out the building in search of his next meal. Those hookers were still there. He felt so good about himself, he thought he would just give them the thrill of their lives with his cock - before he ate them, of course. His deal of old had made him crave flesh and blood. To get his jollies, he had to think up new ways of eating humans, or other supers, if he didn't have a choice, but he preferred humans. Strolling across to them, the hookers turned to each other with a grin. Big roller! They had no problem doing them. They paid so well.

"Hello, girls! You know," he whispered to them, "I have a really big dick!"

He unzipped his pants, and yanked it out to show them. He was really hard. Dinner always gave him a huge hard-on.

The girls licked their lips! He WAS big!

"I have the desire to have a threesome along with all kinds of vulgar things I'd like to do to both of you! I hope you are up for letting me fuck you girls in all kinds of ways tonight? 'The better to eat you with, said the Big Bad Wolf!'" He laughed. "I guarantee the two of you will LOVE it when I eat you!"

He laughed waving his cock at them.

"We love doing threesomes!" The girls giggled in agreement. "But, it costs more."

"I have no doubt of that!" He gave them a wicked grin.

Seductively, he grabbed a breast from each girl, and pulled them out with drool spilling from his mouth. He ducked his head, and licked first one hooker's then the other's. The girls moaned, and giggled with his licks. Leaving their breasts bare, and his cock out for them to see, he slipped between the girls, and tucked their hands in each of his, letting them lead him to their room. Oh, yes! He was going to fuck well, and then, eat well tonight!

Tomorrow, that fucking bitch, Sarah and her fucking offspring would die. And so would Sam!

Three walked into a darkened building, but only one would leave.

"The real prophecy is still to be found," he told her.

"Is it time, my love?" She answered him.

He nodded. "I do believe it is."

"So, who do you have in mind to receive it?"

"Well, I'm not quite sure." He responded. "What about you? Do you have an ideal person in mind?"

"Hmmm." She snapped her fingers. "How about…?"

The White Wolf Prophecy continues with Book 2:

The White Wolf Prophecy: The Hall of Records